A Basket Case

A Maddie Sparks Mystery, Book Two

LESLEY A. DIEHL

CAMEL
PRESS

KENMORE, WA

CAMEL PRESS

A Camel Press book published by Epicenter Press

Epicenter Press
6524 NE 181st St.
Suite 2
Kenmore, WA 98028

For more information go to:
www.Camelpress.com
www.Coffeetownpress.com
www.Epicenterpress.com
www.lesleyadiehl.com

This is a work of fiction. Names, characters, places, brands, media, and incidents are either the product of the author's imagination or are used fictitiously.

Cover design by Scott Book
Design by Melissa Vail Coffman

A Basket Case
Copyright © 2024 by Lesley A. Diehl

Library of Congress Control Number: 2024935783

ISBN: 978-1-68492-220-8 (Trade Paper)
ISBN: 978-1-68492-221-5 (eBook)

As was true of Spiked Punch, the first book in the Maddie Sparks Mysteries, Spike the orange rescue cat plays a role in identifying the murderer in A Basket Case also. This second book is dedicated to those individuals involved in rescuing animals who need a home, particularly to Faithful Friends, Morris, NY and its owner, Nan Johnston who begged us to foster a chubby tuxie cat "for only a month." Her name is Bandita, and she has been with us for over a year. We are her grateful and devoted staff and always will be.

ACKNOWLEDGMENTS

M Y THANKS TO DEIDRE BRETT, intern in Museum Studies who patiently answered my questions about museums, their structure and the work of their employees as well as providing information about the role museums play in the return of artifacts to Indigenous people.

Note: The Native American Graves Protection and Repatriation Act (NAGPPA) became law in 1990. It is designed to return objects of spiritual, religious and cultural importance to the nations or tribes and requires all entities receiving federal funds to comply with the act.

CHAPTER 1

"YOU HAVE SOMETHING THAT BELONGS to my family. I want it back."

I glanced up from behind the plexiglass barrier of the local museum at the figure in front of me: male, tall, well-built, and about fifty years of age. He wore a grey suit with a white shirt. I would have taken him for a businessman were it not for the two, long black braids that hung over his shoulders and down the front of his jacket.

"I want to see Director Carlton." It was not a request, but a command. His eyes were blacker than a moonless night. They paralyzed me.

"Uh . . ." I said.

My granddaughter, Sara, must have spotted my discomfort as she entered the entrance hallway of the museum. She came up behind me. "Can I help with something?" she asked. Sara worked as a museum intern, her final stop before she received her degree in museum studies from a local university.

I managed to swallow the lump in my throat and spoke. "Yes, Sara. This man wants to see Director Carlton."

Sara looked up at the man. Her blue eyes widened, and she hesitated a moment, then smiled at him. "Yes, of course, Mr. Powles. She's waiting for you. This way."

The man gave me a final glance and nodded. He stepped around the museum's front desk where I was seated and followed Sara down the hallway past the security guard stationed next to the director's office. Sara tapped on the door and stuck her head in, announcing Mr. Powles's presence. She gestured to him, and he pushed by her into the office. Sara closed the door, glanced at me, gave a shrug and stepped back into the hallway.

I shivered, not because the museum's air was cold. It usually was. Visitors who entered to see the exhibits kept their coats on even in the winter months when the air inside the museum in upstate New York was warmer than outside. We held the air temperature at a steady sixty-eight degrees and the humidity low to preserve the exhibits. I wore my sweater draped around my shoulders. I was used to the temperature. My feeling of chill wasn't from the air. It came from my brief interaction with Mr. Powles. Despite his being one of the handsomest men I'd ever encountered, something about him unsettled me.

I pulled my sweater tighter around me and greeted the visitors who had just entered. I sold them their entrance tickets, handed them a brochure and directed them down the stairs to the exhibit they indicated they had come to see. A woman with a cane and a man accompanying her punched the elevator button to access galleries on the second floor. I could hear the laughter of children from the basement floor where the museum had set up an interactive display of over-sized soft sculpture animals. Kids loved to bounce on a koala bear, giraffe, elephant, horse and other animals piled together. A family with two children that I had greeted several minutes ago emerged from the hallway to my left. A boy and girl pulled at their parents' hands leading them down the curved staircase to the animal exhibition.

The sun shone brightly through the museum's windows, a perfect autumn day in rural Upstate New York. Everyone smiled and chatted, enjoying the ambience our small museum provided, but their conversations were interrupted by shouting from the director's office. The security guard rapped on the door. Sara and I exchanged worried glances.

Mr. Powles emerged from the director's office, stopping before he entered the hall. "My family and others who support us have a right to it. You intend to satisfy the other claims. Why not ours?" Mrs. Carlton joined him in the doorway. "We know to whom the other items belong. Bring me some evidence to support your assertion about the basket, and I will honor your request."

"A fair request. I will bring you what you need." He strode down the hall with such authority that the guard hadn't time to react before Powles was out the front door.

Director Carlton stood in her office doorway. Mrs. Carlton, a woman in her early fifties, smoothed her salt and pepper hair back into her bun, and gave everyone, who by now were staring at her, a reassuring smile. "Just a misunderstanding. Please, go on enjoying our exhibits."

My curious nature wanted to propel me to the director's office to find out what kind of incident had occurred between her and Powles, but my job as a volunteer at the Meadowbrook Museum was to remain at the desk checking in visitors and providing them with information on the holdings and displays. I glanced at Sara, raising one eyebrow in questioning. She shook her head and mouthed "later."

Sara was my only grandchild, the daughter of my oldest son, Geoffrey and his wife Abigail. My other son, Richard, was unmarried. Sara was tall, blonde-haired like me and with my blue eyes, and much to the consternation of her parents, seemed to have inherited my personality characteristics including a tendency toward nosiness. In the past I authored cozy mystery novels satisfying my snoopy nature and netting me a small income. Much as I enjoyed having a granddaughter with an inquiring mind like mine, I wasn't keen she get herself involved in criminal work as I had done on an amateur basis this past summer. It could be frustrating and . . . dangerous.

Right now Sara was pursuing her degree in museum studies and, having told her my writing of romance and mystery fiction didn't occupy enough of my interest, she convinced me I should volunteer at the museum close to the small village in which I had lived for most of my adult life. I am on the farther side of seventy and what is there to do at that age other than solve murders and fall in love with someone? I'd done both. Along with my present beau, Zack Montgomery, retired county sheriff, we had tracked down a killer last summer. The love remained, but no murders appeared to be in the making. I told myself I was relieved but retiring from snooping left a void in my life. Sara's parents offered me a job at their real estate and management company, but that was more boring than sitting in my backyard watching the weeds grow in what had once been my garden. I was still spry but bending over to tend a garden made my knees and back ache. If I was going to get exercise of any kind, I preferred working out at the local fitness center and bouncing on the bedsprings with Zack, And, oh yes, dabbling in writing romance novels. I'd done more than dabble. In the past two months I'd made progress on my romance entitled *Love Again*, a story of two lovers who found each other again after decades of being separated by family conflicts. A small publisher had offered me a publishing contract with a deadline in March. I sighed. March was next year . . . so far away. I found it more satisfying kissing Zack than writing about my protagonist kissing her lover. The writing was going slowly. My romance with Zack was on fire.

Thinking of Zack made me giggle. I put my hand over my mouth and nodded at Sara. She pursed her lips in a kissy pout. She and I were close enough that she read my mind, even at times I would have preferred she not. She gestured as if drinking a cup of coffee, and I understood we'd talk later at my break.

TWO LONG HOURS LATER, the time seemed to creep by. I could barely hold back my curiosity about Mr. Powles and Mrs. Carlton's argument. I poured tea out of my thermos for Sara and me as we sat in the downstairs room just off the area where collections not on display were stored.

"So, tell me. What's going on?" I practically wriggled my way off my chair in eagerness to hear what Sara had to say.

"It's messy, and I probably shouldn't be telling you this, but I think everything is about to break anyway. Don't be surprised if the story appears in the local newspapers and it could go national."

I said nothing but smiled to encourage her to continue.

"Mr. Powles is from a small Native American family."

"Not from one of the nations that are part of the Haudenosaunee Confederacy?"

"No. His family group has maintained an identity separate from Confederacy nations or any other small nation in this area. My understanding is that they broke with either the Oneida or the Onondaga nation—it's not clear which—over two hundred years ago. The story came from Mr. Powles. The other nations' history doesn't include any reference to his family."

"Broke? You mean there was some kind of an argument?"

"I'm not clear on that, but Mr. Powles and the members of his extended family see themselves as a separate group."

"I don't understand."

Before Sara could enlighten me, someone cleared their throat. Mrs. Carlton stood at the door to the break room. She didn't look happy at catching Sara and me talking about Mr. Powles's visit.

"It's not your job to inform your grandmother or any of the other volunteers and employees here about the situation with respect to that collection. It's mine. Until I decide how to move forward, I'd prefer the topic not be discussed." Mrs. Carlton remained in the doorway for a minute longer, her hands on her hips and her mouth set in a tight line. "Do you understand?"

We both nodded.

"Now, if you're finished with your break, Mrs. Sparks, we could use your help at the desk. There's a line of visitors and we expect a group of school children to arrive in a few minutes. Harold is overwhelmed."

Harold was usually overwhelmed. He had volunteered at the museum as a guide for almost a decade and had strict ideas about how the space should be used and how patrons should comport themselves. He'd said many times that he thought school children shouldn't be allowed in the space unless they kept their mouths shut. You can imagine how he felt about the interactive soft sculpture exhibit. Children, shouting and laughing? Harold wanted none of it. As for many of our exhibits, especially those by women, Black, Hispanic or any non-Europeans, Harold felt they added nothing to the museum. I was certain he would have expressed the same attitude about the Native American objects. Perhaps he didn't know we had those pieces. I'd never heard him refer to them.

I hurried out of the break room with a glance backward at Sara to signal her we could talk later at home. She nodded and gathered her cup and snacks off the table and followed me out of the room. When we got back upstairs, people wanting to purchase tickets to the museum stood milling around the entrance desk. Harold was nowhere in sight. I rushed over to begin taking money and dispensing tickets and brochures.

"Where's Harold?" I asked the security guard, Melvin Potts, who had worked for many years at the museum. He took his responsibilities seriously and always wore a pleasant look on his face when dealing with the public. Melvin seemed to love his job.

"He said he needed a bathroom break." Melvin rolled his eyes. Harold usually had some excuse for bolting when he felt overwhelmed, which was often, too often. I don't know where he got off to on these occasions, but I suspect he was using a bottle to help him through his work at the museum. In contrast to Melvin, Harold never smiled and when asked to perform any task he saw as beneath him such as working at the front desk, his scowl deepened and a complaint was sure to follow.

A bus pulled up in front and children began pouring off.

"This is my job," said Sara. "I'll get them gathered together out front and take them through the side entrance, so we don't overcrowd the front door." She sped off, and with the help of the children's teacher, she led the fifth graders off to the left of the main entrance and down the walkway to a smaller door leading to a hallway connecting to one of our meeting rooms.

As the bus driver pulled his vehicle away from the front of the building, a white van pulled up and then another followed by several cars. People began to emerge and gather on the sidewalk.

Harold surfaced from his hiding place, took one look at the crowd out front and turned tail back to where he had come.

"Harold!" I yelled. "You need to go tell those people they can't park their vehicles out front."

Harold shook his head and ran down the hallway. I heard the door to the men's room open and close.

I glanced at Melvin for help. "Can't do it, Mrs. Sparks. I have to stay here to oversee security inside."

"So who is responsible for out there?" I asked.

"No one that I know. It's never been a problem before now," he replied.

The crowd that gathered was small, no more than twenty or so people. I saw them reach into the van and the cars and pull out several signs written in a language I didn't recognize.

I did recognize Mr. Powles, who stepped in front of the crowd and raised his arms to signal them to be quiet. "This will be a peaceful coming together. Let everyone who arrives here entrance. Don't stand in their way but make certain they see your signs."

I wasn't certain what good that would do if like me visitors couldn't read the signs. That was when I saw each sign had written in English at the bottom, "Give us our basket back."

CHAPTER 2

"**T**HAT'S ALL THEY WANT? A BASKET?" I said to Sara who joined me at the desk.

"It belongs to his family."

"But I thought the Native American collection housed here belongs to the museum."

Mrs. Carlton stood next to Sara. For a moment she looked frazzled, but she took a deep breath to gather herself together.

Mrs. Carlton touched me on the arm as if to reassure me she was on top of things, then stepped past me, out the door and down the front steps. She and Mr. Powles conferred for a few minutes. I couldn't hear what words were exchanged, but he shook his head, crossed his arms and stood firm.

Mrs. Carlton held out her hands, palms turned upward as if she was beseeching him to be reasonable. He looked beyond her and into the museum entrance, his gaze catching mine.

"Whatever he wants, I'd give it to him," I said to Sara who had returned from her errand.

"It's not that simple," she said.

Mrs. Carlton turned, her shoulders drooped as if she'd lost this round of the confrontation. She shook her head and re-entered the building. "I think we'll close the museum early today. The visitors already here can certainly take their time in viewing the exhibits, but I think we shouldn't let any others inside. And we'll open an hour later tomorrow after a staff meeting."

"Will Mr. Powles and his group depart now, do you think?" I asked.

Mrs. Carlton heard my question. "For now, but they'll be back tomorrow and every day until we resolve the issue. And that may take time. I'll call a meeting of the board of directors for tonight. Mr. Graham, the director will not be happy to have his evening taken up with this business." She shook her head and headed back into her office.

Harold reappeared at the desk. "She needs to take a firm stand on this. Our old museum director would."

One of our employees, Francis Marquis, a Black woman in her thirties who ran the gift shop, had entered the hallway from the shop when she heard the noise outside. She also overheard Harold's remark.

"You've never been a supporter of Mrs. Carlton's, have you?" she said.

"This situation requires a strong leader." Harold's face reddened in anger.

"You mean a man, don't you?" said Francis.

As usual, Sara and I had shared a ride to our work. When I pulled up in front of my house, I invited her in for a glass of wine. "I think we could use something a bit stronger than tea, don't you think?" I tossed my car keys in the bowl on the table next to the door and walked into the kitchen. "You're not going to make me wait for tomorrow's meeting for an explanation of what's going on, are you?'

Sara laughed and took a seat on my couch. "Of course not, Gram. I'm not putting my life in danger withholding information from my grandmother who works out at the fitness center three times a week. How much weight can you bench press anyway?"

"Don't be silly. I don't do that. I do light weights for strength and stretches for flexibility. But if you don't tell all, I will withhold this wine from you." I held the glass at arm's length.

We settled ourselves on the couch, me at one end with my feet up on my coffee table, Sara on the other. She slipped off her shoes and sighed. "Why do I wear these?"

"Because they're stylish?"

"And too tight." She rubbed her feet. "Are you familiar with the Native American Graves Protection and Repatriation Act? It became law in 1990."

"A bit. I know it's designed to return objects of spiritual, religious and cultural importance to the nations or tribes, as many whites call them."

"Right. The act requires all entities receiving federal funds to comply with the act."

"And the Meadowbrook Museum holds such items?"

Sara nodded and set her glass on the coffee table. "Yes. We receive funding from both state and federal sources as well as from private individuals."

"I've never seen any such objects on display."

"No. They reside in storage in our collections room. They've never been put on display."

"Intentionally relegated to downstairs or not?" I asked.

"From what I've heard, the director of the museum at that time thought having the collection on display would simply create problems he wasn't willing to deal with. But the issue has been taken out of our hands anyway."

"Oh?"

"The history of those pieces is rather interesting because they were loaned to the museum from a local family, the Taylors. The collection has been sitting in our collections room for a number of years. Not only does NAGPPA stipulate the return of the collection to the nations, but Mr. Taylor, the last remaining member of the Taylor family, specified in his will that the museum return the items to their people. But no one has acted on either of those requirements."

"There was more than one nation involved?"

"Yes. The objects are from the Onondaga Nation and the Oneida Nation. Covid interfered with the return of the objects, but Mrs. Carlton wants to return the collection sometime this fall."

"I guess the director before Mrs. Carlton dragged his feet on the collection, right?"

Sara nodded. "I never met him, but I heard that at first he tried to pretend the collection never existed, then, he said it had been returned to the Taylor family and finally he refused to answer questions about the items. In the years after NAGPPA, there was some movement on Native American objects held in museums, libraries, colleges, and universities, but some of these collections were lost from records. When Mrs. Carlton stepped into the director's position five years ago, returning the collection was one of the first issues she addressed."

"Harold liked the old director from what he said today."

"Oh, of course. Francis was right. Harold is not fond of women in positions of power. Or of minorities either. He does like having young women around, however." Sara cleared her throat and set her wine glass on the table.

"You've had trouble with him, have you?"

"Nothing that hasn't been addressed."

I left to get the remainder of our wine and poured us each another half glass.

"So what's the issue now with the collection? Why is Mr. Powles so concerned?"

"Mr. Powles claims one of the pieces in the collection belongs to his family. He said the item was stolen from his relatives years ago. A member of Mr. Powles's family worked in the Taylor mansion as a housekeeper. She claimed she saw the item amidst the collection in Taylor's library. The Powles's family believed her, but when the family reported it to the authorities, there was no way to connect the theft with the Taylor family. And besides, no one was likely to believe a Native American woman telling a tale of a basket supposedly taken over a hundred years ago."

"But what did Mr. Taylor say about the basket? Do you think he stole it?"

"He said he bought a box of items at an auction and the basket was in it. So, theoretically, he owned it, part of his private collection."

"So why is Mr. Powles making his claim now?"

"Mrs. Carlton's announcement that the museum holds the Taylor collection, and it will be returned to the nations to which it originally belonged, alerted Mr. Powles's family that the basket is probably one of the objects we hold. It's his chance to reclaim his family's possession."

"Have you seen the collection?"

"No, so I have no idea what 'basket' he's referring to. I understand there are many in the collection. Mrs. Carlton told me there is a basket in the collection which was not designated in the Taylor collection inventory as belonging to either the Onondaga or the Oneida people. Mr. Powles contends that's the basket that was stolen many years ago. He wants it returned."

A knock at the door interrupted our conversation.

I popped off the couch. "I'll be back in a jiffy. I want to hear all of this."

I opened the door. On my front doorstep stood the man I loved, Zack Montgomery, and two women, one around his age, the other much younger.

"Zack. What a surprise. I didn't expect you back from your visit to your daughter until later this week. Come on in." I reached out and threw my arms around him, kissing his cheek. He drew back from my embrace. Odd for someone who had romped with me night after night in my bed.

"Uh, maybe I should come back later. You and Sara look as if you're in the middle of something."

"Oh, we are, but she can tell me later."

Sara smiled at Zack. "Hi, Zack. I know Gram is delighted to see you back so soon. I'll leave you to talk. Gram can call me later. And if she doesn't find the opportunity tonight," Sara winked at Zack, "we can chat on the way to our meeting tomorrow morning."

I was torn. The explanation for the trouble at the museum or a night in Zack's arms? But Zack came first. It had been that way since this past summer.

Sara slipped on her shoes and started out the door. "I'll walk home. It's only a few blocks."

"With your sore feet? No way."

"My feet feel fine now." Sara sounded eager to leave. She waved goodbye and closed the front door.

"Maybe I should give her a ride," said Zack.

The younger woman reached out and touched Zack's shoulder as if she was restraining him. "She looks young and healthy. I think she can hold out for a few blocks."

I thought her comment was insensitive and rude.

"I'm sorry. We've never met. I suppose Zack told you who I am. You must be Amy, his daughter."

"Amy, this is Maddie Sparks," Zack said.

"Zack talks a lot about you. He was so looking forward to visiting you. How nice that you came back with him." I gave her a half smile. I was surprised there was no sign of her husband, but I decided not to ask about him.

Well, that explained who she was, but who was the other woman?

Zack had taken off the Stetson hat he usually wore and was awkwardly turning it round and round in his hands.

"Uh, this is Mary Sanders, an old friend of my wife's. And mine, of course."

She stepped forward and held out her hand to shake mine, then stepped close to Zack, placing her hand on his arm. "We've known each other for ages, haven't we, Zackie?"

Zackie? She called him Zackie?

"That was my granddaughter, Sara, who just left. We both work at the Meadowbrook Museum. Well, I volunteer. She is an intern there. Zack, you should show them the museum. It's small, but we're immensely proud of our collections."

"I think we won't be staying here for long, so I'm not certain we'll have the time to do 'touristy' things." Mary made "touristy" sound like they would be attending a theme park. I hadn't liked Amy's dismissal of Sara very much and now I was beginning to feel the same animosity toward Mary. But maybe that was mostly due to her hand which continued to rest on Zack's arm in a too familiar way.

"So, then. Sara and I were just relaxing with some wine. Would you like a glass?" I turned toward the kitchen to fetch another bottle and three more glasses.

"We don't drink," said Mary.

I think my eyes must have bugged out at this pronouncement because I distinctly remember Zack and me having wine over dinner and a few cocktails on other occasions.

I shut my mouth which I realized was gaping open like a guppie facing off against a hungry bass. "I'll put on some tea then."

"I'll help." Zack extracted his arm from Mary's clutch, and he followed me over to the stove.

He lowered this voice. "I'm sorry about all this, Maddie."

"Okay, but I don't understand why you didn't let me know your daughter was returning with you from your visit to her in Seattle."

"It was a surprise to me also."

"But a wonderful one, right, Dad?" Amy had followed us into the kitchen area. "And there's more to come."

"Really?" I didn't like what I saw on her face. Not really a friendly smile, but more the kind of grin you'd expect from the proverbial cat who has swallowed the canary. And speaking of cats, where was my orange, furry friend? He was crazy in love with Zack, so I expected him to be rubbing his body around Zack's legs.

"Yeow!" The scream came from behind us in the living room, from Mary. "Get this beast away from me. He just attacked my leg."

Ah, there was Spike now, and from his reaction, he was not in favor of Mary's presence in the house. I smiled to myself. The cat has wonderful taste in people.

CHAPTER 3

"**B**AD NIGHT?" IT WAS SARA'S TURN to drive to the museum this morning. I slid into the passenger's side and fastened my seat belt.

I stared straight ahead as Sara drove away from my house and turned left onto the highway leading to Andrewsburg, the small village in which Meadowbrook Museum was located.

"I swear I thought I knew Zack, but don't you think he should have forewarned me with a call to tell me his daughter and one of his old friends were accompanying him back here from Seattle?"

"A surprise visit from his daughter. How about that? What's the problem?"

"Well, for one she hates me."

"Kind of strong words for someone you just met."

I told Sara what Amy said when Sara had left the house. "It was a snotty comment especially when I had told her we'd been on our feet all day long."

"She's probably nervous meeting you for the first time."

"Hah! No manners, that's what."

Sara ignored my comments. "And the other older woman with them?"

"Zack introduced her as an old friend, but there was something else there. I think she's an old flame, and Amy has set her up to replace her mother as Zack's wife-to-be."

"That's a lot to figure out from an initial meeting."

I shot Sara a pointed look. "You should have stayed. If you had, you'd be able to confirm what I found out simply by being in the same room with those two women."

"You may be right, Gram, but I hope you didn't say anything to them."

"Hey. You know me. Even if I'm right about what the daughter has in mind, and I am you know, I'm also smart enough to hold back until I can see what she has planned. Zack, like all men, isn't savvy to what's happening, and he won't believe me if I tell him. He has to discover this for himself."

"Didn't Zack tell her about his relationship with you?"

"Yes, of course."

"So this is an intentional interference on her part. I guess his daughter wasn't swayed by his affection for you."

"Obviously not."

We drove on in silence for a few minutes.

I turned in my seat to look at Sara. "And here's the clincher. He booked them into the bed and breakfast he stayed in this past summer when we were working on the Basset murder. And he's booked a room for himself there also."

"But I thought the two of you were staying together in your house."

"We have been. For the last two months."

"Did Amy know that?"

I nodded. "He told her. She brought Mary with her hoping she and Zack could rekindle a romance that ended over forty years ago." I reached into my purse and rummaged around for a tissue.

"You're not crying, are you, Gram?" she asked as I blew my nose.

"Seasonal allergies." I wiped my eyes. "And maybe a few tears. I think I love that man."

Sara pulled the car onto the side of the road and reached out for me. "Oh, Gram. I'm so sorry, but I've seen you and Zack together. He loves you too. You are made for each other. It just took the two of you longer to find each other than it does most people. Mary is the past."

"But his daughter is now. And she favors Mary. Otherwise why bring the woman here?"

"I guess you'll have to fight for the man."

I was sad and scared, but I was also angry. I did a final swipe of my nose and sat up straighter. "I'm good at fighting when I know I'm right."

A FEW OF THE SAME PEOPLE WHO had been present yesterday afternoon were already out in front holding their signs when Sara and I walked toward the entrance. They did not confront us when we came in, but I felt a bit jittery about the impact of their presence. Would visitors be put off by the crowd, turn around, and leave? And the news media was certain to get ahold of the story. They'd soon be outside too with reporters and cameras recording the event. Someone had once said any publicity was good, but I wasn't certain people in the area would agree, and who would want to have to pick their way through protestors and media folks to see our collections? We were a small museum, the smallest among a few others in the area who held better-known exhibits and more of them. People had a choice about which museum they would visit. Besides, if visitors wanted to see Native American work, the collection under question wouldn't be available for viewing.

As with yesterday, the crowd was quiet and respectful. Mr. Powles had joined them and nodded to Sara and me when we entered. He stepped forward and tapped her on the shoulder.

"You go on in, Gram. I need to talk to Mr. Powles."

I was surprised. I didn't know Sara and he knew each other before yesterday's encounter.

I took a seat at the table in the break room where Director Carlton had called a meeting of museum employees and volunteers. The expressions on the faces of the staff around the table told the same story: we were worried about what would come from having Powles' family members in front of the museum entrance.

Sara took a chair beside me at the table. "Later," she said when I raised a questioning eyebrow.

Mrs. Carlton entered the room accompanied by Graham, the head of the board of trustees. I'd never met the man before but had seen a picture of the board members which hung on the wall outside the entrance desk. He had thinning light brown hair and a low forehead.

I leaned over and whispered to Sara. "Board Director Graham. Doesn't he remind you of someone?"

At that moment Harold entered the room and grabbed the chair at the end of the table next to the one Mrs. Carlton had gestured for Graham to take.

Sara grimaced. "He's Harold's cousin. And I think they're cut from the same cheesy cloth."

Mrs. Carlton stood at the end of the table to address us.

"As you know Mr. Powles is requesting that when the museum returns the collection of artifacts we hold to the two nations claiming them, that we give him and his family the basket he claims is theirs. His small group is not federally recognized, and it has never petitioned to be, so we are not compelled by law to consider his claim. However, I do not think the museum should be the deciding party in this dispute. I think the two nations involved and Mr. Powles's family should work this out among themselves."

"How did Mr. Powles find out about the basket?" asked Sara.

Mrs. Carlton shrugged her shoulders. "The story is that one of his ancestors worked for the Taylor family and claimed the basket was in the Taylor collection purchased by Mr. Edmond Tayler at a sale. There are a number of baskets included in the collection willed to us by Mr. Taylor. Most of them have been designated as

Oneida or Onondaga in origin. I've been working with the collection for several months in preparation for returning it to the nations people, but I'm not expert enough to determine which basket may belong to Mr. Powles. Perhaps none of them, but he's adamant that it's among the collection."

"There must be some proof of his claim," I whispered to Sara.

"Has he offered any proof or is this just a wild claim on his part?" asked Mr. Graham.

"We're working on that," Mrs. Carlton said.

"Powles is a troublemaker. Always has been," shouted Harold.

"Let's not argue about this here," Mrs. Carlton said in a calm voice.

Mr. Graham stood. "My understanding is that the collection is made up of objects from the Oneida and Onondaga nations. No other. We need proof. If there is any proof."

"I discussed this last night when I met in an emergency session with the board. You were absent." Mrs. Carlton's tone of voice was sharp and cold.

"I had other important business," said Graham.

"Yes, well. As I told the board members, we need to gather the parties together to talk and make their cases. It's not our call."

"I assume you mean the two nations and Mr. Powles. Do you think that's wise?" Graham asked.

"The board agreed with me. This must be done soon so as not to delay the ceremony for returning the collection." Mrs. Carlton sounded determined to go ahead with such a meeting.

Murray, the security guard rushed into the room. "There are more people gathering outside. It appears some are against Mr. Powles's claim and want to confront his family."

Graham rose to his feet, a look of fear on his face. "We need to call in the state police to protect us."

"Us? Just who are the us?" asked Mrs. Carlton. "You're blowing this peaceful protest all out of proportion. I will handle this." She strode with purpose out of the room. All at the table except Mr. Graham and Harold followed her. I was certain others felt as I did.

If we showed we were all behind her, those gathered would see the approach she proposed to have the interested parties talk was reasonable.

At the front entrance, Mrs. Carlton stepped out the door and stood on the top step. Those in the crowd who had been shouting at one another fell silent and all eyes fastened on her.

"I'd like to talk with representatives from each of the parties gathered here. We will get nowhere in this if we continue to yell and argue. Come into my office and we'll confer." She gestured at the building and said loud enough for the members of the crowd to hear, "Please. We all want to do what's right."

Members of each of the groups began to talk among themselves. A man dressed in a faded denim shirt and jeans strode forward. A Rawhide strap holding a leather pouch was slung over his shoulder and across his chest. His eyes were deep brown as was his skin, his hair pure white.

"I will speak for the Oneida," he said.

"And I," said a woman with long black hair and eyes the color of hemlock bark, "speak for the Onondaga."

Mrs. Carlton nodded in welcome. "Please. Come in."

Mr. Powles stepped forward from the people who had made up the crowd yesterday. "I speak for my family."

Both the woman representing the Onondaga and the Oneida delegate exchanged a glance. With a frown on her face the woman said, "I am familiar with Mr. Powles, but he does not represent one of our nations. We hold no animosity toward him or his claim, but we want to see evidence that his claim is just. Do you have the right to your claim?"

Mr. Powles nodded. "My family does not mean to create difficulty nor to claim what belongs to your nations. We want only what is ours."

The leader of the Onondaga conferred with the other leader.

No one in the crowd said a word, but the tension hung in the air like a blanket of humidity before a rainstorm.

Both nation leaders signaled their agreement to confer by step-ping forward. Mr. Powles followed behind.

After a moment's hesitation, all three walked up the steps, down the hall and into Mrs. Carlton's office. I hadn't realized I was hold-ing my breath. I let it out in a rush of air and grabbed Sara's hand as she stood by me. When I looked into her eyes, I realized she was as tense as I.

The door to Mrs. Carlton's office closed.

"I hope that woman knows what's she doing," said Harold from behind me.

"I'm sure she does," said Sara. "These people respect her."

"Huh," said Harold. "I say box up the pieces, load them on a truck and get them out of here so we don't have to deal with them anymore. I don't understand what's so important about them anyway. They're just old pots, and belts of beads and baskets. Not worth much. And not even pretty."

Sara spun around. "You know nothing. Those objects have reli-gious and spiritual importance to the nation members."

"And it's the law," said Francis Marquis from the gift shop, "whether you like it or not. Thank goodness you're not in charge around here or we'd have tossed out anything not done by a European artist."

"Well, you're wrong, missy. I could go for a good Egyptian mummy or two. That would bring in traffic," Harold said with a sneer on his face.

I'd tolerated Harold's negative attitude for the two months I'd volunteered here, but no more. "Shut up, Harold. You're making a fool of yourself," I pushed past him to set up the entrance desk for patrons.

Sara followed me to the desk. In a low voice she said, "It's as if he's learned nothing in all the years he's volunteered here. Wouldn't it be nice if we could replace him with someone more sensitive and intelligent?"

"Like my friend, Jane. She'd love to volunteer here."

"Why don't you recommend her to Mrs. Carlton?"

"I will. Once all this has calmed down."

We opened the museum an hour later than the usual ten o'clock time. Word must have gotten out that something was going on at the museum because a group of curious onlookers had joined the gathering outside. None of these new folks acted interested in entering to see the exhibits. They were just lookie loonies who were joined several minutes later by media personnel from a local television station and newspaper reporters. I recognized one of the reporters, Agnes Danderfield, dressed in her signature red suit. She saw me through the windows of the front entry way, waved and then began to work her way through the crowd, microphone in hand followed by a photographer.

"I see Agnes is here," said Sara. "That can only mean trouble. If people weren't on edge before out there, they will be once Agnes's intrusive questioning works them up."

"I'm surprised the paper sent her here and that she writes stories that make the front page. I thought she only did that "About Town" column," I said.

"I like Agnes. She tells it like it is," said Harold who had walked up behind us.

"You would," I said.

"Now look here, Mrs. Sparks. You're new around here and don't understand how things work, and you've been rude to me, like today. I could talk to my cousin about you, and you'd be looking for someplace else to work." Harold had his say, turned on his heel and strode off, almost bumping into Mr. Powles as he and the Oneida and Onondaga representatives exited Mrs. Carlton's office. The look Harold gave Powles was filled with disgust. "Watch where you're going, you . . ."

But Harold didn't get the chance to finish what we all knew would be a racist remark because Mrs. Carlton cut in and stopped him with a stern look and "Harold," said in warning.

Was my position here in jeopardy because of Harold? I knew Mrs. Carlton didn't like the man, but he had been here for years, and his cousin was the board director. She might be forced to let me go.

Sara seemed to read my thoughts. "I don't think you need to worry. In fact, I'm not certain how long Harold will remain here."

Mrs. Carlton walked the nation reps and Mr. Powles out the door. Although none of the three leaders she'd met with looked happy about what was said in the meeting, they signaled to their constituents who, while not departing in their cars, took up a silent but peaceful vigil outside once again.

"Ms. Danderfield," called Mrs. Carlton, "I'd like a word, if you don't mind."

Mrs. Carlton knew just what she was doing, bringing the reporter to her office for a talk before Danderfield could create chaos where Carlton had smoothed over the waters. I wasn't certain what Carlton could say to dissuade Danderfield from aggravating everyone or from publishing a story filled with half-truths and outright lies, but if anyone could talk Agnes into a more reasonable state of mind, it was Carlton. She'd demonstrated in her meeting this morning with the nations and Mr. Powles how well she managed controversy and worked with differing points of view to prevent trouble from erupting.

After she and Agnes Danderfield talked in her office, Mrs. Carlton, aware that the peace she had managed might not hold for long and particularly if the crowd out front grew beyond the parties involved, called in two part-time security guards, one to station himself just inside the entrance, the other outside the front door. The outside guard had the advantage of judging the tenor of the crowd and hearing what comments were being made. Like Mrs. Carlton, I was certain the Onondaga and Oneida folks gathered outside would not be the source of any difficulties that developed. Their representatives appeared to have been satisfied with what Mrs. Carlton proposed and had persuaded their people of the wisdom of her approach. Mr. Powles appeared to have reassured his family also. If tempers flared and trouble began, I knew it would be the result of comments made by the curious who came to see how the "Indians" would manage the situation and who might provoke physical confrontation.

Because Sara was the most senior of the interns, Mrs. Carlton had called her into her office to let her know she had managed to set up a series of meetings where the two nations and Powles's family would talk further about the basket and work out a solution to the situation.

Sara told me about the meetings as we drove home after a long tense day. "I know everyone wants this to happen overnight, but Mrs. Carlton is taking it slow to make certain everyone is heard. She's a wonderful leader for our museum. I admire her patience, intelligence and control."

I was eager to get home, put up my feet, make myself a martini and call Zack whom I'd not heard from since yesterday.

"Look who's here," Sara said as she pulled up in front of my house. "I won't come in. I know the two of you have lots to talk about."

Zack's car sat in front of my house.

I rushed into the house hoping he would spend the evening with me and perhaps stay the night. Unfortunately, Zack had other plans. He had a key to the house, so I wasn't surprised to find him upstairs in the room we had shared for the last two months. His suitcase was open on the bed.

"Maddie."

"You think you'll need all your clothes for your stay at the B and B with your daughter and, uh, what was her name?" I tried to keep the sarcasm from my voice without luck.

"Mary."

"Yes. Mary."

"I'm sorry about this, Maddie, but my staying with you is really upsetting my daughter. She's not ready for this relationship."

Why would he not meet my gaze? "I guess she's not the only one."

I wanted him to deny it, wanted him to say he'd tell her how he felt about me, wanted him to take me in his arms. Instead he closed his suitcase, touched me on the arm as we walked out of the room and headed down the stairs.

I followed him. Spike sat at the bottom of the stairs, gazed up at Zack and must have seen something in his eyes that he didn't like for Spike hissed at him as Zack opened the front door and walked out.

Chapter 4

Through the front window, I watched Zack get into his car and drive off. If he thought I would run after him and stop him, he was mistaken. I wouldn't beg—not Maddie Sparks. I had learned my lesson about men the hard way, through a bad marriage to a bad man. If Zack wasn't willing to fight for me, he wasn't worth my time.

Spike came over to me and rubbed his body against my legs.

"You're on my side, aren't you?"

Spike looked up at me with his big, round, yellow eyes and meowed. I wasn't certain if he was agreeing with me or just wanted his food bowl filled, but since it was just the cat and me now, I got his dry food out and poured some into his bowl. Usually it's easier to please a man than it is a cat, but I wasn't going to alienate Spike by ignoring his needs.

He gobbled down his food, looked up at me and then vomited it onto the kitchen floor.

"Did Zack upset your tummy?" I asked.

The cat blinked at me and turned his gaze to the couch. I picked him up and sat, rubbing his head and trying to comfort him. Soon he began to purr. I kissed him on his fluffy head which was oddly wet. Oh, rats! I was crying and it wasn't because my cat had puked his food all over. It was that I had a man problem. I thought I knew Zack, that our relationship was solid, but family came first. I know that. If his daughter wanted me out of his life, he'd have to figure out if that was what he wanted. Unfortunately, the next move in our relationship was his, and I hated not being in control.

Sara had told me when she dropped me off today that on Wednesday the representatives from the two nations and Mr. Powles were scheduled to meet in Carlton's office to discuss again the issue of the collection and especially the disposition of the basket Mr. Powles claimed belonged to his family. Mrs. Carlton hoped whatever evidence of ownership provided by Mr. Powles would be definitive. Tomorrow was Wednesday, the day I had the morning off from volunteering at the museum. Wednesday mornings and late afternoons after I left the museum were the hours I devoted to writing. Sara would drive herself to work tomorrow, and I would drive in later in the afternoon.

In a way I was happy to not be working tomorrow morning, not only because I needed to write but the crowd outside, while peaceful so far, made me anxious, worried something might erupt. I was curious about the meeting, however. Sara would tell me what happened, I was sure. I needed the morning to do laundry and go to the market to get some supplies like bread, sugar and flour. I was not a woman who baked often, but when something upset me, I sometimes took my mind off my worries by making chocolate chip cookies.

After two nonproductive hours at my computer, I made myself a peanut butter sandwich for dinner and accompanied it with a vodka martini, one of my wicked pleasures. As I suspected, Spike came around from his barfing bit with no side effects. I fed him a light supper of tuna delight, and the two of us shared our meal by watching the news on television after which I went to my office and sat in front of my computer screen for another hour or more writing only one sentence of my current work. I didn't feel like creating a passionate scene between two lovers when my lover in real life had dumped me. I turned off the computer, and Spike and I went upstairs, me to read a thriller novel, him to jump on the end of the bed and snuggle next to my feet.

I set my alarm for early the next morning so I could do my shopping and baking, turned off my light around ten o'clock and moved Spike off my feet sometime in the morning hours. He always made them too hot with his warm body temperature, something I couldn't tolerate in the warmer months, but a sleeping position I would appreciate come winter.

I awoke to the alarm and reached over to turn it off, but I couldn't silence it. I then realized it was my phone ringing. I looked at the clock. It read seven in the morning.

"Maddie," said a male voice over the phone.

"Zack?" I tried to produce enough ice in my voice to freeze the phone line, but he continued.

"I want to apologize for yesterday."

I said nothing.

"Are you there?"

"Yes." I tried for icier.

"I know you're angry and you have a right to be. We need to talk. Face to face. I want to explain what is happening."

"Really, no explanation necessary. Your actions yesterday said it all. And I don't have time to talk with you. I'm busy today."

"Busy?"

"Yes. There's my afternoon at the museum. And I'm baking this morning."

I shouldn't have said that. It gave too much away to a man who knew me well.

"I've upset you I know, but I didn't have time to go into detail yesterday. My daughter was waiting for me back at the B and B. Let's do dinner tonight."

"Won't your daughter expect you to dine with her and Mary?"

"I told Amy last night that I wanted to get together with you. If you'll have me, that is."

My heart did a little bounce of happiness, but I tried to control my response. "Okay, but don't expect me to forgive what you did so easily."

He said he'd pick me up at seven. When I put down the receiver, I no longer felt like baking this morning. I turned over and slept another hour.

WHEN I WASN'T WORKING AT THE MUSEUM, other volunteers filled in. Today, Greta Markowitz, a retired schoolteacher, sat at the desk. She wore a sweater in shades of green and gold signaling fall on its way and beckoned me to step inside the plastic barrier around the entrance desk for a private word. "Your granddaughter is downstairs in the break room, and she's upset. I'll remain here to cover for you. I think you should see if you can do anything."

"What's going on?" I tossed my satchel under the desk.

"Well, you name it. About everything today."

"Did the crowd outside do something? Is that what has upset Sara?"

"I don't think so. They've been pretty quiet this morning."

I ran down the hall to the steps to the lower level. When I entered the breakroom Sara sat with her elbows on the table, face down in her hands. She looked up at me and I could see her eyes were red from crying.

"What happened/"

"I'm just so mad, that's all."

"Mad. You look like you've been sobbing."

"Well, I'm sobbing mad." She nodded toward the door to the hallway. "Close the door, would you?"

I took the chair next to her and pulled her to me. "Tell me."

"It's that old goat, Harold. I told him and told him not to stand so close to me, but he's ignored me, gives me one of his lascivious smiles. He did it again this morning, so I pushed him away. Now he says he's going to file assault charges against me. He's talking to Mrs. Carlton now. I know I lost my temper. I know I never should have touched him, but it was just a little shove although he acted as if I'd hit him. I didn't. I just wanted him to get away from me."

"Did anyone see the encounter?"

"No. I don't think so. All the women who work here have encountered Harold's violation of personal space. I'd even bet he's gone farther than that with a few of them."

"Hasn't anyone told Mrs. Carlton about him?"

"I'm sure they have. I said something once to her, but when she asked if I wanted to file a formal complaint, I said no. She wasn't surprised at Harold's behavior and said she'd take care of it. I planned to talk with her again, but now it's too late." Sara pounded her fist on the table. "The pig."

She was furious. Well, good for her. At least she wasn't blaming herself for what Harold had done.

"Maybe it's not too late. Let me talk with some of the women here and see what I find out. If others complained about him, Mrs. Carlton must have kept a record. She might bring it to the board of director's attention, and they can act." I also suspected Mrs. Carlton was observant enough to have seen Harold's behavior toward the female employees.

"But you know he's related to Mr. Graham, the board director. Regardless of what any of us say, Graham won't reprimand Harold."

"Well, we'll see about that. Let me handle this for now."

Sara leaned over and hugged me. "Thanks, Gram. This is more than Mrs. Carlton needs to deal with right now. I think the talks with the two nations and Mr. Powles did not go well. They broke off the meeting after half an hour."

Before we could get up from the table, we heard a pounding coming from the direction of the side entrance nearest the break room.

"Wait here," I said to Sara.

I ran out of the room and down the hallway. Through the glass door I could see several people, angry looks on their faces, shouting and hitting their fists against the door.

"Go to the front entrance if you want admittance," I said, but they continued to shout and pound on the door. One of them took a placard he was carrying and tried to break the glass. Lucky, it was too thick to give.

I retreated from the door and ran back to the break room. Sara wasn't there.

"Sara!"

"Here." Sara stood in the main hallway at the foot of the stairs. I ran to join her, then turned, closed and locked the door where the hall met the main corridor.

"Mrs. Carlton called to me from upstairs. She wants everyone to get to the west entrance and leave through the doors there." Sara grabbed my hand, and we fled across the open corridor into the hallway leading toward the other entrance at the lower level. This exit from the building was less well-used than the one near the breakroom. It led onto a small patio area overlooking the stream that flowed behind the museum. In warm weather, the employees used the picnic table there for their lunch and breaks.

As we fled past the two curved staircases leading upstairs, Sara and I called to the employees working on the main floor, Greta at the desk and Francis in the gift shop. I could see several people from the second and third floors descending the main staircase.

The guard Murray along with the two other guards who worked the upper floors were with the group. Murray was talking on his walkie-talkie.

"There are no visitors on any of the floors, ma'am. All our staff are with me, and I'll get them to safety." Murray spoke with calm and authority, and I was happy for his presence.

He descended the stairs and herded us toward the west entrance, but a crowd of people was already outside, and in an ugly mood. They beat their fists against the door. Several rocks hit the glass in the door, but it, too, was reinforced and didn't break.

"Where is Mrs. Carlton?" I asked Murray.

"She's at the main entrance trying to contact their leaders to get them to speak to the people here from their nations. Maybe they can talk some sense into the crowds."

"Wasn't Harold with her in her office just now?" Sara asked. "So where is he? Outside?"

I put my hand over my mouth to hide my smile. "Oh, I doubt that. I don't see Harold as the kind of man who would willingly confront a mob of unhappy people."

"Well, I need to account for everyone," said Murray. He ran back upstairs. In a few minutes he returned. "Mrs. Carlton is talking to the leaders out front including Mr. Powles. But I can't find Harold."

"Did you try under Mrs. Carlton's desk?" said Francis with a sneer on her face.

"I thought I saw him out of the corner of my eye following us toward the west exit, but he's not here now," said Sara.

I could still hear shouts coming from the other side of the building behind the door I had closed as Sara and I retreated from the breakroom. I looked down that hallway from which we had come.

"A minute." I held up my finger and retreated back down the hall. I looked up at the sign and walked into the room to my left.

"You can come out now, Harold." There was silence from within. "I can hear you breathing, Harold." *Nothing.* "And please put down your weapon, will you?" I waited. The stall door at the farthest end of the Ladies Room slowly opened. Harold stepped out, a heavy sword in his hands.

"Put it down, Harold. Someone could get hurt." I tried to keep the condescension out of my voice.

Murray came up behind me. "How did you know he was here?" I rolled my eyes.

"Oh, heh. I get it. But the sword?"

"I noticed it was missing from the wall in the lower main corridor." I said.

I thought he was going to hand Murray the weapon, but instead Harold grabbed ahold of me and brandished the sword at Murray.

"Out of my way. I can deal with this." Using me as his shield, Harold put his hand around my neck and walked me back out into the hallway. I punched him in the ribs with my elbow and he let go of me, but then ran toward the main stairs and up the lefthand staircase. Murray and I rushed after him.

Mrs. Carlton stood at the top of the stairs.

"Everything is okay, Harold," she said in a soothing voice.

Looking up the staircase I could see through the entranceway that the crowd there had quieted. Harold pounded toward the entrance, sword at the ready, and confronted Mr. Powles just outside.

"Out of my way or I'll take off your head." Harold waved the sword in front of him.

Mr. Powles gestured him past with a flourish of his hand and almost a cavalier's bow, then stuck out his foot and tripped him. Harold fell at the feet of the two nation leaders. The sword flew from his hand and banged harmlessly on the sidewalk.

"I hope you haven't ruined one of exhibits, Harold," said Mrs. Carlton with a straight face, but I could see one side of her lips twitch.

CHAPTER 5

I FOUND IT EXHAUSTING TO GET IN MY CAR and drive the few
miles home. Who knew volunteering at a local museum could
be so filled with unexpected disruptions? Spike greeted me at the
door with a concerned look on his furry face as if he knew how
difficult my day had been. When I plopped down on the couch, he
joined me and bumped his fuzzy butt against my hip and made his
eyes big and round, doing his "aren't I cute" act.

I needed to go upstairs and take a shower to get ready for my
date with Zack, but all I wanted to do was crawl into my bed,
curl up (like Spike) and sleep until next week sometime. Mrs.
Carlton had calmed down everyone outside the building who
were riled up about the collection. My admiration for her had
increased tenfold after I saw her in action once again with upset
demonstrators. What had gone from a quiet, peaceful gathering
of people asking that their needs be addressed had erupted in a
few days into an unpleasant and potentially dangerous situation.
Mrs. Carlton had prevented that from occurring and had pro-
tected her employees as well as listened respectfully to the people trying to gain access to the museum. Afterwards, she told us
the crowd who yelled and tried to break into the museum wasn't
from the Native American groups concerned about the return of

the collection, but rather made up of outside people interested in making trouble and gaining publicity. Ah, I thought to myself, white folks, who knew little about the Native American issues. I wish we did better to educate ourselves about the culture and history of the nations whose land we took.

I laid my head back on one of the cushions, slipped off my shoes and lifted my legs and feet onto the couch. Spike's purring soothed not only him, but me and the next thing I heard was a knock on my door. I awoke confused about where I was for a moment. Then I realized I had fallen asleep on the couch and had only an hour or so to get ready for my date with Zack.

I ran to the door and threw it open to Zack on my doorstep, a bouquet of flowers in one hand and a large shopping bag in the other.

"I'm so sorry, Zack. I lost track of time. The day . . ."

"I heard on the news. Your day has been horrible. I figured you wouldn't be up to going out, so I brought dinner." He held up the bag and I smelled something delightful emanating from it.

Spike jumped off the couch and came over to us.

"Hiya, buddy," said Zack. "You miss me?"

Spike didn't hiss at him, but neither did he greet Zack with his usual body figure eight around his legs. He looked up at Zack and meowed.

"Whatever you have in that bag has grabbed his interest."

"Chinese."

"You're a lifesaver. I'll make some tea to go along with it."

We sat at the kitchen table and ate. Zack, realizing that he had some repairs to make on his relationship with Spike as well as with me, dropped morsels onto the floor where Spike gobbled them up.

"Well, it appears I know how to win back a cat's affection." Zack reached down and patted Spike's head.

"I may not be so easy," I said.

"I know, but I also know you're reasonable and compassionate woman, Maddie. Hear me out, would you?"

I nodded. "Let's begin by tidying up. I'll make some decaf and we can talk in the living room."

We tossed the take-out cartons and napkins in the trash and put our teacups in the dishwasher. I started the coffee. Zack took my hand and led me to the couch. His touch sent tingles up my arm. Did he know what he did to me? He sat on the couch. I scooted as far away from him as I could. I wasn't about to give into anything amorous. He'd hurt me and angered me. He seemed to understand what I was experiencing because he withdrew the hand he had extended to touch mine.

"I'm worried about my daughter," he said.

"And she's worried about me."

"I think she's more worried about me. She's terrified she'll lose her father. She already lost her mother three years ago to cancer. She's my only child. She and my wife were remarkably close. Amy did not deal with her grief well. She ran off to Seattle right after the funeral as if she could flee from the reality of not having her mother. Amy and I have always loved each other, but I could not replace her mother in her heart. No one can." Zack paused to clear his throat. I could see tears well up in his eyes.

"I'm so sorry for both of you. I knew your wife died, but I didn't know how devastated your daughter was by her mother's death."

"There's more. While she was in Seattle, she met some people who got her into drugs. She married one of them, although the marriage didn't last more than a few months. When I heard about what had happened, I flew out there to be with her, but she convinced me after she got clean that she had found a job and made new friends. That she was doing fine. I believed her."

"But she wasn't fine?"

He shook his head. "She started using again, went back into rehab and called me a few weeks ago. That's why I flew out there last week. Again she insisted she was fine and told me she had high hopes for a new life." Zack paused and ran his hands through his hair. "But I'm not sure if she's as happy as she says she is. 'I've got a surprise for you, Daddy,' she said on the phone. And when I got to the airport, there she was with Mary. 'Look who's here.' I was in shock, but glad to see Amy and Mary, my old friend, at her side."

"But it wasn't that easy, was it?"

"I told Amy all about you. She would simply smile at me and say, 'We'll see.' I didn't want to push her, so I let it go."

"But now you understand what she plans her 'new life' to be. Mary, whom she's known since she was a kid and who she knows loved both you and her mother, will become her new mother and you will be her father. Right?"

"I'm not sure I get it. Why is she pushing Mary on me when she knows I care for you?"

"Because your daughter feels comforted by the familiar. She doesn't really want a "New Life." She wants her old life with someone she loves and trusts as her mother. I'm a stranger to her."

"But I love you."

"Amy doesn't love me."

"She doesn't know you yet. Maybe small doses of you and she'll come around." There was so much hope in his voice that I didn't want to dissuade him from what he was thinking and planning, but Amy needed much more than "small doses" of me. She needed real help that only competent intervention could give her.

"So here's what we'll do." Zack forged ahead with his plan for lunches, movies, picnics so Amy could get to know me.

Finally, I reached out and placed my fingers on his mouth to stop the flow of words. "What about Mary?"

"What do you mean?" It was almost as if Zack had forgotten about Mary altogether.

"Amy talked Mary into coming here, but do you think Mary understood the relationship you and I have? I doubt Amy told her I was anything but a friend."

"She knew we were living together."

"Did she? Or did she believe we were sleeping together, just another randy, lonely pair of seniors."

Zack's mouth dropped open. "I don't . . . I'm sure Mary understands that . . ."

"Why should she? You came dashing back here the next day, grabbed your clothes and moved into the B and B. That doesn't spell commitment between us, does it?"

Zack ran his hand through his hair. "What do I do? My daughter needs me."

"Your daughter may need more than you."

Zack jumped up from the couch. "She's had help. Lots of it."

"Drug addiction is more than getting off the drugs. You know that because you've seen it in your work. It's a lifelong issue. I think you know what you need to do, and I'm not the person to tell you what steps you should take. I'm not even certain I'm the person you should be talking to right now."

"Who then if not you? Maddie. I love you."

"I love you too."

I got off the couch and walked into my office to find my address book. Yes, being an old-fashioned gal, I kept an old-fashioned address book with names, telephone numbers and addresses written inside. I flipped through it and jotted down a name on a sticky pad.

"Here." I held out the yellow note to Zack. "This may be the place to start. Ask for John Tennent. He's an old friend of mine."

"'Project 400.' I've heard of them I think."

"Of course you have. I'm certain in your years as county sheriff in the neighboring county you and your officers dealt with them on more than one occasion. They're a drug counseling service."

"So. Help for Amy, but what about for Mary, as you pointed out, and me?"

"John will provide you with all resources the three of you will need. Use him. Use what he recommends."

"What about us?"

"We'll come through this. You'll see."

Zack left soon after we had our coffee. Neither he nor I knew what "we" would become, but it was clear Zack had to take care of his daughter. She needed him. I loved him but I had the strength to get on with my life until Zack and I decided what we could have together. Amy had only begun the emotional work she needed to accomplish, and she should have her father at her side. I knew that. Oh, drat. I sometimes hated what life had made me: a strong, level-headed woman.

I ROLLED OUT OF BED THURSDAY MORNING feeling as if I had a bad hangover. I hadn't had anything to drink, but serious relationship issues can do that to someone—give you a headache and make your bones ache. Add the possible loss of love to the aging process and I felt as if my body creaked with each step I took.

Sara picked me up, and we sped off to the museum. Other than "good morning" I said nothing to her about last night.

"Do you want to talk about it?" she asked.

"Maybe later."

"So," she said, as we turned onto the highway leading to the museum, "what will today bring, do you think?"

"More of the same. Why do people want to interfere with what isn't their business?" I said, referring to those in the crowd who were not nation members but who liked stirring the pot outside yesterday.

"I guess some don't understand how important it is for nation members to have their cultural, spiritual and religious items returned to them. And some of the items might be recognized as belonging to a particular family, items that had been handed down for generations and then, for unknown reasons, disappeared and found their way into the Taylor family collection."

"Like my grandfather's glass decanter which I keep on my liquor cabinet. I'd be furious if someone took it and told me I couldn't have it, that it should be placed on display in some museum somewhere."

Sara pulled into the drive that led up to the museum. There was a small gathering of people there, and they appeared to be nations members. Mr. Powles stood nearby and nodded at us as Sara drove the car around the museum's drive to an employee parking area behind the building.

"You know him well, don't you? You said you'd tell me about him, but we haven't had the time to talk about it." I didn't want to push Sara into talking about something she wasn't ready to discuss, but she had skirted this issue before. It was time to talk.

Sara pulled the car into a parking space and shut off the engine, then turned to me. "He's the father of the man I hope one day to marry."

I took a deep breath. "Oh."

Sara laughed. "Why Gram, I'm surprised you don't have more to say. You aren't one to hold back your words."

"I don't know what to say. I don't know the young man to whom you refer."

"That's so sweet and wise of you to say, Gram, but let it out. I'm sure you have more to say."

"Not me."

"Say it, Gram."

"Do your parents know?"

"There it is. And no, they don't. They know I've met someone. Leonard is coming to dinner on Sunday."

"That will be nice."

"Do you want to come, too? You can meet him."

I shook my head. "Let's not overwhelm him with the 'meet the family thing.'"

"Like I said, Gram. You are so 'sweet and kind.'"

My oldest son Geoffrey and his wife Abigail were wonderful people and terrific parents to their only child, Sara. They had raised her to be broad-minded, generous and accepting of people. Yet I worried that neither my son nor his wife was quite ready for their daughter's chosen to be the son of as public and outspoken an activist as Mr. Powles. Sara shot me a look that said it all: she wanted me there on Sunday in case she needed ammunition to plead her case with Leonard; but there were more than Sara's parents to consider. How would Mr. Powles and his family feel about Sara? And if the museum's decision about the basket went against the family claims, how would the family feel about Sara as someone associated with the museum?

"Let me think about this," I said. "We can talk during our coffee break."

The morning rolled by with no trouble from the crowd that had gathered outside. I worried that those who had created trouble yesterday would return this afternoon. The two nation delegates and Mr. Powles were again to meet with Mrs. Carlton in the afternoon. Ellie, one of our high school volunteers would spell me at the entrance desk around ten. We had several high school students who worked a few hours each week. Part of their responsibilities included filling in for volunteers and employees taking coffee breaks. Sara came by the desk to go with me to the break room.

"Ellie not here yet?" said Sara.

"She will be soon. Ellie was in the gift shop while Francis took her break. I just saw Francis return, so Ellie should be here soon. You go on ahead."

"Oh. I almost forgot. I've got a treat for you. Mom baked yesterday. Blueberry muffins." Sara held up a container and headed down the stairs.

I saw Ellie leave the shop and head into the women's room on this floor. When she came out, she saw another intern, Jeremy Westin, heading down the hallway toward an exhibit room across from the gift shop. He was a handsome young man, blue-eyed and blonde, over six feet tall and carried an air of certainty about him.

"Jeremy!" she called.

He turned and let her catch up with him.

I watched the two of them together. Everyone in the museum knew Ellie had a crush on Jeremy, and everyone knew Jeremy had a crush on my granddaughter, Sara. Ellie said something to Jeremy and then reached out and touched his arm. He shrugged her hand away, spun on his heel and continued into the exhibit room. I knew

Sara had gone out on a few dates with Jeremy last year, but she told me she wasn't interested in him and had said no to another date. I wondered how let down he was by her refusal.

Ellie looked down at her feet for a few minutes, seemed to gather herself together and headed my way.

Hoping to lift her spirits, I said, "If there are any muffins left, I'll bring you one back from break."

"Oh, yummy." Ellie was a high school senior this fall. She wore her long brown hair in a braid down her back. Her eyes were chocolate brown and she always wore a smile. She was a very pleasant young woman who had expressed an interest in a program in museum studies—or was it Sara she was emulating? Jeremy had applied to a museum program also.

I almost ran down the stairs, eager to get to the promised muffins. Abigail was quite a baker, and her muffins were sweet and tangy with the taste of fresh blueberries in every bite.

"I've got the tea." I held up my thermos and called to Sara who was standing in the doorway of the break room. I was surprised she wasn't already in the room.

She didn't turn at the sound of my voice. "What's wrong?" I asked.

Finally, she did a half turn and pointed into the break room. "It's Mrs. Carlton. I think she needs help."

Mrs. Carlton lay on her back on the floor in the middle of the room. The sword Harold had brandished yesterday stuck out of her chest and blood had seeped onto her clothing and the floor where she lay. I gently pushed Sara back from the door.

"Call the police," I said, "and keep everyone out of here."

"What about . . .?" Sara pointed to the tall figure standing on the far side of the break table.

"Just do as I say, Sara."

"Mr. Powles. What are you doing here?" I asked.

"Not what you might think," he answered.

CHAPTER 6

"I DIDN'T KILL HER," HE SAID.
But there was blood on the front of his shirt and on his hands. He looked down at himself. "I tried to help her."

"We both need to stay where we are and not touch anything." I felt uncomfortable standing in the room with Mr. Powles because, if he had killed Mrs. Carlton, I stood in the way of his leaving the room. I had put myself in his path.

"I'll wait then." He looked again at Mrs. Carlton's body, a look of sorrow on his face. He then turned to stare at the artwork on the far wall.

Our museum guard Murray rushed into the room with Sara at his heels. He knelt by Mrs. Carlton and felt for a pulse, a futile effort considering all the blood on her clothes and the floor.

"Did either you or Sara touch the body?" asked Murray. He didn't ask Mr. Powles the same question assuming, I guessed, that the blood on Powles' shirtfront meant he was responsible for her death.

How did Mr. Powles get into the museum, I wondered? As if reading my mind, he turned to me. "Mrs. Carlton let me in through the side entrance."

Did she? Should I believe him?

"I told her yesterday I had proof the basket belonged to my family. She asked I show the evidence to her before the meeting of the two nations leaders, me and her this afternoon."

What was this proof and where was it now? I opened my mouth to ask Mr. Powles but he turned his back on me. Our conversation was over.

Murray stepped in. "I want both of you out of the room. I called the sheriff's department when Sara told me how she found Mrs. Carlton. They will be here soon."

Sara started across the room toward Mr. Powles, then apparently thought better of it. She followed me out the door. Board Director Graham and Harold stood in the hallway along with Jeremy and other people, most likely visitors to the museum.

"Mr. Graham," said Sara. "I'd didn't expect you here."

"Mrs. Carlton asked me to sit in on the meeting with the nations people." He glanced into the room over Murray's shoulder. "And Mr. Powles."

Murray blocked the doorway to the room. "Let's everyone step back."

Looking up the open staircase, I spied museum personnel lining the banister and peering down at us. Sara climbed the stairs and called to the second-floor guard to escort any visitors into the corridor outside the gift shop where there were a few benches where people could rest. I followed her up to the first floor.

"And say nothing to anyone about what has happened, either people in here or anyone outside in the crowd," she said to the guard.

"Good thinking, my dear," I said, patting her shoulder. "The authorities will want to interview everyone here, but what about those outside?"

"I can't see how anyone there could have gotten in the museum without passing you or Ellie at the desk. Besides, there are cameras out there recording any activity." Sara had taken charge of the situation. I was proud of how calm and authoritative she was despite having discovered Mrs. Carlton's body. Well, after Mr. Powles did. Or the murderer. Were they one in the same?

Many questions about Mrs. Carlton's murder whirled around in my head. It was not my job to find out what happened and yet curiosity drew my mind back to the scene of the director's body and the presence of Mr. Powles next to it.

I heard sirens, and several sheriff's vehicles pulled up in front of the museum's main entrance. A woman wearing the brown uniform and wide-brimmed hat of the sheriff's department stepped from the first car.

"Maddie," said Anita Burroughs, our county sheriff. She was a tall, lean woman with short blonde hair. "What are you doing here?"

"I'm a volunteer. I work at the front desk. Murray, our head guard will take you downstairs to, uh, the scene." I was going to say, "the body," but that felt so cold.

Anita nodded and she and her uniformed deputies followed.

Anita had been sheriff only since this summer when the county board had appointed her to the position until an election could be held this November to fill the position. I'd heard she was running, and I hoped she would be elected. She'd demonstrated her ability and competence when she brought in the killer of a village resident this past summer. Before her appointment to the office, Zack had been interim sheriff. I'd asked him later this summer if he wanted to run for the position, but he said, "I'm retired, and I'd like to keep it that way." I was delighted at his response since it meant we could spend more time together. Now, however, that plan was on hold.

After several minutes, Anita reappeared, leading Mr. Powles in handcuffs. An officer put him in the back of a sheriff's car, and they sped off.

"That man is going to need a good lawyer," Anita whispered to me and gave me a pointed look. I sighed and extracted my cellphone from my pocket.

"Richard," I said, when my youngest son answered my call, "I've got a case for you."

Richard, my youngest son was a defense lawyer, and the two of us had been in a similar situation only months before. Then I had called him to defend his brother, Sara's father, on a murder charge.

"Mom. Good to hear your voice but why does it have to be because you want me to take on something legal that you've got your fingers into? Why not, a 'Hi, son. How about dinner?'"

"Because you're always too busy for dinner. And I don't have my fingers into anything. It's really a museum issue."

"Is it? Hmmm. Here I thought you volunteering at the museum would mean issues of a criminal matter wouldn't be on your radar. I think the rest of the family thought that also. Just, you and a bunch of art and, Zack, of course." I heard Richard chuckle.

"Well, it is a museum thing. It's murder." I explained to him what I knew of how Mr. Powles was connected to Mrs. Carlton's murder.

"Maybe he already has in mind someone to represent him."

"Maybe, but given the volatile situation here, he's going to need the best. That's you, of course."

"I'd say because you're my mother that you're biased, but, yes, I am the best." He said this not in a bragging tone but in a realistic manner. My son called it as he knew it to be.

"I'll see what I can find out and let you know if your services might be needed. Anita thought so."

There was silence on the other end of the line. Richard and Anita had dated before she married, but since she was now divorced, I thought the two of them were once more an item, but perhaps not. I dared not ask him for fear he would think me an interfering mother, which, of course, I was.

"Let me know, but I have to tell you my schedule is packed."

Sara came up to me as I finished the call. "Was that Uncle Richard?"

"Yes."

"And is he willing to represent Mr. Powles?"

"Mr. Powles has to want him as his legal representative," I said.

"That could be a problem. I heard him say he already had the best representation."

"Someone from one of the nations or a family member? Who could that be?" I asked.

"He said he'd be representing himself."

I groaned. That was a poor plan. "You must talk to his son and have Leonard convince his father of how foolish that would be."

"I will. I'll call him now." Sara walked several steps away and put her cell to her ear, waited for a minute and then shook her head.

Anita's officers began to question everyone in the museum, staff and visitors. Anita talked to Sara and me first and let us go home soon after.

"Did you get ahold of Leonard?" I asked Sara as we walked to the parking area behind the museum.

She shook her head. "He's working on his MA in accounting at the university. He's probably in classes all afternoon, but I'll keep calling and drop by his apartment. He should be there soon."

"How about his mother and other family members?"

"I'll ask Leonard. He should be the one to tell other family members, don't you think?"

"Yes, of course. And he'll want to visit his father as soon as possible. And he should. Someone needs to talk sense into the man. Representing himself if he's accused of murder? Only an idiot does that."

"Or someone who doesn't trust the justice system and white lawyers. Like Mr. Powles."

Given the history of how Native Americans had been dealt with historically by treaties which removed their land, by government agencies and other white dominated groups, he had reason to be distrustful.

"Can you persuade Leonard that your uncle will fight for his father with the same energy and attention that he would anyone, or does Leonard share his father's mistrust?"

"I think Leonard has reservations about white people, but, if we can persuade Richard to meet with Leonard and Leonard can see how dedicated Richard is and how unbiased, maybe Richard can convince him his father needs an experienced lawyer."

"On the surface it looks bad for Mr. Powles He was in the room with Mrs. Carlton and no one else was there, well, no one we knew of. The district attorney will believe he was the murderer. Richard will have to mount a convincing case for someone else having killed her. That means Richard will need some seasoned investigators."

"I can think of one person who fits that description," said Sara, throwing me a cautious look.

I also knew of a person who could ferret out the truth about Carlton's murder, but he was too busy trying to save his daughter. My chest heaved in a deep sigh. I remembered how well Zack and I worked together this past summer to track down a killer. I didn't have the experience Zack had, but I had proved myself to be intuitive as well as logical, putting together clues that pointed toward the identity of the murderer. Zack and I made an effective team. Would we ever work together again? Would we ever be able to be together as we had been this summer, not merely an investigative team, but also lovers who cared deeply about each other?

"Gram? Where did you go? You seemed to wander off in your thoughts." Sara touched my arm and brought me back to the present.

"Sorry. Find Leonard and I'll talk again to Richard. Leonard might already have heard about his father and is on the way to the jail to see him."

We stood together in the parking lot next to Sara's car. She tried again to connect with Leonard. She smiled and held up her finger. "Got him. Leonard? Oh. Yes, of course. I'll meet you there." She ended the call. "He's on his way to the jail now. Someone from the family was at the museum this afternoon and came to the campus to meet him on his way out of his last class of the day."

"You go on now. I'm going to nose around here for a while. See what I can find out."

"But you need a ride home."

"I'll wait for Ellie."

Sara cocked one eyebrow and looked at me. "The authorities will not let you back in the building, not even Anita, despite being your friend. Her duties come first."

"I know that, but I want to casually hang around. I might hear something useful. I'll tell the officer stationed out front that I have to wait for Ellie, that she's my ride. They can't deny transportation home."

"And you'll grill everyone who comes out of the building, won't you?"

I tried for an innocent look, but knew I'd failed when Sara added, "Be cautious or the authorities might throw you off the property despite your looking like an innocent senior lady."

"Oh, of course, my dear." I waved her good-bye and walked back to the building's entrance. I knew some of the nations people had left as soon as they heard the police sirens. Others had remained and been questioned already by Anita's officers.

I met the two nations leaders as they walked to the visitor parking area and introduced myself.

"Hi, I'm Maddie Sparks and I work at the entrance desk here. You may have seen me over this past week?"

They nodded.

I tried for a casual remark. "I can't believe Mr. Powles could have killed Mrs. Carlton."

"He was upset about the issue of ownership of the basket," said Mr. Nader, the leader of the Oneida delegation.

"Have you seen the basket?" I asked them.

They both shook their heads and the second leader, Mrs. Sands of the Onondaga spoke, "We want what is ours and we have waited for many years to have this made right. We need to see evidence of his claim."

"I assume that Mr. Powles's family are or were members of one of your nations. Do you know which one?"

"There are stories that his ancestors came from both our nations many years ago."

"But nothing in writing?" I said.

They both shook their heads and Mr. Nader sneered. "Of course not. That's the problem with white people. They have no respect for oral tradition."

"Mr. Powles said he was going to provide us with proof of his claim this afternoon," said Mrs. Sands.

"And if that's so, why would he kill Mrs. Carlton before he could present his proof to all of you?" I asked and then wanted to call back my words. I should have been more circumspect with my comments.

"Ask him," said Mr. Nader. "We fear the murder will have an impact on returning the items to us and we have already waited too long." They nodded and walked past me. Mr. Nader was correct: without Mrs. Carlton to mediate this dispute, the issue of the basket would remain unresolved. Her death stopped the negotiations. Was that what Mr. Powles intended? It didn't make sense that he would kill her prior to presenting the evidence for his claim.

What did I expect I would learn from the nations leaders? They didn't know me, I was white, a museum employee and the entire situation made them suspicious.

Ellie and Jeremy exited the front entrance and came down the sidewalk toward me. This time Jeremy appeared more interested in Ellie than he had in their recent hallway encounter. He leaned toward her to listen to what she said to him, then reached over and put his arm around her shoulders. To my surprise Ellie pushed him away. Jeremy's face turned red with anger but when he saw me in front of him, embarrassment replaced irritation.

"Well, see you later." He hesitated a moment, then arched an eyebrow at Ellie as if he wanted her nonverbal agreement on something.

Ellie turned her back on him to face me. "Need a ride home, Mrs. Sparks?"

"That would be great."

She and I proceeded down the path toward the parking lot from which I had come a few minutes earlier. Jeremy had gotten in his car and drove past us but didn't glance our way.

"I thought you had a bit of a crush on him, but just now you blew him off. Was he being too forward for you?"

"I always wanted him to be attentive, but he never was. Then just now he acts as if he suddenly likes me, but he's trying to use me."

"Use you?" I said.

"Yes. He wants me to say he and I were together in the alcove outside the gift shop just before Mrs. Carlton's body was discovered. But that's not true. I tried to stop him then in the hallway to talk, but he ignored me. He wants me to be his alibi." Fear crossed her face. "Do you think he might have killed her? Why would he kill Mrs. Carlton?"

I paused to reflect on any motive Jeremy might have. "Unless . . ."

Sara wrinkled her brow in confusion. "What are you thinking, Mrs. Sharps?"

"I heard Jeremy ask Mrs. Carlton for a recommendation for his graduate study."

"Would she give him a bad one?"

"I don't know, but I do know that Jeremy was often late coming in, and he spent more time on his phone than he did working on the exhibits."

Ellie looked frightened. "You think he might have killed her to prevent her from saying something bad about his work at the museum?"

"I don't know. He seemed very keen on pursuing museum studies."

Ellie frowned. "I think he was only keen on it because he was more than a little interested in Sara."

We walked the rest of the way to her car in silence. She used her key fob to click the car doors open. "But I did overhear Mr. Powles and Mrs. Carlton talking about the basket he claims belongs to his family."

"Yes?"

"They were talking outside her office earlier today. She said she would keep the proof of ownership safe. He said, 'I'm trusting you to do that.'"

"Was he threatening her?" I said.

"I don't know. Maybe. He makes me uncomfortable."

"It's his manner. He speaks with authority."

Was I right to defend him or had she not lived up to his trust in her? Proof? What kind of proof?

CHAPTER 7

Ellie pulled up in front of my house, but before I got out of the car, I said to her, "I think you should tell Sheriff Burroughs what Jeremy asked of you."

"I hate to do that. It feels like tattling."

"Ellie. A woman is dead. Murdered. This is more than telling on a friend."

She nodded. "I know. You're right."

I waved goodbye. Before I got to the door, my cell rang. It was Sara.

"Can you talk Uncle Richard into meeting Leonard tonight? We just got off the phone with each other. He told me he visited with his father at the jail and, if he was charged with murder, which he expected would happen, Mr. Powles wouldn't hear of anyone defending him but himself. I told Leonard he should talk to Richard."

"I'll call Richard and set up a meeting tonight at my place unless you think Leonard wouldn't want me there."

"I've told Leonard so much about you that he feels like he already knows you. Are you certain Richard will be interested in the case?"

"He will be after he eats a dinner of my meatloaf and then hears you and Leonard tell him about the murder."

I called Richard on my landline when I got into the house. "We haven't gotten together for such a long time. How about a meatloaf dinner tonight?"

"You know I can't resist your meatloaf. And I probably won't be able to resist hearing about the murder at the museum from you and Sara."

"And from the son of the man who is now in custody and will probably be arrested for it—Mr. Powles."

"The fellow who thinks he can defend himself in a murder trial."

"If it comes to trial with him as the accused. I'm sure you can prevent that from happening."

"Not without a good investigator." Richard paused. "Aren't you going to recommend Zack?"

"He would be my first choice, but he's busy with family problems, so you'll have to put that question to him yourself."

"I hope this doesn't mean you and Zack are also having problems."

I ignored his comment. "Tonight. Dinner at six. Bring wine and your appetite."

Richard and I had finished cleaning up the dinner dishes and I'd brewed a pot of decaf when Sara and Leonard showed up. We made introductions all around and sat down in the living room with coffee and cake, not homemade, of course. I could cook a mean meatloaf, and I sometimes made cookies, but cake? Never.

Leonard was tall, mahogany skinned like his father, but his hair was cropped short, and his clothes were similar to those worn by all college students, faded jeans and a tee-shirt. His eyes were softer than his father's but still projected a stern and unwavering gaze as he shook hands with Richard and me.

Once Sara and I had filled in Richard and Leonard on what we discovered when we entered the break room this afternoon, Leonard nodded.

"My father believes the authorities will not look beyond him as a suspect because he is a Native American. That is why he wants to serve as his own lawyer."

"Why wouldn't he trust a lawyer from one of the nations people? There aren't many, but I can recommend a few who have good reputations," said Richard.

"For the same reason. Father says regardless of what a Native American lawyer might do to defend him, the verdict would be the same."

"My son is the best lawyer around here." I said.

Skepticism was written all over Leonard's face. "He's your son, so you would say that."

Richard started to speak, but I held up my hand to stop him. "Yes, I am biased as his mother, so I recommend you talk with some of the nation lawyers and see what they say."

Leonard, hands clasped in front of him, looked down at the floor and then met Richard's gaze. "The final decision is my father's. Will you meet with him tomorrow?"

I glanced at Richard, worried that because he was busy and because of the doubt Leonard had expressed about him that Richard would refuse to talk with Mr. Powles. What lawyer wanted to take on a case where the defendant thought he was biased against him because of his cultural background and over two hundred plus years of prejudice against Indigenous people? Richard was not so narrow-minded, but would Mr. Powles believe that of him?

"Of course I will."

I let out the breath I didn't know I was holding. The meat loaf had worked. I wondered if I could sneak some of it into the jail tomorrow to help induce Mr. Powles to give up the idea of defending himself and instead take on the man I knew could find out the truth about the murder.

Sara and Leonard left soon after while Richard stayed for another cup of coffee.

"What do you think?"

"You tell me, Mom. You and Sara found him in the same room as the murdered woman. With her blood all over him. No one else was there. He is the prime suspect in this case. So what do you think? What does your gut tell you?"

I thought for a moment before answering. "His quiet and uncompromising manner puts people on edge, even the two nations leaders with whom he shares a history. However, I think he is an honorable man. I think he tells the truth as he sees it. And Sara believes he has raised a son with whom she wants to share her life. And you are the only man I know capable of presenting a strong defense to a jury."

"If he agrees to using me as his attorney, as I said earlier, I'll need the best investigator I can find."

I grabbed a piece of paper and wrote some numbers on it. "You have Zack's cell, don't you? In case he doesn't answer, here's the number of the bed and breakfast. You can leave a message there for him. Call him and see what he says."

Richard nodded and put his arms around me and hugged me. "I may need some of that meatloaf of yours to talk Zack into working this case."

If my meatloaf was that persuasive, I'd bake pounds of it and serve it to the jury.

CRIME SCENE INVESTIGATORS WERE STILL WORKING the scene the next day, so the museum was closed. However, Graham, the head of the board of directors, called a meeting to decide how to proceed with running the museum. They met at Andrewsburg town hall. Sara called me mid-morning after they had called her into the meeting.

"Trouble?" I asked when I heard she had met with them.

"Not really. They want to appoint me to take over many of Mrs. Carlton's duties until they can open a search for another permanent director."

I couldn't read Sara's mood about that offer over the phone. "So what do you think about that?"

"I haven't been at the museum as long as some of the other employees, but I'm the only person with a formal background in museum studies and extensive experience in other museums as well as at Meadowbrook. Even Mr. Graham, who I never thought liked me much, said he was eager to have me in the position. It makes sense. It just means a lot more hours there."

"And what about your coursework for your degree?"

"No courses until next semester and I think by then the board will have found someone to fill the directorship."

"Could you apply for it on a permanent basis?" I asked.

"I could, but I'd prefer another placement, a larger museum where I could expand my background."

I didn't want Sara to leave this area, and I was certain her parents felt the same way, but her career goals were important to her. I wondered how Leonard felt about the possibility that she might go elsewhere.

"But I'm worried about something else, Gram."

"Tell me."

"I'm the common link between the museum and Mr. Powles. If I take on the directorship, I make that link more official. Some of the museum employees have been there much longer than me and, although they don't have the credentials, they might resent my taking on the position. And the relationship between Leonard and me will get out sometime. That's another reason some at the museum won't like having me as director."

"You mean people like Harold."

"Him. And maybe a few others. And then there's Mr. Powles's family. Once they know about Leonard and me, how will they feel about my position as museum director?"

"But Mr. Powles already knows about Leonard's feelings for you, doesn't he?"

"Yes, and he has his reservations about me because I'm white. This could tip the scale against me."

"You don't think Leonard would end his relationship with you?"

I heard Sara's breath catch in her throat as if she was suppressing a sob. "Leonard's family, their traditions, culture and history are important to him. His father is the person he most respects."

"Talk to Leonard. You're guessing about what he's feeling."

"Good advice, Gram. I'll talk with him this afternoon after Richard has seen his father. And let me toss that advice back on you."

I was confused. What did she mean? "Huh?"

"Talk with Zack. I don't know what's happening between you two, but I suspect it had to do with his daughter and his wife's friend."

An insightful observation on Sara's part. Family concerns for both Sara and me might impact both of us and the men we loved.

THAT EVENING I WAS AT THE COMPUTER in my small office off the living room when I heard a knock on my front door. Darn! For the first time since Zack and I had parted ways, I was making progress on my manuscript, and someone was interrupting my flow. Could I just not answer the door? That wasn't an option because my car was in the drive. Anyone I knew could tell I was home.

I started toward the door and the person knocked gain.

"Mom. I know you're there. It's Geoffrey."

Geoffrey, the older of my two sons and Sara's father. Oh, oh. Sara would have told him about the murder of Mrs. Carlton, but I should have followed up with a call of my own. I'd been so distracted with the murder and with Zack, and, actually, I hadn't wanted to talk with Geoffrey because I knew how protective he was of his only child. I was sure he'd want Sara to resign from her internship. I wasn't up for that conversation just now. I took a deep breath and opened the door.

"How could you keep this from us? I tried to call you yesterday evening when I heard about the murder and this morning. Why aren't you answering the phone? Abigail and I are worried about Sara. Aren't you?"

"Worried? No more than about anyone else at the museum. Between my volunteering at the museum, my membership on the Historical Committee and my writing, the murder and, uh, other things, I'm a busy woman. I had planned to talk with you and Abigail later."

"Maybe you should give up some of these activities. Your family needs you. Sara adores you and will listen to what you say."

"Let's talk about this inside." I ushered Geoffrey into the living room. His face was flushed with worry, and he looked disheveled, his tie hung loosely around his neck, his suit jacket rumpled as if he had slept in it, not Geoffrey's usual neat and tidy appearance.

Geoffrey threw himself onto the couch, extracted a handkerchief from his pocket and wiped his brow. "Sara is in danger. You know that don't you?"

"Take it easy, son. Have you talked with Sara?"

"I have, and I read in the paper this morning that the authorities have arrested one of the Indian rioters. Is it true?"

"The nations people prefer the term "Native American." And they were peaceful demonstrators." Well, the nations people were anyway.

"So it's taken care of then?" Geoffrey looked relieved and gave me a weak smile. "I was so, so worried Sara was under threat." He paused for a moment. "Uh, and of course that you were in danger also."

"Of course not. We're both fine. I'm sure Sara told you that." I had calmed him down with a few bits of information and some reassurance. I mentally kicked myself for not having called him and Abigail the evening of the murder. Geoffrey was a worrier. I knew that.

"She told us not to worry about her, but you know how it is."

I did know. Despite my sons being in their forties, adult men who took care of themselves and, in Geoffrey's case, his wife and daughter, I still felt the need to problem solve when they ran into difficulties. Most of the time I tried not to intrude, to let them work through the issues, but sometimes, being the nosy woman I was, I inserted myself into their lives, and they weren't appreciative of my meddling.

"Tea?" I asked. "I have some cookies from the bakery." Naughty me trying to work Geoffrey out of his worrying by offering him sweets. I knew Abigail worked to help control his weight by restricting his intake of sugar.

While I brewed tea, Geoffrey slid back into the couch. I felt doubly guilty for not talking with him and Abigail. He looked exhausted as if he had been up all night, troubled over his daughter's safety.

"And there's another thing on my mind," he said.

"Oh?" I brought a tray with the tea and two cookies on a plate and set it down on the coffee table.

"Sara told us the other day that she had a boyfriend and she wanted us to meet him. We knew she was seeing someone, but she's been secretive. You know we don't try to pry into her life, unlike some parents do." He stopped and shot me a pointed look. "But we're curious about him because their relationship has been going on for a while and we don't even know his name. Anyway, Abigail invited him over for Sunday dinner. So, I'm wondering. You talk to Sara almost every day. Did you know about this fellow?"

"Uh, well . . ." I tried to stall. I didn't want to lie to Geoffrey. What should I tell him?

The sound of a car door closing followed by a knock on the door distracted us. Good. I was saved from confessing what I knew about Sara and her boyfriend, at least for now.

I jumped up and ran to the door, swung it open. Sara and Richard stood on my doorstep.

"Hi, Mom. We just got back from visiting Mr. Powles and thought we'd stop by to update you," said Richard. "Oh, good. Tea. And you're here, too, Geoffrey."

Well, Richard might have been delighted to see Geoffrey, but Sara and I exchanged looks of concern.

"Hi, Dad." Sara gave her father a hug and sat beside him on the couch.

Geoffrey returned her hug, but then a look of confusion crossed his face. "I don't understand. Update? About what?"

"Oh, right. I guess you didn't know I talked with the man accused of Mrs. Carlton's murder today. The authorities have arrested him for the murder. He was going to represent himself in the case, but I convinced his son that I should talk with him. He's Native American and doesn't trust the justice system, but Sara and I with the help of the son convinced him he should have legal representation. Well, I guess Mom had a hand in this too."

Geoffrey was silent throughout Richard's explanation and as Richard talked, he became aware that he was revealing more about how he came to represent Mr. Powles than he should have.

Finally, Geoffrey said, "Okay, but how does Sara figure into this?"

Sara, Richard and I exchanged glances. Who should tell him? I started to open my mouth, but Sara held up her hand to stop me from speaking.

"Mr. Powles's son, Leonard, is my boyfriend."

Geoffrey put the pieces together and it was clear he didn't like the final picture.

"No," said Geoffrey. "He's not. Not anymore. And you're not going back to that museum to work." He got off the couch and slammed out the front door.

CHAPTER 8

R ICHARD, SARA AND I COULD HARDLY MEET each other's eyes. Now Geoffrey was angry as well as frightened for his daughter. I tried to lighten the gravity of the moment. "I guess that means no guests for Sunday dinner at Geoffrey and Abigail's." No one laughed.

"We should talk to him. Explain." Richard said.

"All of us together will look as if we're ganging up on him. I'll go, and calmly explain everything to him and Abigail." I grabbed my sweater and bag and opened the front door. Zack stood on my front steps about to knock on the door, someone I should have been happy to see, but only if he had resolved the situation with his daughter and his wife's friend.

"Zack." My head pounded in anticipation of what he would say to me, and I reached out to touch him. Instead of leaning toward my touch, Zack took a step backward. "Richard left a message on my phone and told me to meet him here."

Zack avoided looking at me. Instead his eyes locked with Richard's. "I understand you have a business proposition for me."

I dropped my hand and nodded my head toward Zack to signal him into the house.

Richard caught the awkwardness between the two of us. "I hope you don't mind, Mom. I mean, as long as Zack is here."

"Fine. I'll leave you two to talk. I'm going into my office to work. Sara, you should go home. I'm sure Leonard will want to talk to you. I'll deal with your father later."

Sara hugged me. "Thanks, Gram. Call me, would you?"

"You'll need a ride," said Richard.

"I'll give Leonard a call. He can pick me up out front." She waved at all of us and scurried out.

Zack held his hat in his hands and scuffed his foot against the floor. "I've stepped into it, haven't I?"

"It's a situation I created with my brother. He just left. This is your house, Mom. We can leave and talk somewhere else."

I turned at the entrance to my office. "Maybe I should stay to hear what's going on."

Zack's lips lifted in a tiny smile. "Good idea. Given her snoopy nature, she'll either eavesdrop on our conversation or she'll bother both of us until we tell her about it."

I crossed my arms over my chest. "You think I can't guess what's afoot. You said it before to me, Richard. If you're taking Mr. Powles on as a client, you're going to need a top-notch investigator on your team. And that's Zack. Am I right?"

"Of course you are." Richard smiled at me then turned his gaze to Zack. "So what about it. Interested?"

"Tell me what I need to know, unless . . ."

Enough of this. I dropped my arms to my side in exasperation. "Oh, sit down, both of you. There's still some tea left."

"Anything stronger?" asked Richard.

I marched over to the liquor cabinet, the carved piece of furniture from Hong Kong that my father had given me, reached in and pulled out three glasses and a bottle of scotch. My feet almost danced across the room in anticipation of being allowed in on what Richard had to say about the murder and the case against Mr. Powles. I worked at the museum so of course I was interested. But that wasn't all. There's nothing I liked more than puzzling out clues in a murder case. Zack and I had done that together this past summer. For this case I wouldn't be as intimately involved, but I could be a resource to Richard and Zack. I knew everyone at the museum, I knew the situation that had unrolled because of the basket, and I'd been on the scene when Sara found Mrs. Carlton. I was already making up a list of potential suspects in my mind.

Richard briefed Zack on the murder, the events at the museum leading up to Carlton's death and on Mr. Powles's presence in the room when Sara found Mrs. Carlton's body.

"He had her blood on him?"

"He told Sara and me he had tried to help her." I said.

"She was stabbed with a sword?" said Zack.

"Fingerprints on it?" asked Zack.

"Anita, uh, the sheriff said it was clean. No prints." Richard said.

"Where did it come from?"

Before Richard could reply, I butted in. "It looked like the one that hung on the hallway that led to the break room."

"So anyone in the museum could have grabbed it off the wall?"

Again I interrupted. "Someone already had done that. The day before when members of the crowd tried to enter the side doors to the museum, one of our volunteers snatched it from the wall, ran up the stairs with it and confronted the crowd gathered outside."

"One of the volunteers grabbed the sword the day before the murder. Who was that? Tell me about the situation. It sounds like a melee with the crowd, press, visitors and museum employees." Zack reached into his jacket and removed his pen and black notebook and flipped it open.

"It was confusing and frightening. I think Harold thought he was defending the museum from the crowd outside." I hesitated and cleared my throat. "Well, of course, first he ran into the bathroom at the lower level. The women's bathroom."

Richard and Zack looked at me, puzzled looks on their faces.

"Well, anyway, after I shooed him out of the bathroom, Harold, sword in hand, charged down the hall and upstairs through the entrance into the crowd, where he fell, and it flew from his hand. I don't remember noticing where it landed because I was focused on the crowd gathered outside."

"Interesting," Zack said. "Harold attempted to use the sword once. Could he have decided to use it again on Mrs. Carlton? Where was Harold when Mrs. Carlton was attacked?"

"I don't know. He was in the hallway with others after Mrs. Carlton was found. But let me tell you this. I don't think Harold is capable of killing anyone despite dashing into a crowd of people. He might well have been trying to escape, not attack anyone. There were people intent upon breaking into both side doors. I think he was bent on flight and saw the sword as a way to defend himself by getting people to move out of his way. He was as likely to have dropped the sword once he broke through the crowd if he hadn't tripped on Mr. Powles's foot."

"Harold is clumsy?" asked Richard. Watch how many times you use so.

"Well, yes, but in this case, no. I'm sure Mr. Powles intentionally tripped him." I said.

"So Mr. Powles stabbed Mrs. Carlton, got blood on himself from stabbing her and then, wiping the sword clean, remained in the room with the dead body. Doesn't make any sense," said Richard.

"I'll need to talk with Mr. Powles as well as reinterview all those people who were at the museum the day of Mrs. Carlton's murder. And what about her family members, friends?" Zack asked.

"She was divorced. She had two children, both girls, both grown. The oldest followed in her footsteps and works in a museum in France as curator. The other lives in Italy. She had a few friends. Sara might know better than me who they are," I said.

"I hear you have a friend and your daughter visiting you, Zack. This is a big job, interviewing and checking all the people at the museum." Richard didn't ask Zack if he could fit investigating the murder into his schedule, but it was implied.

"I can help," I said. Both men gave me a stern look. "Now don't say no right away. It's just that I work there, and it would be natural if I talk with everyone about the murder. I could find out a lot more than an investigator could. I'm their friend. Everyone would answer any questions I asked them and wouldn't see me as being too nosy."

"Even Harold?" asked Richard. "Sara told me he's got personal space issues. He might be more interested in making the moves on you than chatting."

"I'm not his type," I said. "Too old for him. He prefers them Sara's age." Which gave me another thought. Harold harassed Sara and, from rumors around the museum, others too. Francis was in her forties, too old also, but Ellie was young. She'd confide in me and might know something about Harold's movements the day of the murder.

Richard and Zack exchanged glances, then Richard said, "Okay, Mom, but be careful. People generally expect you to be a bit snoopy, but don't push the questions too much. The chances are the killer works in the museum."

Good. Richard believed Mr. Powles was innocent even though he was in the room with the body before Sara entered the break room.

"Anyone I should focus on? Did Mr. Powles see anyone he recognized near the breakroom? And what was he doing there, anyway? Did he tell you when you talked with him, Richard?"

Zack chuckled. "She's already on the case except she's interrogating the wrong people."

I gave him an angry look and turned my attention to Richard. "Well, did Mr. Powles see anyone near the break room?"

"He said he thought he saw someone run down the hallway toward the main stairway," Richard said.

"I didn't see anyone coming up the stairs. I wonder if Sara did," I said.

"I haven't had the opportunity to talk in detail with Powles. He's not a talker, not even to his lawyer. I'll have to work on him to get the full story. How did he get into the building?" asked Richard.

"He told me Mrs. Carlton let him in the side door," I said.

"Do you believe him?" asked Richard.

I nodded. "He may not be the chatty sort, but I don't think he lies. Maybe Leonard can help you break through his silence."

"Okay. For now let's follow the leads we have. You work tomorrow at the museum, right, Mom?"

"If the sheriff's office allows us to open. I hope so. Sara needs to meet with everyone before we open the doors."

Richard and Zack looked puzzled.

"Sara has been appointed acting director until they find a replacement," I said.

"I don't like that much," said Richard. "I'd prefer both you and Sara not be the focus of anyone's interest right now."

"You think Mrs. Carlton's murder was related to her position at the museum?" asked Zack.

"I'm not eliminating that possibility, and neither should either of you. I'll talk to Sara tonight. Make certain she keeps alert," Richard said.

I thought about what I had promised Sara earlier. "Well, don't talk to her with Geoffrey and Abigail there. Geoffrey is already upset enough that he wants Sara out of the museum and out of her relationship with Leonard. I should get over to their house now and see if I can calm him down."

"How about if I come along? Perhaps I can help reassure him of Sara's safety." Zack gave me one of his sweet smiles and also a wink.

Of course I agreed to having him with me. It meant we could be together. I missed him.

"SHE'S AN ADULT, HONEY," SAID ABIGAIL after Zack and I had talked with Geoffrey for over a half hour. "She has the right to make up her own mind about where she works and who she sees. She won't take any unnecessary risks." Abigail sat on the couch beside Geoffrey stroking his arm gently.

"What do you think, Zack? You know about these matters. Is she safe?" asked Geoffrey.

"I'll talk with her and insist she not stay at the museum beyond working hours. She and Mom share a ride back and forth."

"But Mom only works part-time. Some days Sara drives herself."

"I'll be there full-time. We're down one person, so everyone will need to put in a full day's work," I said.

"What about when she's home at her apartment?"

"She could stay with me until we solve the murder." I knew Sara would have preferred Leonard stay with her at her apartment but suggesting that to Geoffrey would just set him off again.

"Okay, I guess. You really don't think Mr. Powles is the killer?"

Despite Powles being Richard's client, I knew Geoffrey would have preferred that Powles be the killer tucked safely behind bars for Sara's safety. Although I found Mr. Powles a somewhat intimidating person, he was using what the law provided to fight for the rights of his family. Murder wouldn't help him in his battle. Unless he thought the proof of the basket's ownership, whatever that was, wasn't persuasive enough.

Having done all we could do to reassure Geoffrey and Abigail, Zack and I left, me to drive myself home and Zack to drive to the B and B to be with his daughter and . . . that other woman.

When I pulled into my drive, someone awaited me on my front doorstep. At first, I didn't recognize the woman, but then I gasped. What was Mary Sanders, Zack's old flame from Seattle, doing at my house?

"I must talk to you," she said.

"If it's about Zack, I don't think we have anything to say to each other."

"Oh, but we do. We both want what's best for him and his daughter, don't we?"

I wondered how many times I'd heard that line used to persuade someone of the necessity of engaging in a conversation they wanted to avoid.

"I'll just stay here until you let me in."

She wasn't winning my sympathy with her approach, but I heard the steel in her voice and wouldn't have been surprised if she sat on my steps for the remainder of the night.

"Okay. Five minutes. That's all. And only because I care for Zack and know how worried he is about his daughter. If I can be of help to him with her, then I'll talk to you."

I gestured her into the house. Having heard my voice outside, Spike stood on the upstairs landing waiting for me.

"Have a seat."

Spike must have thought I was entertaining a friend because he bounced down the stairs and approached Mary. Mary shoved him away with her foot.

"Get this mangy thing away from me. I'm allergic."

Obviously recognizing her from his first encounter the other day, Spike crouched and growled at her.

"Is he going to attack me?"

"No." But what a good idea that would have been.

I picked him up. "C'mon, sweetie. Let's get you upstairs where you're safe."

"Safe? From me?"

I hurried up the stairs and locked Spike in my room then returned to confront Mary.

"Since you took up half your allotted time molesting my cat, now you've got less than two minutes to tell me why you're here."

"It's about the baby."

CHAPTER 9

"**B**ABY?" I COULDN'T HELP MYSELF. Who could after someone delivered a line like that? "What baby?"

"It's a long story. May I sit?"

My first instinct was to toss her out of my house. I didn't like this woman, but my curiosity got the best of me. I gestured toward the couch, and she took a seat.

"I don't suppose you know much about Zack and his wife, do you?"

"I know she died several years ago. Cancer, I believe."

Mary crossed her legs and smoothed her skirt. "Yes. Let me fill you in on what you should know about the man you've had in your bed for several months."

I know I should have stopped her right there, but I didn't. The more she talked, I told myself, the more I'd learn about the kind of woman she was and what she wanted. I thought I already knew what kind of man Zack was. Nothing she said would alter that.

I simply blinked and let her get on with her story.

"His wife, Zack and I met at Cornell College in Ithaca when we were undergraduates. Her name was Odalie. She and I were roommates. Zack and I dated for several months before my junior year, but the relationship never went anywhere. I left for a study abroad program in the fall and Zack and Odalie started seeing one another. By the time I returned from Europe in the spring, they were engaged. They married that summer." She squirmed around on the couch and cleared her throat. "Sorry. Could I have some water? My mouth is so dry."

I grabbed a glass from the kitchen and poured water into it from the pitcher I kept in the fridge.

She gulped down half of it and set the glass on the coffee table. "Thanks. This is hard for me to say, but on one of our dates Zack and I got drunk and we, uh, slept together. I got pregnant."

"And you went to Europe not to study abroad but to have the baby?" I was stunned at her revelation but kept my surprise to myself.

"Yes, I brought the boy home with me, thinking I could talk Zack into renewing our relationship, but when I saw how much in love he and Odalie were, I gave up the idea and put the baby up for adoption. I wanted him to have a loving home."

"Zack never knew about the child then?"

She shook her head. "We all went on with our lives. I married and moved to Seattle but kept in touch with Zack and Odalie. When she died, I came back here for the funeral. Amy was devastated by her mother's death. Zack hid his grief from her by plunging into work. Amy wrote to me soon after her mother's death, saying she needed to get away. I invited her to come stay with me in Seattle. My husband had died several years before Odalie did. We had no children. I introduced Amy to her husband and for a time they were happy, but Amy's depression soon spiraled into drug use. Her husband left her. I did everything I could to help her. Zack knew about Amy's drug problem and wanted to come out to help her, but I assured him she was doing well. Recently she told her father she was again having issues with addiction. That's why he flew out to visit. He wanted to bring her back, thinking he could help. She's been in and out of rehab programs. She and I have become close. She's like a daughter and I'm like a second mother to her. She wants Zack and me to be together, she wants us to be a family."

I listened carefully to her story. There were so many aspects of it that I questioned. Of course Zack was once young, and they might have slept together, but I couldn't see Zack drunk enough and careless enough to make love with someone without taking precautions. And why wouldn't she tell him about the baby? By her account they had been seeing each other for a number of months. Zack was the kind of man who would have wanted to know. Her story differed from Zack's, but I kept my doubts about it to myself. But I knew what she was after.

"You want to tell Zack about your son so he can help you find him. Am I right? He must be, what, forty by now? Why after all these years would you try to locate him?"

"The time is right, right for Zack, Amy, my son and me to be together."

"Your child may not want to connect with his birthmother. He has a family of his own who raised him and loved him. What then if he doesn't want you in his life?"

"Zack will help me one way or the other. That's the kind of man he is. You must know that."

Oh, I did. I knew of his generosity, his intelligence, his kindness. His commitment to helping his daughter overcome her addiction was evidence of that. Zack must have felt as if he had failed his daughter after her mother died and Amy began using drugs. Now was Zack's moment to make that up to her. Would he also feel he should go further, find a son he didn't know he had and bring everyone together as Mary wanted?

"Have you talked with Zack about this yet?"

She shook her head.

"He's just taken on a position as investigator on a murder case, and he has his daughter to support. This may not be the time to tell him."

She grinned, a kind of self-satisfied smile. "I can wait. I've waited all these years for everything to be right and now it is. A few weeks or so won't matter."

The look in her eyes warned me to be wary of her plans. There was something unhealthy in her commitment to bringing Zack back into her life. I didn't share these thoughts with her. I needed time to turn everything over in my mind. I couldn't tell Zack what she had revealed. It was her story to tell, not mine.

AFTER MARY LEFT, I CALLED SPIKE down from upstairs. "How about a tuna nightcap?"

He meowed his interest, and I filled his bowl while Mary's story swirled around in my head. Was her visit a confession designed to get me on her side in her search for Zack's companionship and in locating her son? I mentally shook my head. Somehow it felt more like a warning to me, a kind of "I'm holding almost a half-century of connections with Zack, and you have only a few months. Don't get in my way." And she planned on updating the past by bringing it into the present with the search for her son. And what of her story of helping Amy with her drug addiction? Something about that didn't quite feel right. What I could do was to ask Zack if he had used the drug counselor contact I'd given him and, if not, encourage him to get in touch with John. I'd do that tomorrow before Sara and I left for the museum. My day at work promised to be busy. I had potential suspects to gently interrogate.

THE SHERIFF'S DEPARTMENT HAD ALLOWED the museum to open Saturday. A restless crowd again gathered out front, and probably because people's curiosity had been tickled by news of the murder, we had a record number of visitors. I didn't get a chance to talk with anyone after the meeting Sara convened with volunteers and staff before we opened the museum doors. Soon after ten thirty, the influx of visitors slowed, and Ellie took over for me at the entrance desk. I grabbed my bag with my thermos of tea and headed for the break room.

Sara was already there waiting for me. "Close the door. I don't want anyone to overhear what I have to say."

I poured us two cups of tea and we sat next to each other at the break table. "You look worried. What's up? Is it something about Mrs. Carlton's death?"

"No, I mean I don't think it is. Look, Gram, I'm only in the director's position until they find someone more qualified to fill it, and I haven't even finished my degree yet, and I only have a few years' experience under my belt, but . . ."

"Sara, I trust your knowledge and instincts. What's wrong?"

"Some of the objects in our collections aren't real."

"As in?"

"They're fakes. Good fakes, but fakes. When I first took the internship here, I examined some of the objects we hold in storage, and I know they were genuine. We were preparing a collection in storage to be moved into one of the display cases, so I reexamined a few of the items again early this morning. One of two pieces of jewelry has been replaced by a copy and the other piece is missing."

I held my breath, suspecting I knew what she was about to say.

"I haven't had the time yet to look at the Native American collection we are about to return to the nations people, but what if some of them are also copies?"

"Could you tell?"

"I'm not an expert on the Onondaga and Oneida objects, but my professor at the university is."

I thought for a minute. "I want to discuss this with Richard and with Zack, but I think you should have your professor examine the collection."

"Without letting anyone on the board or the museum employees know? You think this is connected to Mrs. Carlton's murder?"

I nodded. "If she found out items in any collection had been replaced, she could have suspected who did it. And they killed her to keep her quiet."

Sara visibly blanched and her hands shook. I grasped her fingers in mine.

"That's why I don't want anyone else to know about the thefts. Unfortunately, Sara, I hate saying this, but your father might be right. You are in danger. If the thefts are connected to Mrs. Carlton's murder, now you know what she knew and she might have been killed for that knowledge."

"And so are you if the person or persons responsible finds out I told you."

"I'm going to phone Zack and Richard right now and see if I can get them over here today, soon."

Someone banged on the break door room. "Hey, open this door. It's locked and it's time for my morning break. Mrs. Sparks, are you in there?"

It was Jeremy Westin.

"Just a minute." I got up, unlocked the door and opened it. Jeremy stood outside looking upset.

"I only get fifteen minutes, you know. Why is the door locked?"

"Girl talk." I gave him a coy look. He didn't question why we would be talking girly stuff in the break room two days after a murder but pushed past me.

"There's a new group of visitors at the desk. Ellie is feeling overwhelmed. Some of them are holding complimentary passes provided by one of the hotels near here and she doesn't know how to manage it." The frown on his face disappeared into a smile when he looked at Sara.

"Got it." I slipped my thermos into my bag and rushed toward the door. As if continuing our discussion, I said to Sara. "You're right, Sara. Go ahead and call your mom." I held up my cell phone as if I was suggesting Sara call home to talk with her mother, but while Jeremy continued to focus on Sara, I nodded at my cell to let her know I'd be calling Zack and Richard.

Upstairs I showed Ellie how to manage complimentary museum tickets hotels offered to overnight quests. Satisfied that she understood the procedure, I stepped away from the desk and signaled to her that I needed to head outside for a moment. I walked beyond the crowd, down the drive and toward the pillars flanking the driveway entrance. I contacted Zack first to let him know what Sara had discovered.

"I'll call Richard. Eventually we'll have to notify the authorities, but I think you did the right thing for now, telling Sara not to discuss this with anyone at the museum." He disconnected.

Before I could reenter the museum, Richard called. "The missing jewelry has got to be connected to Mrs. Carlton's death. But before we take this to the authorities, we need confirmation that the genuine museum item has been replaced with a fake. Sara's professor can do that, I gather."

"But there's another problem, Richard. We don't know how many items have been stolen or replaced. Especially sensitive is the Native American exhibit."

"Zack and I will meet Sara in her office. Is there any way you can get away from the entrance desk to join us? In an hour or so?"

"I'll find a way." I disconnected and noticed Agnes Danderfield, the reporter for the local paper, standing under one of the maple trees on the lawn not far from me. What had she heard? I hoped she was far enough away that she hadn't caught my reference to "stolen or replaced."

I caught her eye and walked over. "Mrs. Danderfield. I thought you got most of your story the other day when you were here. There can't be much to report on now."

She was a gangly-looking woman, all arms and legs with a loping walk. Her auburn hair always looked as if she had forgotten to comb it when she got up or as if the wind had blown it around, probably both.

"Problems inside?" she asked, knowing I worked at the entrance desk.

"No. Just catching some fresh air."

She paused for a moment, and I thought she was about to walk off, but she stepped nearer to me. "I think there are some issues at the museum that need resolving."

I remembered Mrs. Carlton drawing Agnes into her office on the first day the crowd had gathered outside. I assumed Mrs. Carlton had cautioned her about writing an article that might stir up resentment in the community, both the local community and among the nations people. But perhaps there was more to the conversation the two of them had in Carlton's office. I tried to think back on that day. What was the expression on Carlton's face? Was she going to warn Agnes about overstepping her journalistic boundaries or did Mrs. Carlton appear to be looking for someone to talk to, like a friend? Were she and Agnes friends? I didn't know, but I decided to see if I could get Agnes to reveal the nature of her relationship with Mrs. Carlton.

"I guess you're pretty broken up about your friend's death." I tipped my head to one side and put a sympathetic look on my face, hoping to invite a confidence from her. "How long had the two of you known each other?"

At first Agnes gave me a confused look but followed it with a change of expression. Her eyes took on a cold glare. "What do you know about the two of us?"

Agnes spun on her heel and walked away.

I wasn't as clever as I thought. I couldn't tell what the relationship between the two women was, but Agnes' question to me about difficulties in the museum made me wonder; did Agnes suspect something, and was it related to Carlton's death or the thefts? What a story that would be for Agnes's column.

LATER THAT AFTERNOON, RICHARD AND ZACK arrived at the museum. I had Ellie take over the desk again while Sara, Zack, Richard and I went into the director's office to plot our strategy for dealing with the thefts.

"It's only paint over pot metal," said Sara, taking her nail and chipping off the gold color from a late nineteenth century broach. "But the bracelet is missing." She held out the broach so we could examine it.

"Isn't it reckless to replace an original with a cheap fake? The stones could fall out or the clasp break, not something you'd expect from a fine piece of jewelry," said Richard.

"It would be if these were items that are handled every day, but they're not. They sit behind glass. No one but the individuals placing them into the display cases get that close," Sara said.

"And who would be placing them into the exhibit cases?" Zack asked.

"I would, along with another museum worker, Jeremy or Ellie, or another intern."

"Would they have noticed an item missing or the substitution of a fake for a genuine object?"

"Maybe Jeremy would have. He's had more coursework in the program than Ellie, but I don't know if he has any specific knowledge about that period or this particular collection."

"Who decided this collection would be moved out of storage and put on display?" asked Richard.

"Mrs. Carlton made that call. We were going to feature jewelry and other pieces of art from the period, specifically pieces from the Albertson home where one of the area's prominent families lived until the house burned down several years ago. Some of the jewelry worn in the late 1890's by Mrs. Eugene Albertson had been removed from the house prior to the fire and other pieces such as vases and furniture had survived the fire. We had been holding the collection until we rotated another collection into storage and brought the Albertson collection out."

"Do you know why Mrs. Carlton decided to put the Albertson pieces on display?"

"We have a number of items in the museum from families around here that we've been featuring under our "Our Neighbors Collection 1850-1930."

"So these pieces were up in that rotation?" I asked.

"I'm not certain," said Sara. "Mrs. Carlton made those decisions. I don't think the Albertson collection was due to be displayed until early next year." Sara lowered her gaze and cleared her throat. "But," she said, "the family might have contacted her about these pieces, or they might have made a donation to the museum and expected the items from the family to be displayed soon."

"A nice way of saying bribery or pressure," I said.

Sara gasped. "Gram. How can you say such a thing?"

"What does it sound like to you? The family gave some money to the museum and in return expected their family collection would be put on display now rather than later," I said.

"I can't believe Mrs. Carlton would give in to that kind of request. I could tell more if I could take a look at the notes from the museum's ledger, but the authorities took it after the murder," Sara said.

"We need to look at the ledger," said Richard.

"Without telling the sheriff why. At least for now," Zack added.

"Sara, call the sheriff and tell her you need the ledger because entries in there have bearing on the day-to-day operation of the museum. Can you do that and make it sound legitimate?" asked Richard.

Sara nodded.

Sara picked up the phone on her desk and connected with the sheriff's department. While she talked, I leaned close to Richard and whispered, "What we're doing in withholding information in a murder case isn't legal, is it, dear?"

"Don't worry, Mom." Richard put his arm around me and hugged me.

But that was my job. Parents always worried even if their sons were smart. If we were found out, even a clever defense attorney like my son would have difficulty making our actions appear innocent.

CHAPTER 10

U NTIL THE LAW CAUGHT UP TO what we were doing, I had a few other items that were bothering me. There was Zack. There was always Zack. I gave him a look and he caught my gaze in his.

"How are you doing, Maddie?" he asked.

"I need a word."

I poked my head out of Sara's office door and looked up and down the hallway. There was no one in sight. "I had a visitor yesterday. Your friend Mary. She told me the two of you had been an item before you married your wife."

"Uh, yes. We dated. But why did she stop by your house?"

"Just wanted to chat. She's very close with your daughter, isn't she? How is Amy, by the way? Was my friend helpful?"

"Amy is not very keen on going back into a rehab program."

"What then? How is she going to manage her addiction?"

"I think Mary will be helpful."

"Mary doesn't have the credentials or the experience to give Amy the kind of help she needs."

Zack stared at me, then, a stern note in his voice said, "Mary has been at Amy's side for years."

"Years? Then maybe your daughter needs another approach."

A muscle in Zack's face twitched. He gave me a look of annoyance, then stepped back into the office. "I'll meet you outside, Richard." Without another word to me, he left.

"Mom?" Richard said when I reentered the office.

"You heard some of that. Yeah, yeah, I know. I'm butting in where I'm not wanted. She's Zack's daughter. It's his call, but . . ." I shrugged and didn't finish my sentence.

"Drug addiction is a hard one. All you can do is be his friend."

"I thought I was, but I'm not certain he sees me that way now that he has Mary at his side."

"Give him some space, Mom. He's got a lot to think about." Richard gave me a one-armed hug.

I had a few concerns of my own.

I wanted to finish my talk with Agnes Danderfield. She knew something about the museum she hadn't told me . . . yet.

"Gram? You seem distracted," said Sara.

"Oh. Well, I suppose I should get back to the desk or someone will think the four of us meeting here is suspicious."

As Sara opened the office door to let Richard and me out into the corridor, I caught the flash of something blue disappear around the corner. Someone had been trying to eavesdrop. What had they heard if anything?

Richard must have caught the flash of color too. "Who was wearing a blue shirt, pants or dress today?" he asked.

I thought back to the morning when all of us had met in Sara's office. No one wore jeans to work, so the clothing had to be a pair of pants, shirt, dress or blouse. Let's see. My mind's eye ran over everyone in the room. The guards wore black uniforms, Jeremy had on a blue shirt and dark blue tie, Francis sported her usual vest with autumn leaves on it over a white blouse, and Harold had donned his navy-blue blazer to appear more official. I looked over at the desk I usually sat at. Ellie was there in a blue blouse and navy skirt, but she had to have been at the desk while Zack, Sara, Richard and I met in Sara's office. Ellie wouldn't leave it with no one to sell tickets and greet visitors, would she? It had to have been

Jeremy unless it was a visitor innocently walking around the corner toward the gift shop.

I shared my suspicion with Richard. "Jeremy. It was Jeremy."

Just then Jeremy walked out of the men's room, wearing a white shirt and blue tie. "What?"

"Jeremy. I thought for certain you had on a blue shirt today," I said.

"I did, but I spilled some mustard from my sandwich at lunch on the front of it. I had to dash to my car for a change. I always carry a back-up shirt with me. Why are you asking?"

"I thought the shirt was a particularly smart one." I smiled and nodded.

Richard held out his hand and introduced himself as Mr. Powles's lawyer. "Were you acquainted with him?"

Jeremy shook his head. "I only know of him, never had the opportunity to meet the man."

"Have you seen the collection of items that will be returned to the nations? And the basket that Mr. Powles claims belongs to his people?"

"No I haven't. No one except for Mrs. Carlton had viewed the collection. I'm anxious for the day the items are handed over and everyone can view them in the hands of their rightful owners." Jeremy shuffled his feet back and forth. "Uhm, is Sara free now? I need to speak to her."

"Give a knock on the door," I said.

"Nice to meet you, sir," Jeremy said to Richard and gave me one of his engaging smiles, then headed toward the director's office.

As I accompanied Richard to the entrance, he asked, "How well did you know Mrs. Carlton, Mom?"

"She wasn't one to socialize outside of work, so I don't think many of us felt we knew her as other than the competent boss she was. Although now that I think of it, I believe she was married at one point. She and her husband divorced years ago."

"Contentious divorce?" Richard asked.

"I don't know."

"Say, Mom. You're pretty savvy on the internet. See if you can track down Mrs. Carlton's ex. Find out where he lives. And when you do, give the address to Zack, would you?"

Me? Give Zack the information? Richard, you sly devil. I know what you're up to. You're giving me an excuse to contact Zack and repair the misstep our relationship had taken.

I grinned. "Sure. With the assignment you already gave me to talk with the staff and other volunteers and now this one, I feel like I'm part of the investigative team."

Richard gave me a sharp look. "Don't get ahead of yourself. Be discreet in what you talk about with the others at work."

"Of course, dear. I wouldn't think of being too pushy. You know me."

His sharp look continued.

"Off to work." I tapped Ellie on the shoulder and relieved her at the desk.

Spike and I were sitting on the couch later that evening sharing a pint of chocolate ice cream. Well, I was eating the ice cream. I knew better than to give chocolate to Spike. It would make him sick, so he had albacore solid white tuna in his bowl, the expensive kind, caught on lines and packed in water. Like me, Spike didn't care for the chunk light stuff. My phone rang and Spike looked up at me and gave me one of his clacking sounds, the kind he made when he was annoyed.

"Eat your fish. I'll get the phone."

Spike meowed and continued licking his bowl.

"Gram?"

I could just make out Sara's voice.

"Speak up, honey. I can hardly hear you."

"I think there's someone outside."

"Did you dial the sheriff's office?"

"Yes."

"Okay, honey. Stay on the line and I'll call Zack on my cell phone. He can be with you in a matter of minutes." I knew it would take forever for the sheriff to get to Sara's house unless there was an officer in the area.

I made the calls, then got back with Sara. "Zack is on the way. Me, too."

"Gram, no. It could be dangerous."

"Go into the bathroom and lock the door. I'll be with you in less than five minutes."

I shoved my ice cream container in the freezer, grabbed my coat and bag and headed out the door to my car.

What if I got to Sara before Zack? Just what did I think I could do? Especially if the person prowling around Sara's was armed?

When I pulled up in front of the house, I recognized the car parked next to the curb was Zack's. I jumped out and banged on her front door.

Sara opened the door, her face filled with fear, her cheeks drained of all color.

I tossed my bag on the couch and wrapped my arms around her.

When she stopped shaking, I asked, "Where's Zack?"

"He went around back. C'mon in."

Outside, a sheriff's car pulled up blue lights flashing and siren wailing. Sheriff Anita Burroughs hopped out of the car and rushed up the sidewalk and into the house. Zack walked through the kitchen door in the rear of the house.

"Find anything?" asked Anita.

"Looks like someone was prowling around the back of the house, trying to peer into the window. There might be some tracks there, but we need a better flashlight to see." He and Anita walked back outside.

When Anita and Zack returned, I was doing my usual Gram-comfort thing, making tea.

Anita's cell twanged. She listened for a minute, then disconnected.

I could tell from the concerned expression on her face that the sheriff's department had another emergency.

"Can you take care of things here for a while, Zack? I'll send another officer over later, but right now I'm needed at the museum. There's been an attempted break-in."

Zack nodded. "We'll be fine. I'll talk to Sara and see what she can tell me."

Anita turned and rushed out to her car.

"Now, Sara, are you doing better?" Zack asked.

"I'm fine now."

"Good. Tell me what happened."

"I heard a noise coming from the back of the house. I couldn't tell if someone was in the yard back there, but I worried they might try to get into the house, so I called the sheriff and then Gram."

"Interesting choices," Zack said. "Why not just the sheriff's department?"

"Because I know how short-staffed they are. There's only one full-time officer on at night," Sara said. "I was going to call Leonard, my boyfriend, but I decided that wouldn't be the best choice."

"Smart woman," said Zack, "but what did you think your grandmother could do? She isn't armed."

"I knew Gram would take action. She called you, didn't she?" Sara sounded a bit put out that Zack thought her call to me was misplaced.

Zack turned to me. "You aren't armed, are you?"

"Don't be silly. But I knew you would be. That's why I called you. The B and B is right down the road. I hoped I wouldn't be 'disturbing you.'" I said the last with a coy look on my face.

"How long ago was it that you heard someone prowling around the house?" asked Zack.

"About half an hour ago, I guess. Maybe less."

Zack's cell chirped. He talked for a few minutes, then turned to Sara. "Sheriff Burroughs wants you to come to the museum. Someone tried to punch in the alarm code, but had the wrong numbers, so they tried to jimmy the side door. The alarm went off in the sheriff's department, but by the time the deputy in the field tonight got there, he found no one. There were marks on the door, but no sign of entry."

Sara blanched.

"The sheriff would like Sara to come to the museum and walk through with her to make certain everything inside is as she left it when she locked up this evening."

"I'll drive you, Sara, and bring you back here when you've finished. Grab whatever you need." Zack started toward the front door.

"Nope, no way. Sara is not coming back here to stay. She's not safe," I said. "Even though it looks like a peeping Tom, these things can escalate." When Zack, Richard and I had talked to Sara's parents, we had told them Sara could stay with me, but somehow that idea had gotten lost in everything that continued to focus attention on the museum especially the concern over the stolen items Sara had discovered.

"Good point. Maybe we should we call your parents?" asked Zack.

"No, no. We can't do that. Dad will go crazy."

"She's right. Geoffrey already wants her to leave her position at the museum and break up with her boyfriend. If he finds out someone was snooping around here, he'll want her to move back in with them," I said.

"I could go stay with Leonard."

Zack and I exchanged glances.

"I don't think that's a good idea until everything is sorted here and with the museum," Zack said.

"You don't trust him because of his father." Sara's voice was shrill with accusation.

"We discussed this before, Sara, and convinced your parents you'd be safe staying with me, if necessary," I said. "And for now, let's keep your parents out of this until we know more."

Sara looked relieved.

"The incident here will find its way to the police blotter, but the attempted break-in at the museum coming on the heels of the murder will hit the local news sometime soon," I warned.

"One step at a time. Let's go, Sara." Zack escorted her out the door.

Sara locked up and Zack gave me a worried look before they left for the museum. Was it a general look of uneasiness about the recent events associated with the museum or was the expression of concern on his face for me? If so, it warmed me. He was anxious about my well-being. I could take care of myself. I had an attack cat at home whose claws needed clipping. Between Spike and my grandfather's brandy decanter which I'd used as a weapon on one occasion before, I was perfectly safe. But my granddaughter might not be. Her new position as museum director might have made her the target of whoever killed Mrs. Carlton.

Back home I decided to spend some time in front of my computer working on my manuscript. Spike joined me to help, taking his usual seat on the chair next to my desk. My cell rang a half-hour later.

Agnes Danderfield was on the other end.

"I know this is late to call, but I'd like to talk to you if I could. Can we meet somewhere tomorrow?"

Her voice sounded shaky.

"What's this about, Agnes?"

"You asked me about my friendship with Mrs. Carlton. I thought I should clear up any questions you might have. Meet me for lunch tomorrow at the Billinghouse Restaurant. I'll tell you then."

Before I could ask any more questions, she disconnected.

CHAPTER 11

THE CALL FROM AGNES DANDERFIELD puzzled me. She and I weren't friends. I hardly knew her beyond recognizing her as a reporter for the newspaper. Her articles written under the column entitled "About Town," were not really newsworthy unless you were into local gossip, which I wasn't. Well, I was, but I knew enough people that I got my gossip in person and didn't have to read it in the newspaper. Besides, Agnes' information was often not trustworthy.

I went to the kitchen to retrieve the ice cream I hadn't finished and was taking the last spoonful of it when Zack and Sara returned.

Dark circles had appeared under Sara's eyes.

"Let's make this short. Sara needs sleep," I said.

"I'll leave you two alone. Sara can fill you in." Zack turned to go.

"I didn't mean to chase you away."

"No. I know, but Mary will be worried as will my daughter. I'll talk to you tomorrow." Zack leaned in as if he meant to kiss me as we used to, but he must have thought better of it. My feelings about him were so confused, I didn't know if I wanted to hug him or yell at him. He stepped back from me, gave me a rueful look and left.

Sara saw the interchange and looked concerned. "What's with you and Zack, Gram? Suddenly the two of you act so awkward around each other."

"I'll tell you some other time, but now I want to know what's going on at the museum."

Sara sighed. "It appears someone did try to break in but was unsuccessful." Sara grabbed my arm and pulled me to her. "Oh, Gram. I don't know what to think. Someone snooping around my apartment along with an attempt to break into the museum? And the thefts? Paired with Mrs. Carlton's murder, I'm feeling shaky about taking over as temporary museum director."

"I can understand your fears, love. We'll sort this out tomorrow. For now, I'll drive you to your apartment and you can pick up anything you need to get you through spending the night here with me. We can return tomorrow after the museum closes, and you can pack the items you'll need for at least a week." I thought about telling Sara about my conversation with Agnes Danderfield, but decided she didn't need to worry about anything else at this point.

We drove over to Sara's apartment, and she packed an overnight bag. We were back at my place in less than half an hour. I could tell she was feeling better because she accepted my offer of ice cream. I had a second pint in the fridge and decided I could use another helping to soothe my nerves too. Soon, tummies filled with our chocolate treat, we headed upstairs, Spike accompanying us and settling himself at the end of the bed in the spare bedroom.

"Do you mind him sleeping with you?" I asked. "His purring is so loud he might keep you awake."

"No danger of that. I'm exhausted, Gram. Thanks for letting me stay with you and Spike."

"He makes a good watch cat. He'll keep us safe."

"I'm going to call Leonard and let him know where I am and what's happened tonight."

"Good idea especially if he dropped by your place and didn't find you home. He'd be worried, I'll bet."

"Good night, Gram." Sara settled back onto her pillows and reached for her cellphone.

"Make the call brief. You need rest. See you in the morning." I shut the bedroom door, leaving it open just enough that Spike could leave the room if he needed the litter box or a drink of water from his bowl downstairs.

I heard soft murmurs from Sara's bedroom for several minutes, but then the sounds ceased. I assumed Sara fell asleep right after her call. I took longer, tossing and turning, my thoughts bouncing from my concerns about Zack to wondering why Agnes Danderfield wanted to talk with me.

I DROVE SARA AND ME TO THE MUSEUM the next morning, letting her know I had a lunch appointment and arranging with Ellie to take over the entry desk for an hour and a half while I met with Agnes. I hurried off to the restaurant, arriving a few minutes after noon. Agnes wasn't there. I grabbed a two-top table to wait for her, but after half an hour, it appeared she wasn't going to show. I checked the number on my cell she used to contact me last night and called her back. There was no answer, so I left a voice message asking her to get in touch with me. I put in my lunch order to go and left the restaurant. Before I returned to the museum, I called Sara and asked her to check Mrs. Carlton's desk to see if she could find an address for Agnes.

"What's up, Gram? You sound worried," said Sara. "Oh, here it is. Agnes lives in Stone Side, not far from the Billinghouse Restaurant." She read off the address to me and I told her I'd be back at the museum in half an hour.

I pulled up in front of a white frame house, small, two maple trees ablaze with red leaves on either side of the sidewalk leading to the front door. There was no garage and no car parked in the gravel parking area next to the house. I knocked on the front door, but the house was silent. I cupped my hands over my eyes to hide the glare from the sun and peeked through the front windows into the living area. It was deserted. I walked around back and mounted the steps to the back door and looked in the kitchen window, but saw no one. A hand tapped me on the shoulder, and I jumped.

"Looking for Agnes? Not interested in robbing her or selling her something she doesn't want, are ya?" said an elderly woman, white hair pulled back in a tight bun, eyes bright blue and filled with suspicion. She carried a rake which she held in front of her like a shield . . . or a weapon.

"Oh, yes. I'm sorry." The truth seemed the best way to assure the woman I meant no harm to her or to Agnes' property. "Agnes and I were to meet for lunch, but she never showed. Have you seen her today?"

The woman shook her head. "The last I saw her was last night. I live over there." She waved her hand toward a red brick house across the street. "I saw her porch light go on, then someone knocked on her door. She let the person in and turned off the porch light a few minutes later. That's all I know."

Given how quick she was at appearing at the back door when I tried to peer in, I was certain she knew a lot more. She was this area's version of a geriatric neighborhood watch. I'd bet there wasn't much around here that went on without her knowing about it.

"Man or woman?" I asked.

"How would I know?" Her tone was snippy.

"If the light was on and she let the person in, you'd have a perfect view of the individual."

She blinked. "Hmmmph. Man. He wore a dark coat, was tall, with longish hair."

"Did he arrive in a car?"

"Now how would I know that?" She dropped the end of the rake onto the ground and planted her other hand on her hip.

"If Agnes answered the door, she was in and would probably have parked her car in the drive, so if he drove here, there would be two cars in the drive or one near the curb."

"You a cop or something?"

"No, but I sometimes collaborate with the police." It was almost the truth, not really a lie.

"Only Agnes's car."

"Did you hear Agnes drive off last night or this morning?"

"Nope. I went to bed after her visitor arrived. Her car was gone when I got up this morning."

"Thanks for the information." I started down the steps, but then reached into my purse. "If you see anything else, call the number on the card." I handed her one of Zack's business cards.

She read it. "Private eye? Hey, this is a guy's name."

"He's the fella I work with." It was another partial truth, but I had hopes we'd work with each other again in the future. Well, actually I had hopes for more than that.

"I'm Maddie Sparks, by the way. And your name?"

"Edith Denton."

Right. Edith Denton, probably one of Agnes' sources for her gossip column. I smiled and said good-bye.

"Enjoy your lunch?" Sara met me as I hung my jacket in the coat room near the entry desk.

"I got stood up." I held my takeout bag aloft. "I'll be back in a moment. I just need to put this in the fridge in the break room."

When I got to the break room, I ran into Jeremy and Harold, their heads together as if they were sharing a secret. They looked up when I entered, looking guilty.

"Boy talk," said Jeremy, a smug look on his face, using a similar phrase to that I'd used when Jeremy had interrupted Sara and me talking. I laughed. Jeremy did also.

"I'll be right out of your way so you 'boys' can continue with your chat."

I'd never noted the two of them were friendly and I hoped, given Harold's manner around young women and his attitudes toward minority groups, that Jeremy didn't get too chummy with him. He wasn't the kind of man who would provide Jeremy with a good role model.

When I got back upstairs to the entrance desk, Ellie was anxious to leave.

"Not have lunch yet?" I asked her.

She smiled and giggled. "Jeremy's waiting for me downstairs. We're eating together."

I took up my position at the desk, noting there were few visitors this afternoon and that even the numbers of the nations people had been reduced from last week.

Sara emerged from her office and leaned down to whisper in my ear. "I hope I did the right thing. I put off the return of the Native American collection until later this year. By then I hope the issue of who killed Mrs. Carlton will be settled. Meantime, I'm meeting with the two nations to notify them of the delay. I know they won't like it, but I hope they understand how upsetting Mrs. Carlton's murder has been to a formal exchange."

"What about the claim of Mr. Powles's family and the basket?" I asked.

"I'm going to the jail after work tonight. I hope you can come with me. I want to talk with Mr. Powles. He said he had proof. I want to find out what it is, and I'm going to persuade him to appoint someone to represent him in the continued discussions among the nations and the museum."

I shook my head. "This is so, so messy."

Sara nodded and then turned to reenter her office. Before she closed the door, she slapped her forehead with her hand. "Oh, and here's another wrinkle. Mrs. Carlton agreed to address the local historical society tomorrow night. I should step in for her, of course, but I'm sure the society will be more interested in the murder and its relationship to the arrest of Mr. Powles, and I certainly can't talk about that. I hate to cancel, but . . ."

"Call them and let them know the murder isn't a topic you can discuss because of the ongoing case. They'll understand.

How about talking about the upcoming exhibition, the "Our Neighbors" show?"

"Not as exciting as a murder." Sara's eyes filled with tears. "I do miss Mrs. Carlton. She was a wonderful mentor and a strong, intelligent and creative woman. She'll be hard to replace."

"Yes, she will, but until the museum finds another director, you'll oversee everything well. And you know everyone is here to help you." I hesitated, thinking of Harold and wondering if his cousin, Mr. Graham, the president of the board of directors, shared his view of women, especially young women.

Sara must have been thinking the same thing. "Maybe not everyone thinks I can do this job." Then she seemed to shrug off the thought. "Great idea, Gram, speaking to the Historical Society about the "Our Neighbors" exhibition coming up soon. It might help attract people to the museum. For the right reason, not to gawk at the site of a murder."

I smiled to myself. Sara might have doubts about whether she was the right choice to temporarily serve as director of the museum, but I did not. She was smart and stronger than she thought she was.

My cell rang. I grabbed it out of my purse and looked at the number and name on the screen, my son, Sara's father. I usually ignored calls on my cell while I was at work, and I wanted to let this one go so I wouldn't have to talk to Geoffrey, afraid he might ask me questions about Sara I didn't want to answer, but that was cowardly of me and not very responsible as a parent.

I sighed and answered in a cheery voice. "Geoffrey, dear. What's up?"

"I've tried and tried to contact Sara on her cell, but she's not answering. I stopped by her house this morning and her car was there, but no Sara. Did the two of you go to work early this morning?'

"Yes, Geoffrey. We went in together in my car. Sara has so much more on her plate now that she's heading the museum that . . ."

"What do you mean, 'she's heading the museum?'"

Oh dear. I had counted on Sara telling her parents about her new position, but, like me, she obviously didn't want to worry her father who wasn't happy with either her professional life or her personal one.

"The board needed someone with both the experience and the education in museum studies to take over until they could mount a search for another director."

"But she doesn't have her degree yet, and she's not safe there. I told her that."

I hated to lie, but I needed to calm Geoffrey down. "Why would anyone want to hurt Sara?"

Geoffrey sputtered into the phone. "I hope the authorities have arrested the right man, but what about all those people rioting outside the museum? Sara is right in the middle of that. And people around here are having second thoughts about whether the museum should be returning that collection to the uh, Native American folks."

"Geoffrey! What are you talking about? There has been no rioting, just people expressing concerns about their property."

"Obviously, you haven't read the article in this morning's newspaper, the article by Agnes Danderfield. That's not what the article says."

"Agnes Danderfield doesn't do crime stories. She does gossipy things in her "About Town" column."

"Well, this time she's tackled the murder. Read it. It's on the front page."

I gulped. More publicity for the museum. Not what was needed. "Overstatement, I'm sure."

"Will you get a message to my daughter? Tell her to call me. I'm on my way to the museum now."

Well, of course I knew Geoffrey wouldn't "drag" Sara out of her office, but I wanted to prevent him dropping by. The crowd of people out front would upset him, and he was already in such a state I knew he wouldn't contain his concern and would have words with Sara, loud enough that everyone would hear. That was the last thing Sara needed and, if anyone here had doubts about her ability to do the job, a screaming mad father wouldn't be reassuring. What was Geoffrey thinking? But I knew what he was thinking. He wanted to protect his only daughter. I understood that. I gestured to Ellie who came up the stairs from her lunch break.

"Watch the desk for me, would you?" I dashed off to Sara's office.

I knocked and opened the door without waiting for a reply. Oh, good. Sara was on her phone. With her father? She held up a finger to signal me and mouthed, "I'm talking to Leonard."

I shook my head and grimaced.

"I'll get back to you," she said into the phone.

I was about to tell her to call her father, when someone grabbed the door from behind me and threw it open.

"Geoffrey!"

"Daddy!"

Too late, and Geoffrey had brought reinforcements with him. Abigail pushed her husband out of the way and rushed over to Sara enveloping her daughter in her arms.

Sara and I exchanged looks of despair. How could we manage a pair of helicopter parents?

CHAPTER 12

M Y IMPULSE WAS TO JUMP IN and chastise Geoffrey and Abigail for intruding into Sara's life, but she had a different approach.

"How nice of you two to come visit me. I've been so busy that I haven't has a chance to call you and tell you about changes in my duties here."

Oh what a clever girl, calling her appointment as acting director a "change in my duties."

"I don't think you've ever been to the museum before, have you? I've got some time in my schedule right now so let me show you around. Unfortunately, we haven't finished mounting our upcoming show, so that space is empty at this time, but I'm sure you'll love the other displays." Sara came from behind her desk and ushered her parents into the hall, continuing to talk about the displays, steering them into the ground floor exhibit of photography of the Adirondacks. I watched in awe at how she oversaw the situation. It was clear she didn't need my help to manage them. I returned to the front desk. When they exited the photography display, the concern about their daughter's safety written across their faces earlier was now gone replaced by proud looks from both parents.

Sara glanced at me and winked, then continued to walk them down the hallway toward a collection of local artists' works.

"Remember Marie Arnold who lived down the street from us years ago? She has several of her watercolors here. Let me show you. Then, if you'd like, we can return to my office for a coffee break. I'm sure you came here with questions about my work." Sara nodded at our first-floor guard stationed near her office door. "This is Murray. He's been with us for over five years. Murray, these are my parents." Geoffrey and Abigail exchanged greetings with the guard. "We have guards on all three floors as well as volunteers to answer questions."

Sara shot me another glance, this one filled with a look of relief. Sara's posture of professionalism coupled with a sense of relaxation and pride in the museum reassured her parents. This was her place, one where all the employees worked together in harmony. Nothing to worry about, she seemed to be saying . . . and they bought it. Thank goodness.

A half hour later, the door to her office opened and Geoffrey and Abigail exited, Sara saying, in her most reassuring voice. "I know you have some doubts about Leonard, but I'm certain, when you meet him, you'll see what a wonderful person he is."

"But his father is in jail for killing Mrs. Carlton," said Geoffrey, some of the old anxiety returning from the sound of his voice.

"No one here believes he's the killer. Why else would Richard take on his case if he thought Mr. Powles guilty? I'm certain all this will be cleared up soon."

"But if you're right, then the killer is still out there," said Abigail. "It's probably someone who works here. Otherwise, how did they get in?"

"I trust everyone who works here," said Sara. "The killer could have accessed the museum the same way you did. Through the front door."

"That certainly doesn't set my mind at ease," said Geoffrey. "I still think you could be in danger working here."

"And what about Gram? Should she give up her job here, too?" Sara asked.

Geoffrey locked glances with me. "Do you feel safe here?"

"Of course I do. Not that Mrs. Carlton deserved to be killed, but most murders aren't random. The killer is usually someone the victim knows, a targeted killing. If you don't believe me, ask Richard. That's why he's hired Zack to investigate the murder. He's looking into Mrs. Carlton's enemies, if she had any, or someone with a grudge against her. And Mr. Powles was certainly not an enemy. She was working diligently to address the issues among the nations and Mr. Powles's claims on one of the items in the collection."

Abigail reached for Geoffrey's arm. "We can't lock her in her room, dear. She's a grown woman."

Geoffrey shook his head, almost convinced Sara could oversee the situation. Lucky for Sara the crowd of nations people were fewer in number today and had withdrawn to the shade provided by the maple trees on the front lawn. Geoffrey stared at them through the door.

"You're not worried about them?" he said, waving his arm toward the group.

"Not at all. In fact, I'm due to meet with them in a few minutes to arrange an appropriate time for turning over the collection to each nation."

"Okay then," said Geoffrey. "How about you and Gram come to dinner? Soon. Maybe tonight?"

Sara hesitated in answering, poor girl. I knew how stressed she was with her new position and what happened last night at her place and the museum. She wanted time with Leonard, too, but not everything she had said to her parents to convince them of her safety was strictly true. The two nations thought the date for turning over the items had already been set, but Sara had decided to delay it. She was about to tell the representatives that now, and when she did and they let their groups know of the delay, the peacefulness of the gathering might be shattered by the news. And then there was what Sara had not told her parents: someone had been snooping around her apartment and another person had tried to break into the museum.

"Sure, Dad. Dinner would be great."

"Okey dokey, you two. Let's let Sara do her job while you run along home. We'll see you tonight." I rushed them off to their car and waved them goodbye.

"Thanks, Gram," said Sara.

"No. Thanks to you for being so level-headed. But tonight we need to let them know you're staying with me and why."

"Have you talked with Zack today? Does he have any idea who tried to get into the museum?"

"No, but I'll bet he's been looking into it as we speak. I'll give him a call."

I wasn't certain Zack would answer, but his cell rang only once.

"Hi, Maddie. I was about to call you about the events last night."

"You know who was responsible?"

"No, but I have some thoughts on it. Can we talk later, maybe after you get off work? I can stop by your place."

"Sure, but Sara will be there, you know."

"That's fine. If you don't mind, I'll see if Richard is free also along with Anita Burroughs. I think it's time we let the authorities know about the replacement of some museum items with fakes."

"Is that what Richard thinks too?" I asked.

"Yes. We were going to talk with Anita later today about it, but I think it makes sense to have all of us in on a discussion about the attempted break-in and the thefts of museum items sooner rather than later. I don't believe in coincidences—a murder, art objects stolen, the prowler at Sara's and the attempt to break into the museum. All of these must be connected somehow. We need Anita's office to be in on these investigations. I can't try to find Mrs. Carlton's killer as well as look into the other crimes. Anita's office has limited resources, but she will want to dedicate one of her deputies to these crimes."

"Okay, then. Sara and I will stop by the pizzeria on the way home and pick up a pie for us. No one can solve a murder on an empty stomach."

Zack laughed. "See you then."

The family dinner at Geoffrey and Abigail's would have to be postponed. I punched Geoffrey's number to let him know Sara and I wouldn't be coming. "Hi. Change of plans. Richard, Zack, the sheriff and I need to meet to talk about, uh, things."

"What things?"

"You know, stuff at the museum."

Assuming I meant Mrs. Carlton's murder, Geoffrey said, "Why are you and Sara going to be in on this discussion about the murder? Is there something we should know?"

"Oh, no. They just want to go over some questions Richard has about the events of that day." I wanted to keep the reason for the meeting vague and not let on about the events of last night.

"Tomorrow night then?"

"If we can make it a short dinner. Sara is the speaker at the historical society meeting."

"Fine. Maybe I should ask Richard if he'd like to come also. Make it a real family get together."

"Good idea, Geoffrey, but you know Richard can't talk about the case."

"But he can discuss it with you, Sara and Zack?" Geoffrey sounded indignant.

"Zack is Richard's investigator on the case. They just want to ask Sara and me some questions."

Geoffrey made a hmmmphing sound into the phone. "And I suppose you're playing amateur detective with him." With that jab at me, he disconnected.

THAT EVENING AT MY PLACE, Zack, Sara, Anita, Richard and I shared a pizza for dinner and then got right down to talking about the break ins.

"We know someone tried to enter the museum. I think whoever it was had burglary on their mind. Do you think one of the nations people got tired of waiting for the museum to return their property and decided to steal the items?" asked Anita.

"Until this afternoon when I announced the return of the items would have to be delayed, everyone thought the ceremony would be this fall as announced earlier by Mrs. Carlton. Why try to steal what would be theirs in a month or so?"

"So the burglary attempt was unsuccessful, and the museum's property is intact," said Anita.

Sara fidgeted in her seat and shot a meaningful look at Richard. Anita noticed her discomfort. "Is there something else, Sara?"

Richard nodded at Sara. "Go ahead and tell her."

"Some of the museum items aren't real," said Sara.

"What do you mean?" asked Anita.

"According to Sara, at least one is a fake and another is missing." Richard cleared his throat. "We think Mrs. Carlton may have known about them."

Anita's face reddened with anger. "And you didn't think this information was significant enough to tell me?"

"Everything has been in an uproar around here, Sheriff Burroughs. And the events last night only made it worse," said Richard. That was a pretty lame excuse for not informing the authorities about something that might be related to the murder of Mrs. Carlton, but it was the truth. Nothing had been normal since the murder.

"When I discovered the fake, I was most worried about the objects in the Native American collection, so I called my professor at the university to pay us a visit tomorrow and check on those objects and others I found questionable. I'm no expert in Native American artifacts, but he is." Sara shrugged her shoulders and looked sheepish. "I'm sorry I didn't tell you sooner."

"Maybe it's just as well. I have no way of determining a fake artifact from a real one. Your professor's expertise will be necessary in determining if anything from that collection has been stolen or replaced." Anita did not look happy about learning of thefts, the fake and of the delay in telling her about them.

"The contents of the entire museum will come under scrutiny and calling in more experts to decide what's real and what's not will take time. If the public thinks the museum may be displaying fake collections, it could ruin us. I'd like to keep this as close to home as possible." Sara's voice was filled with worry.

"As well you should. Do you trust all your employees?" asked Anita.

Sara sighed and shook her head. "I'd like to say yes, but I can't. I checked Mrs. Carlton's museum ledger which your office returned when I asked for it. As for the possibility that the Albertson family donated money to the museum to have their items in the "Our Neighbors" displayed earlier than intended, the ledger revealed that Mrs. Carlton wanted the collection to be displayed this fall as a draw for museum patrons. There's no evidence that the Albertson family had any role in that. Also there's no notation to indicate Mrs. Carlton was aware of the switch to a copy or of the thefts, but she knew something was going on. She hinted to me that she was worried about the security of our collections, but she wasn't specific. I thought she meant we should be more cautious about locking up items after they had been brought out of locked security and used for study."

"For study?" asked Zack.

"Yes. Under the supervision of a guard or one of our employees and in special circumstances, college and high school students interested in exhibitions are allowed hands-on study of the art."

"I can see what an issue this is. For now, call in your professor to examine the Native American collection. Let's not alert anyone outside this room that we believe items are not genuine or stolen. I now suspect Mrs. Carlton was killed because she knew the truth." Anita turned her eyes to Sara. "That worries me about you and the prowler last night at your place. Who knows that you discovered the thefts?"

"Only Gram." Sara's eyes wouldn't meet mine and the sheriff caught the hesitation in Sara's expression.

"You told someone else?" asked Anita.

"I told Leonard, but he doesn't know anyone associated with the museum except for Gram and me, so who would he tell?"

"How about his father?" said Zack.

"Who might tell his family members." Richard shook his head. "It may be too late to contain this information."

"And if it is, then Sara is in danger," I said.

"You both may be targets." Zack reached out and patted my shoulder.

Richard arose from the couch. "I'll talk to Leonard's father and see what he knows. Meanwhile, Sara, can you convince Leonard not to tell anyone about the museum items?"

Sara nodded, but she said she didn't know if he had already talked with his father or others in his family.

"It's the best we can do for now. I'm on my way to visit Mr. Powles tonight."

"Can I come with you, Uncle Richard? I need to tell him that I've changed the date for turning over the collection to the nations people. And to him, of course, assuming he can establish the basket belongs to his people."

"I'll come along, too, if you don't mind," I said.

Richard started to shake his head.

"Not even if I promise to remain silent and not ask a lot of questions?"

Richard laughed. "That's a promise I know you can't keep. He is reluctant to talk to me and I'm his lawyer."

"And I'm Sara's grandmother. His people respect their elders. He may find me a more acceptable presence than a legal representative. What's the harm?"

So Sara, Zack and I piled in Richard's car. Anita left ahead of us. Would Mr. Powles agree to see all of us, and would the jail allow it?

Anita must have paved the way for our visit because the guard ushered us into a visitors' room and even found two extra chairs for Sara and me, then escorted Mr. Powles into the room. His face registered nothing other than the usual grim expression he'd shown when I'd seen him at the museum and standing in the room across from Mrs. Carlton's body. I almost felt as if we were intruding, yet he had been informed about the identity of his visitors and had agreed to our visit.

He locked eyes with Richard. "Do you really need your investigator, my son's girlfriend and an old woman to plan your defense?"

I wanted yell at him for calling me an "old woman," but instead I leveled a stern look at him and said, "Be respectful of your elders as your culture demands."

His eyes turned flinty for a moment, then he threw back his head and laughed. "Yes, Grandmother."

Mr. Powles's response took Richard aback for a moment, but Richard adroitly followed up on Powles' acceptance of my presence. "This is my mother, Mrs. Sharps," Richard said.

"I know. Many in this area know her and her penchant for ferreting out the truth. And I have been informed that your granddaughter is now acting director of the museum." He then turned his attention to Sara. "My son tells me your path ahead in this position may be difficult."

Sara's face grew sad. "Your path and that of your fellow nations may also hold difficulties. I have had to push back the date for the museum's return of the collection until later this winter."

We all held our breath waiting for Mr. Powles' reaction to Sara's announcement.

But he merely nodded. "Because of Mrs. Carlton's death. I understand. And so, I ask all of you: knowing that such an act would impede the progress of the return of the collection, why would I, or any of the nations' members kill the person most responsible for helping return those items to us?"

"No one of the nations people or you would kill her. We know that," I said.

"And if you know that, why am I here?"

Richard spoke up. "Because you were found in the room with her body."

"And I told you I entered that room after she had been attacked. I knelt to see if I could help her and, when I could not, I stepped away from her to give her the dignity she deserved in death."

"I'm curious," I said, "You told Mrs. Carlton you had proof the basket belonged to your family. What kind of proof?"

Mr. Powles knitted his brow in puzzlement and hesitated to answer my question, but finally said, "You really don't know?"

"No, but if you can provide that proof, it may help your case," Richard said.

"I'll think about it. Is that all you need from me?" Powles rose to his feet signaling he had nothing to add.

"For now," said Richard. "If you can think of anything else before tomorrow, let me know."

"I'll let your mother know." The corners of his mouth twitched as if he wanted to smile, but instead they returned to the firm line that was his signature look.

"Uhm, you don't have any way to contact me," I said.

"I can find a way."

He turned his back on us and knocked on the door behind him. The guard standing on the other side opened it and Powles left without another word.

CHAPTER 13

RICHARD, SARA, ZACK AND I STOOD OUTSIDE the county jail after our meeting.

"Well, that went well, don't you think?" My voice was filled with sarcasm.

"He's not very forthcoming," said Zack, "and considering what has happened, I can't blame him."

"I wonder why he looked puzzled we didn't know what he meant by 'proof' of his claim." I said.

"The nations' people never appeared interested in the basket. They were concerned with the artifacts they knew with certainty belonged to them. They appeared willing to consider Mr. Powles's claim on a basket in the collection." Sara stood with her arms wrapped around herself. She shivered a bit as the autumn wind picked up and tossed leaves into the air. "I'm worried that basket or other artifacts in the nations collection may have been replaced with fakes. I'll feel better once the expert I've called in takes a close look at the collection when he arrives tomorrow. Until Mr. Powles is willing to tell us what he means by 'proof,' we at least need to know if everything in the collection is genuine."

I agreed with Sara. Mrs. Carlton's murder, the attempt to blame it on Mr. Powles, and the missing museum pieces were all related. But their connection to one another was yet unclear. Not helping point to the solution was Agnes Danderfield's disappearance, which I had kept to myself. I made a mental note to get on the internet tonight to look for any connection between Agnes and Mrs. Carlton as well as explore Mrs. Carlton's past. I needed to do my part in this investigation as I had promised Zack and Richard. Tomorrow at the museum, I'd talk with museum volunteers and employees to see what they knew about Mrs. Carlton. If I had the time, I wanted to stop by the neighborhood watch dog, Mrs. Denton. She might be the best source for information about Agnes, especially if I loosened her tongue with a gift of some kind.

But first things first. It was time to tell Abigail and Geoffrey about why Sara was staying with me without alarming them too much.

Once home, I sent Sara to bed. The circles under her eyes had darkened and gotten puffier. She looked as if she might drop before she managed to get to her bedroom.

"I'm sending Spike up with you to keep you company." I gave her a gentle push toward the stairs and, assured that she had fallen asleep soon after, I called Geoffrey and Abigail.

Abigail answered. "It's kind of late, Mom."

"I know and I'm sorry. I got caught up with my writing." That was the first lie I'd tell her tonight. "Just wanted to let you know that Sara is staying with me for the time being." That was the truth, but what was to follow was not quite the truth. "Oh, don't worry. It's really nothing. There have been some kids in her neighborhood staying out late and tearing the neighborhood apart. I convinced Sara she'd get better sleep at my place." It was sorta the truth. "And the museum is upgrading their security system. I thought you'd prefer Sara stay with me until the upgraded system was in place," which was mostly a lie, but close enough.

Abigail sounded relieved. "Geoffrey and I would prefer she be with us, but you do have plenty of room, and I suspect she'd prefer having you supervise her visits with her boyfriend rather than her parents. She views you as more indulgent than us. Just make certain she doesn't take any chances."

"Oh, of course."

"Can I talk to her?"

"With all her new responsibilities, she's exhausted and is sleeping."

"Yes. I understand." There was a pause. "And how is your boyfriend? Are the two of you still, er, together?"

"No. His daughter is here visiting, so he's back at the B and B where she is also staying. We thought he'd have more time with her that way."

"Let me talk to her." Geoffrey came on the line. "We're still upset over the murder at the museum."

"Yes, well, not to worry. Richard and Zack are working on that."

"They're working to free the man who did it, aren't they? What help is that to anyone, to let the killer go free?"

"He's not the killer. Why would he kill Mrs. Carlton?"

"The DA thinks he did."

"Richard does not and neither does anyone else."

"The story in the newspaper points the finger at Mr. Powles. The evidence against him is pretty solid according to Danderfield's sources."

"Geoffrey, honey. Agnes Danderfield is not a crime reporter. Let Richard and the authorities work on the case. Anyway, I assure you, everyone at the museum is perfectly safe."

I was too exhausted to spend any time on the internet searching for the relationship between Agnes Danderfield and Mrs. Carlton. Maybe tomorrow. I peeked in Sara's room before I headed to bed. She was sleeping, Spike curled at her feet. Everyone here tucked in their beds, safe as I had assured Abigail and Geoffrey . . . or so I thought.

MONDAY, SARA AND I RODE TOGETHER to work in my car. There were no people outside the entrance when we pulled around the front and parked behind the building. We both looked at each other and smiled. Maybe things were getting back to normal . . . well, except for a murder, a prowler, an attempted break-in and missing museum pieces. Yet, somehow, not having a crowd of people outside holding vigil until the museum returned what those people had been deprived of for generations made the atmosphere at work close to a typical day.

Sara paced the hallway outside her office until the expert she had called to examine the nations collection appeared midmorning. He was a short, broad man, skin the color burnt sienna. His dark hair was cropped short, and he wore an air of competence and assurance.

"Dr. Walker." Sara held out her hand to greet him. "Good to see you again. Let's talk in my office." Sara told me in the car this morning that Walker had a Ph. D. in museum studies and was the perfect individual to examine the artifacts. His mother was Oneida, his father Onondaga. She had enrolled in several courses with him during her museum program studies. Sara hadn't needed to explain much about returning the collection nor how sensitive an issue of fake items would be. Other than Sara, I was the only person working at the museum who knew why Walker was here. I gave a deep sigh of relief when Sara closed the door to her office and she and Walker conferred inside, but my relief was short-lived as I spied Mr. Graham, the head of the museum's board of directors, stride up the front sidewalk and into the entrance.

He flapped his hand at me dismissively and walked past my desk toward Sara's office. "I need to speak with Ms. Sparks. Now." He opened the door without knocking and entered.

I jumped in surprise as I felt someone's hot breath on my neck.

"Harold. What are you doing?" I pushed back my chair, forcing him to retreat a few feet.

"What's my cousin doing here? And who was that other guy?" Harold left my desk and approached Sara's office. He leaned toward the door as if he meant to eavesdrop.

"Mind your own business, Harold," I said.

"I do, but I've heard you don't," he said. "It's not important. I can ask my cousin about it later."

Inviting Dr. Walker to examine the collection was to be kept quiet so as not to alarm the nations' people about the security of their property. To that end I knew Sara had not informed Mr. Graham of her invitation to Dr. Walker. Could Sara and Walker make up a story to keep Mr. Graham from knowing about the missing objects? If he found out and told his cousin, there would be no end to who knew. Discretion was not something Harold was familiar with, and I didn't think his cousin was either. They not only looked alike, but it was rumored they both liked to gossip. We were in trouble.

An hour later, Sara, Graham and Walker emerged from Sara's office.

"Just a routine survey of the collection about to be returned to the nations' people. The sensitivity of the handover means we want to make certain everything is in order for the upcoming ceremony. And, particularly so, with the recent events here." Dr. Walker spoke in a reassuring and authoritative tone, and it looked as if Graham bought it.

The director smiled, shook Walker's hand and patted Sara on the shoulder. "You're doing a fine job. I'd love to show off the collection of Native American artifacts I own."

At the word "own," Dr. Walker frowned.

Graham cleared his throat and backtracked, "I mean, all of my items were gifts from friends. All perfectly legal."

"Except," Dr. Walker said, "you don't know how your 'friends' obtained them."

"Some of my friends are Indigenous people, so they can gift me an item without violating the law, can't they?" There was acid in Graham's voice, and his lips were drawn thin in anger.

Instead of reacting to Graham, Walker changed course. "I might take you up on your invitation and drop by to see what you have. I would find it interesting."

Graham's lips relaxed. "Sure. Anytime."

I could tell Graham regretted issuing the invitation to Walker but couldn't back down. He gave a curt nod, walked out the door and got into his car which he had parked in the handicapped spot in front of the museum. There was no tag on his rear-view mirror to indicate he had a handicapped parking permit. He had assumed he could take advantage because of his position on the museum's board of directors. Graham had a reputation for being difficult and stubborn. Sara told me he wanted to buy the old stone hotel in town but wasn't willing to pay the price the owner asked. Graham's father had once operated the hotel and Graham thought the monthly rent his father paid to the owner when the hotel was up and running should be viewed as rent-to-own money although there was no evidence of a legal agreement of that.

"Graham acts as if he owns this village," Sara had once confided.

"Maybe that's his intention. I understand he's the landlord for many of the rentals in the village. Lord of the Manor," I had quipped to Sara that day.

Sara turned to Dr. Walker. "Thank you for being so discreet about the reason I called you here." Although there were still dark circles under Sara's eyes and her skin looked gray with exhaustion, her eyes seemed brighter with Walker's presence.

Walker smiled at her. "Let's get started, shall we?"

Sara walked him down the stairs toward the collection area.

"I don't like that guy snooping around here." It was Harold again, leaning over me, intruding into my personal space.

I spun around in my chair. "Don't you have a job to do, or is sticking your nose into something which isn't your business part of your job description?"

Harold gave me a black look. "I hear tell that you're one of the nosiest women in the village."

"There's a difference between nosy and curious. I plead guilty to the latter."

I thought my sharp retort would chase Harold away, but instead he leaned closer. "So Ms. Curiosity, do you know what's going on around here? You and your granddaughter are always whispering about something. Does it have to do with the collection? Is something missing from it?"

Now that was an interesting suspicion on Harold's part.

"If something is missing, how would you know about it?"

He shrugged. "I hear stuff."

"What 'stuff'?"

Harold smiled as if he knew a secret and wanted me to beg him to reveal what it was. I wasn't biting.

"Look, if you know something important, you should talk to the sheriff. It could be related to Mrs. Carlton's murder."

"Do you think so?"

"Look, Harold. What you heard could be relevant to the murder. I wouldn't go around talking about it."

What Harold heard could be significant in the murder, and if so, it did put him in danger. I wasn't kidding about that. Or was Harold telling me he overheard something about missing items as a way of protecting himself because he engaged in theft, replacement of artifacts or even murder? Naw, I told myself. Harold wasn't clever enough to cover himself by using me to throw the authorities off the scent.

I didn't trust him. What was Harold really up to and would he get himself killed sticking that pointy nose of his where it wasn't wanted?

CHAPTER 14

HAROLD'S EAVESDROPPING LEFT ME WITH some questions I thought I might be better at answering than he would, so I asked Ellie to work the entrance desk for a few minutes and knocked on Sara's door.

I told her what Harold had said.

"Keep this information to yourself. I don't know what Harold is up to, but I intend to discuss it with Zack. For now, however, I have an errand to run that may help in the case. Ellie can sit at the desk for an hour or so, can't she?"

"Sure, Gram, but I want to know what this errand's about." Sara looked suspicious.

"Oh, nothing, really. I thought I'd run by the bakery and buy some cupcakes for our afternoon tea."

"And that's all you're willing to say. Cupcakes? Really?" Sara put her hands on her hips, tilted her head to one side and rolled her eyes. "You will tell me what you're up to when you get back. Right?"

"Oh, sure." I dashed out the door, grabbed my sweater off the chair, told Ellie I would be back in an hour and ran to my car.

NOT EVERYTHING I TOLD SARA WAS A LIE. I did stop by the bakery and purchase donuts, cupcakes and blueberry scones, but only part of my bakery haul would go to the museum's employees.

I pulled up in front of Mrs. Denton's house. I saw the front window curtain move as I walked up the sidewalk, so I knew she was home. The door opened before I could knock.

"Whatcha got there?" she asked.

"I thought you might like an early tea." I turned and took a look across the street. Agnes's car wasn't in her drive. I sidled past Mrs. Denton into her living room, saw the door into the kitchen and carried the bakery box in, setting it on the counter.

"Bribery is what you mean," Despite her snide remark, she grabbed a tea kettle off the stove, filled it with water and put the burner on underneath it, then she flipped open the lid to the pastry box.

"Like anything there?" I asked.

"They all look yummy, but I've got nothing to report on Agnes Danderfield. No movement around her place. Do I still get a goodie?"

"Take whatever you like. This is more by way of thanks for talking with me yesterday."

She gave me a suspicious look. This was one old lady not easily fooled.

Once tea was ready and Mrs. Denton had poured us each a cup and chosen one of the blueberry scones to accompany hers, she sat back in her chair and sighed. "This is real nice, neighborly, like." She reached for a chocolate frosted cupcake, but I pulled the box out of her reach.

"No, tell me the truth. Did Agnes come back to her house?"

"How would I know?" Mrs. Denton tried her best to make her blue eyes all round with innocence.

"Don't try to fool me."

"I'm not lying," she insisted.

"How about her visitor from the other night? Have you seen him again?"

I pushed the pastry box back toward Mrs. Denton. She took her chocolate cupcake, peeled off the paper and took a dainty bite out of it. "Maybe he returned last night. I don't spend all my time spying on my neighbors, you know."

"Was it the same guy?"

"Could be. Probably." Mrs. Denton continued to stare at the pastry box.

"You've been immensely helpful, my dear. Keep an eye out, will you? You'll be doing the authorities a favor."

Her eyes lit up. "Really? Like I'm on a stake out?"

"Like that."

I closed the pastry box and started to leave. "Sorry, but I need to take these remaining treats back to work for our afternoon break."

"How about just one more for me? I didn't get to try the cream-filled donuts."

I nodded and Mrs. Denton reached into the box and snatched two donuts.

"I hope you're not diabetic," I said.

"Nope."

Before I got back into my car, I gazed at Agnes' front porch step. I found no morning paper there. Now what good newspaper employee wouldn't have the newspaper she worked for delivered each morning to her house? I continued to scan Agnes' house and felt as if someone inside was watching me back. Only a hunch on my part, but I'd find out later, or my neighborhood snitch would find out for me.

I DROPPED THE PASTRY BOX OFF IN THE BREAK ROOM and was about to return to my duties at the desk when Sara brought Dr. Walker into the room for tea. Like the museum employees, he too appreciated the sugar fix.

"Everything going well?" I asked.

"This is my grandmother, Mrs. Sharps. She can be trusted completely. She knows why you're here."

Walker nodded. "So nice to meet you and to know there's someone to whom Sara can confide. I spent the morning and early afternoon with the nations' collection. Everything is genuine, nothing missing. The Taylor inventory lists nineteen baskets and they're all there. One of them must be the basket Mr. Powles' family is claiming. I wish we had an idea of which one."

I breathed a sigh of relief.

"Mr. Powles said he had proof one of the baskets was his, but he's not cooperating with the authorities nor his lawyer about this proof. And I can't show him the collection because he could simply claim a basket. I need to see some evidence for which basket belongs to his family. He's a very stubborn man."

Dr. Walker gave Sara a sympathetic smile. "Can you blame him? You know he has good reason to mistrust white justice."

Sara gazed across the room with a look of sadness on her face. "I do understand, but he can't advance his claim on the basket without some kind of evidence his family has a right to it, but just as important, that evidence might help uncover the identity of Mrs. Carlton's killer."

Sara appeared to shake herself out of her despair and then said, "I think we can now set a firm date for the return of the artifacts. I've also asked Dr. Walker to examine the 'Our Neighbors' collection due to be put on display soon. That's where I discovered the fake brooch. He'll do that work the remainder of the afternoon and Tuesday morning."

"And then?" I asked.

"We'll see. It would be quite the task to go through everything in the museum. I'd hate if it came to that." Furrows deepened on Sara's forehead. "But at least, we know the nations' collection is intact. It will be a relief to have those items returned to their rightful owners. It should have been done long ago."

Walker nodded his agreement. "Despite the law having gone into effect over thirty years ago, there are still artifacts housed in libraries, universities and museums. The relocation of these important works has been painfully slow."

"And not just because of the pandemic. We've had decades to

move on returning the work. I assume there are items all over the nation housed in storage areas that no one even knows about," I said.

Walker nodded again. "Well, I have a lot of work ahead of me. I'd better get to it."

"I'll show you the 'Our Neighbors' collection." Sara waved to me as she and Dr. Walker left, then turned and said, "You are coming with me tonight to the historical society meeting, right?"

"Yep. An early dinner with your parents and then we'll be stopping by to give my friend Jane a ride also. Your parents will drive themselves and meet us there."

Sara gave me a weak smile. I knew having her parents in the audience made her nervous, but they were so proud of her work, they wanted to support her in any way they could despite their reservations about her safety in her new position.

THE HISTORICAL ASSOCIATION HAD JUST TAKEN OVER the building in town that had housed the American Legion, and officers in the association had repaired, repainted and cleaned the facility. This was the first meeting in the renovated building.

Attendance had tripled from the meetings I remembered, probably because of the new facility and also because having the museum's acting director as a speaker attracted a larger crowd. Of course, one couldn't forget the recent murder at the museum drew the curious who hoped Sara would refer to the event and perhaps discuss it in more detail than provided in the newspaper articles, but Sara talked about the upcoming "Our Neighbors" exhibition and said not a word about the murder except to express her dismay at the loss of Mrs. Carlton as museum director. Hands shot up after Sara finished her speech, several people asking about Mrs. Carlton's death. Sara politely told them she could not discuss that while the authorities investigated her death. Sara's presentation was engaging, and several members of the audience stayed even after refreshments were served. Only one of them continued to try to wheedle information about the murder out of Sara, a persistent older man wearing a rumpled suit and a camouflage patterned ball cap. Zack was in attendance, and he stepped in and maneuvered the too curious and unpleasantly aggressive man out of the way. Sara reached out and patted Zack's arm in thanks for moving the man away from her.

"The public has a right to know what happened to the museum director. We know that Indian has been arrested for the murder. Are you trying to protect him?" The man, face red with anger, continued to badger Sara as Zack physically walked him out of the room.

"Time to get you home, sweetie." I grabbed Sara by the arm, nabbed her jacket from the coat rack near the door and led her outside to the car. Jane followed us. Zack waved good night and got into his car.

"Wait a minute. There's someone I want to talk with." Sara approached a woman and man who had sat together in the front row. She talked with them for a few minutes, reached out and pointed at the woman who smiled and nodded, touching something on her jacket. While they were talking, I noticed a familiar figure get into the passenger's side of a car and drive off. Hmm. My earlier suspicion had been correct. I thought I had seen Agnes Danderfield mingling with the crowd in the back of the room. Obviously, she was back in town. Perhaps I could slip out of the house after Sara went to bed and have a talk with her.

Sara ended her conversation and then came back to Jane and me.

"Who was that?" I asked.

"They introduced themselves as Joan and Mitchel Tompson. She wore an unusual brooch, a starburst pattern, each arm of the star filled with tiny rubies. Didn't you notice it, Gram?"

"No. Should I have?"

"It was similar to the one I showed you from the "Our Neighbors'" collection."

"You mean the fake one?"

"Yes, but this one was not fake."

"You mean . . ."

"It has to be the one from the collection."

"Did you tell her?"

"No. I simply said it was eye-catching and asked where she got it."

"Where?"

"She said her husband bought it for her from a jewelry store in New York City. When she told me this, her husband looked uncomfortable. I thought he was lying and, sure enough, when she joined a few women for a chat, he came over to me and confessed he bought it at a pawn shop in Syracuse. 'I didn't want her to know it was pawn, so I led her to believe it was from a high-class jewelry store,' he said."

"Why did he confess this to you?"

"I think he was worried that because I was associated with the museum, I knew something about jewelry and might follow-up with her and tell her it was pawn jewelry. I told him I would keep his secret as long as he told me which pawn shop it was."

"But if it is the broach from the museum, you won't keep quiet, will you?" I asked.

Sara smiled. "He told me the name of the pawn shop. It's in Syracuse."

"Well then, my dear. We need to visit that pawn shop as soon as possible."

"I'll tag along," said Jane. "I mean, in case you two need back up."

Sara chuckled. "Now I know why you and Gram are friends. You're as nosy as she is." Sara threw her arms around the two of us and we planned for our early morning trip to Syracuse tomorrow.

"Do you want to talk to Zack and let him know what we have in mind?" asked Sara.

Jane and I exchanged glances. "No need to get anyone else involved. We're only going to look at secondhand stuff, like visiting a thrift shop. Men find that kind of shopping boring, don't they?" I said.

WE DROPPED OFF JANE, PROMISING TO PICK HER UP the next morning around nine so that we could be the first customers when the shop opened. Sara, apologizing for the lateness of the call, contacted Francis to let her know she and I would be an hour or so late coming into the museum.

Sara gave Francis the access code to the museum's outer doors as well as the one needed to get into the collections room. "Dr. Walker should be in first thing also. You can let him into the room where we're preparing the 'Our Neighbors' exhibition. I don't anticipate any drama tomorrow before I get there, but if you need me, you have my cell. Or, in case of an emergency, call the sheriff's department."

I heard Francis agree. "No problems, Sara. I won't let you down."

And she wouldn't. Francis was a no-nonsense kind of woman. If anyone probed for why Sara and I weren't there to open tomorrow, Francis would tell them it was none of their business in her firm but polite manner. But who would give her grief? Oh, yeah, maybe Harold.

When we entered the house, Spike was hungry as usual, and told us so, loudly. I filled his bowl with his favorite dry food and gave him a pat on the head.

"That cat adores you, Gram."

"Does he? I think her adores his food more."

"Well, as I understand it, that's the way of cats. But he's a good companion for you, isn't he?"

If Sara was trying to wheedle information out of me about my relationship with Zack by her "companion" reference, I played dumb and gave her a nod of agreement.

She waited for a minute, then gave up her subtle probing. "I'm beat. I'm going to bed. See you in the morning." She gave me a hug and climbed the stairs followed by Spike to take up his usual place at the end of her bed.

I waited half an hour, busying myself with checking the kitchen door to the back deck, starting the dishwasher and then heading upstairs as well, but instead of changing into my pajamas, I chose a pair of jeans and a sweatshirt, then crept quietly down the stairs and left the house. Time to pay another visit to Agnes Danderfield's house. I was certain I'd find her home. I had a few questions I wanted to ask her about her conversation with Mrs. Carlton the day before the murder as well as why she called me eager to talk but then stood me up for lunch.

THERE WAS A LIGHT IN THE FRONT WINDOW when I pulled up in front of Agnes' house and her car had returned to the driveway. I glanced across the street toward my snoopy friend, Mrs. Denton, who, as I expected, was peeking through a slit in her curtain. I gave a cheery wave to her and stepped onto Agnes's porch and rang the bell. It was late to be making a call on someone who wasn't a close friend, not even much of an acquaintance, but I didn't want to take the chance Agnes would bolt again and I'd miss talking with her.

I heard voices inside followed by silence, and I worried that Agnes had decided not to answer her door. I heard the lock turn, and she opened the door.

"I knew better than to ignore you, Maddie Sparks. You're a persistent woman. I worried you'd just sit in your car outside until I came out tomorrow morning. You might as well come in."

Sitting in her living room on the sofa was a man, tall, slender, balding, his brown eyes met mine with a look of curiosity. He wore a knit shirt and a pair of jeans.

"This is Al, a friend of mine," Agnes said. "Maddie, the town snoop."

He smiled, got up and came to shake my hand. "I've heard about you."

I cocked my head to one side. "Really? Do you live around here?"

"I used to."

My glance traveled from him to Agnes and back. "You're friends."

"We are."

"Might as well tell her, Aggie," Al said.

"We were more than friends years ago." Agnes picked at her skirt, uncomfortable confessing this to me.

"When did you say you got back in town, Mr, uh . . . Al? I didn't catch your last name."

"I arrived the other night from Illinois."

"And then you and Agnes left. Where did you go?"

Al settled back onto the couch and sighed. "I'm Brenda Carlton's half-brother, not that she told many people about me. My name is Al Lawton. We never got along, and she stepped in when I tried to marry Agnes. My sister thought I wasn't good enough for her friend Agnes. The family backed her opinion of me, so I left. I haven't had contact with either Agnes, my sister or the family for years."

"But brotherly love brought you back here when you heard about your sister's death."

"Of course. I wanted to attend the funeral, pay my respects to her daughters and friends."

I looked at Agnes to confirm Al's story.

"That's right," she said. "When he got here, I realized there was no food in the house, so we left to go to the all-night supermarket."

While Al seemed fine with the story, Agnes continued to pick at the nonexistent lint on her skirt. She looked up at me and rested her hands in her lap.

"Fine, fine. Maddie. You got me. I didn't want anyone to know Al was here, so we went to Syracuse and got a motel room to sort things out."

"You mean you weren't comfortable having Al in the house or even around town, so you drove him to Syracuse and got him a motel room there."

Al got off the couch and came over to Agnes. He put his arm around her. "I'm trying to persuade her that we belong together. I think I'm winning her over. Right?"

Agnes looked up at him and her eyes softened. "Maybe."

"I gather you and Brenda Carlton remained on friendly terms even though she talked her brother out of marrying you."

"We remained on speaking terms." Agnes cleared her throat and started pulling on the material in her skirt again. Why so nervous, Agnes?

I wouldn't get anything else out of either of them, so I left it at that although I knew they were lying to me. Was it condolences, love finally winning out or something else that led Al back here? And just when did Al get into town? He never answered my question about that. He had a reason to dislike his half-sister. She had stood in the way of him and Agnes getting together. He could have killed her, but why now after all these years? And what was Agnes so keen to talk with me about over lunch? And then she was a no show.

CHAPTER 15

I SNEAKED BACK INTO MY HOUSE rousing only Spike who thought he deserved another bowl of food. I complied with his demands to quiet his meows which I worried would wake Sara, as she needed her sleep.

Although I felt tired, unlike Sara, sleep didn't come easily and when it did, I awoke several times during the night, the relationship between Agnes and Al on my mind. One question after the other chased themselves around in my mind: how did Al find out about his sister's death? Were he and Agnes in touch all these years and she told him? If so, and they now took up where they left off years ago, why did it take them so much time to hook up again? Was Al so easily defeated by the family that he left Agnes, the woman he professed to love and wanted to marry?

When the sun finally rose over the creek between five and six, I decided to get out of bed, take a quick shower and call in someone who could help answer my questions.

I went downstairs, fed Spike and put on a pot of coffee. While it was brewing, I called Zack. He sounded groggy.

"I hope I didn't wake you."

"What time is it anyway? Is something wrong, Maddie? I'll be right over."

"No, no. No need. I just have something I'd like you to do for me."

"Anything for you. You know that."

"Good. You're a peach. How is your daughter?"

"Struggling, but Mary is a real help."

I didn't ask him if he had called my friend John Tennet, the man who knew more about drug rehab than anyone I knew and who had helped people get clean. I suspected the answer to that question was no. Why was Zack so keen on keeping Mary in the picture, and had Mary told him about her, or their son? I told Zack about Al Lawton and asked him if he could find out anything about the man.

"I'll get back to you. Meantime, how about we get together for coffee? I'd like to discuss something with you."

"Something about the case or is this personal?"

"More like personal."

"Zack, it either is personal or it's not. There is no 'more like.'" I heard Sara come down the stairs. "Sorry. Sara is up. I've got to run." I ended the call, not having to answer Zack's question about getting together. Collaborating with him on this case was one thing. A personal reason for coffee? I didn't have an answer for him right now.

Sara poured herself a cup of coffee and leaned against the counter, a tiny smile on her face. "Talking with Zack, were you?" her grin suggesting she was pleased Zack and I were in touch. I decided to let her believe what she wanted.

We ate a quick breakfast, picked up Jane and headed on the two-hour drive to the pawn shop in Syracuse.

DEV'S PAWN WAS LOCATED IN A STRIP MALL in a seedy part of the city. The mall had housed five or six shops, but now there was only the pawn shop and another shop at the other end of the mall, a convenience store. The other store fronts were closed. Garbage bins stood at one end of the building, trash spilling out onto the sidewalk. Some had blown around the parking area and into the strip of unmown grass between the lot and the busy street in front. A man pushing a cart filled with black garbage bags and assorted items, probably his life's possessions, stopped to watch us as we turned off the street and pulled into the parking slot in front of Dev's.

When we got out of the car, the man with the cart yelled at us. "Dev's not in yet. Too early." He wheeled his cart into the lot and up to our car. "Got a smoke?"

We all shook our heads, anxious for him to leave, but he leaned against the cart and continued to stare at us.

"How about a ten?"

Jane reached into her purse, pulled several bills and held them out to him.

"That won't buy me nothin'." He scowled but grabbed the money.

Jane added a five to the bills. "Get yourself something to eat and stay away from the smokes."

He clicked the heels of his ratty sneakers together, gave her a snappy two finger salute, turned his cart around and headed off down the sidewalk, the wheels of the cart wobbling and squalling.

"Kind of you, Jane," I said, and Sara smiled at her.

We turned our attention to the pawn shop, which as our cart friend had informed us, was not yet open.

"It says it opens at noon. We've got an hour to wait," I said.

The creaking sound coming from the shopping cart's wheels suddenly ceased. The fella pushing the cart stopped in front of the convenience store, and we watched him wave the bills over his head, pull open the door and push the carriage into the store.

"The money should get him a pack of smokes and a can of Fosters. I wasted my money and my advice." Jane shook her head.

We continued our wait, our eyes trained on the store front as if our gazes could somehow make the pawn door open faster. The squeaking of cart wheels from the convenience store area caught our attention.

"And here he comes again," said Jane. "As if I'd give him anymore cash."

"Hey, gals." He stopped next to us and dug into a plastic bag sitting on the top of his cart. "I got me a foot long sub and an extra-large icy drink. Here's your change." He handed Jane a handful of coins. "Much obliged."

He pushed the cart into the parking area, then turned back toward us. "And before you think I'm reformed, I bummed a smoke off the clerk in the convenience store." He chuckled, shoved the cart across the lot, gave us a wave and turned down the sidewalk. I craned my neck to see where he was going. Beyond the strip mall stood a vacant lot where a few people had pitched tents. I watched him divide his sandwich among them, including tossing a portion to a small dog.

"Your money was better spent than we expected," I said to Jane who watched the group tuck into their lunch.

She draped her arm around my shoulder. "Just shows you how wrong we can be about people."

The man with the cart spoke to those gathered and gestured toward us. Everyone smiled and waved. Even the dog looked happy about the offering and gave a bark of gratitude, or so we believed.

The noise of someone moving around in the store caught our attention. The lights inside came on and we heard the door lock click.

"C'mon in, ladies." A man smoking a cigarette pushed open the door and gestured us in. "I'm willing to open early for good lookin' women." He winked at us and smiled, showing a set of almost too perfect, neon white teeth, obviously dentures and not his own teeth. "Looking for somethin' special?" His hair was pulled back in a thin, greasy-looking ponytail. He let forth a smoker's cough and smiled, flashing his dentures once more.

Jane leaned toward me and whispered, "How are we going to play this? He won't give us any information if we straight out ask him."

"We are, as you said, looking for something special. One of our friends was here a few days ago and bought a lovely Victorian broach. My sister is having a birthday soon and it's the kind of thing she would adore. So do you have anything like it?" I gave him my most engaging smile.

Sara took a notepad and pen from her purse and drew the broach worn by Joan Tomson last night at the historical society meeting.

He glanced at the drawing and when he looked back at us, the welcoming smile was gone from his face. "You guys cops?"

"Oh, of course not, just shopping for a friend's special occasion." I widened my innocent smile.

"Got nothin' like that. I deal mostly in war memorabilia."

When I looked around the small shop, it appeared he was right. Swords, old army uniforms, knives and a few muskets filled the place.

"You might try Cal's. It's closer to downtown. He handles lots of jewelry." He reached for the door handle and opened it for us. The smile appeared back on his face, but his eyes said he wanted us gone.

"Thank you so much for the information." I nudged Jane and Sara out the door. Back on the sidewalk, I heard the door's lock engage.

"We scared him. I wonder why?" said Sara.

"He thought we were looking for stolen merchandise. That's why the remark about our being cops."

"He only glanced at my drawing of the broach, but I'm sure he recognized it," said Sara.

As we opened the car doors to leave, our shopping cart fellow waved goodbye to us. Glancing over at him and his pals, I saw something in his cart I hadn't noticed before.

"Wait a minute," I said to Jane and Sara. "I'll be right back."

I rushed over to the guy with the cart, nodded hello to his companions and said, "That's a nice bag you got there."

"This?" he said, holding up a plastic bag with a logo I recognized on it.

"Yep. I work at the museum that bag came from."

"Hey, I didn't steal it. I found it."

"Where?"

He pointed to the dumpster next to the pawn shop. "In the dumpster."

"Do the convenience store and the pawn shop both use that to dispose of their trash?"

He shook his head. "Nope. Only the pawn shop. Convenience store has a bigger one around the back of their place."

"So, can I buy that bag off you?" I asked.

"Sure, but if you can get them from the museum where you work, why do you want mine?"

"Uhm." I thought quickly for a reasonable story, "because we got new designs on the bags now and they're not as interesting."

I don't know if he believed my story, but I pulled a fiver out of my purse and held it up.

"It's yours." He dumped the contents of the bag including a paper receipt onto the collection of clothes and other items in his cart and handed the empty bag to me.

"I'll take that receipt, too."

He gave me a curious look but shrugged. "Fine. All yours. Anything else you want from my cart?"

"Not right now, but I may be back." I turned to Jane and Sara.

"You bought a plastic bag off that guy?" asked Jane.

"Yes, I did. Take a look at it." I handed the bag to Sara.

"It's from the museum."

"Yep. Our friendly shopping cart guy found it in the pawn shop's dumpster. I figure someone from the museum or someone who bought merchandise from the museum carried items to be sold here in it. What I suspect is Dev bought the items and tossed the bag they were carried in into his trash. Our friend there—I nodded my head toward the grocery cart man who waved at me again—grabbed it from the garbage."

"But that may have nothing to do with the broach," said Sara.

"I know it's a long shot, but look at the receipt from the bag, also from the museum and obviously overlooked by the person carrying items for sale into the shop. Maybe we can trace the receipt to someone."

"And then?" asked Sara.

"Then we get Zack to question that person."

"What if the person paid cash?"

I sighed. A roadblock to finding who pawned that broach, but I was still hopeful. "Then I get Zack back here to question Dev."

I dropped off Jane, and Sara and I continued to the museum, arriving just before noon.

"Got all your errands run, the two of you?" asked Harold suspiciously.

"Did you miss us?" I asked.

Harold ignored me and turned his attention to Sara. "That Indian fella is about finished looking through 'Our Neighbors' collection. He asked me to tell you he needed a word when you got back."

Harold," said Sara, "Dr. Walker is Indigenous and the tribes you're referring to are nations people." I could tell from the sound of her voice that Sara's patience with Harold was almost at an end.

"Whatever." Harold turned on his heel and headed down the hall.

Sara followed him, then veered off to take the main stairway down to the collections room where Dr. Walker had been working. Several minutes later, Sara reemerged and signaled me to follow her into her office. She closed the door after I entered.

"Dr. Walker is continuing his examination of the "Our Neighbors" collection because we know the genuine broach was taken from there. I want to work this in steps hoping we don't have to have all our work in storage examined." Sara sank back into her desk chair, sighing deeply.

"You're doing a fantastic job, honey. Now it's my turn to help you. I'm going to call Zack and tell him what we discovered from our trip to the pawn shop this morning."

"Did you have time to take a look at the receipt?"

"Yes. Unfortunately, it was a cash purchase for a book, but the date was on it, so I'll ask Francis if she remembers the sale and the person making the purchase."

Several hours before closing, Zack entered the museum and asked to have a word. I called Ellie from the third floor to mind the desk. Zack and I knocked on Sara's door and we entered, but not before I saw George sidle down the hall toward Sara's office door.

"I think we should talk in whispers. Harold may have his ear at the door."

Sara smiled, got up from her chair and quickly opened the door. Sure enough, Harold stood outside, but he wasn't alone. Jeremy was with him.

"Aren't you supposed to be leading a tour, Harold?" I asked.

"Right. Jeremy and I are only chatting for a second."

"The two of you can talk after Harold finishes the tour. Your tour members are waiting downstairs, Harold. I suggest you hustle." Sara closed the door as they left, then we gathered on the far side of the room away from the door and the possibility of anyone else eavesdropping.

"I have some good news, at least for Mr. Powles and I think for the murder case in general. They have let Mr. Powles go. Lack of evidence. The sheriff again will be interviewing everyone who was at the museum the day of the murder," Zack said.

"The DA can't be happy about freeing Mr. Powles. It puts the investigation back to the beginning," Sara said. By the troubled look on her face, I knew she was as worried as I about the identity of the murderer. Who wanted Mrs. Carlton dead and why? And what did it mean that her killer was still out there? Were there more victims in his sights and were employees at the museum in danger? When the public heard the news of Mr. Powles's release, people would be upset. Worst of all, Sara's parents would worry about her safety. I had to convince them she was safe staying with me.

CHAPTER 16

Zack walked me down the hall to the front desk where Ellie awaited my return.

"Could you wait a minute while I check on something?" I said to Zack.

"Sure. I'll be right here."

I made certain Ellie didn't mind remaining at the desk while I went to the gift shop where Francis was finishing ringing out a customer.

"Hi, Maddie. What can I do for you?"

I handed the receipt to Francis. "I know this is a long shot, but would you remember this?"

She looked at the one item on the bill and the date. "Let me check on the inventory number of the book to see which one it was." She punched a few keys on her computer.

"Here it is. It was the last book we had on Victorian style. I ordered more in preparation for the 'Our Neighbors' exhibit coming up because I thought people viewing the exhibit might want to know more about the era."

"The receipt indicates the customer paid in cash. I wish it were a credit card so we could track the identity," I said.

Francis chuckled. "No need to. I remember the sale. It was Jeremy. He argued that because he was a student, he should be given a discount on the book, but I told him I'd have to clear that with Mrs. Carlton. It was the end of the day, so I said I would hold the book for him and talk with Mrs. Carlton the next day about a discount. He told me to forget it. He paid full price, wasn't happy about it, but said he was in a hurry. I bagged the book for him, and he rushed off. I forgot all about it until just now."

"Thanks, Francis. You've been a tremendous help."

I sent Ellie off and resumed my seat at the desk. Zack reentered the front door and stepped over to me. "Find out something important, Maddie?"

"Maybe. Jane, Sara and I visited a pawn shop this morning in Syracuse."

"What were you doing there?"

I explained about the broach and finding the plastic bag with the museum's logo on it.

"I agree with the three of you. There has to be a link between the murder and the replacement of a museum item with a fake. It looks as if we need to talk with Mr. Jeremy Westin," said Zack.

"Maybe . . ."

"Maybe what, Maddie?"

"Maybe we need more than the purchase of a book to encourage Jeremy to tell us what he knows."

And that's how Zack and I arranged to revisit Dev's pawn shop the next morning.

BACK AT MY HOUSE, I TOLD SARA about Jeremy's purchase and made her promise not to let on to what Zack and I had in mind.

"I feel so useless like I should be doing something to help find Mrs. Carlton's murder and track down the origin of the fake broach," Sara said over dinner that night.

"People need to play to their strengths in this case. You called in an expert to examine the museum holdings."

"I know, and I also accompanied you and Jane to Syracuse this morning, but . . ." Sara slid back into her chair and folded her arms over her chest in a gesture of frustration.

The phone rang and I got up to answer it.

"Hi, Maddie. It's Jane. Have you been able to track down the person who carried the museum bag to the pawn shop?"

"Yes. We think it's one of the student interns at the museum."

"Well, good. I'll tell you what I would do now. I'd go back to Dev's pawn and show him a picture of the fella, get him to confirm this Jeremy guy was the one who brought the broach in."

"That's exactly what Zack and I are planning to do tomorrow first thing."

There was a pause on the line.

"You and Zack. What about me? I was the one who gave the grocery cart guy the money, drawing attention to him and his stash of stuff." She sounded both hurt and angry.

"Oh, yes. Of course. I was just about to call you and ask if you were busy tomorrow morning."

"Oh, Goodie. Same time as this morning?"

"Sure. Sure."

Sara listened to my end of the conversation. "So I assume that interviewing pawn dealers is Jane's forte, is it?"

"Sara, you know full well that if your parents knew how involved you have become in this case, they'd kidnap you and send you off to a nunnery or something. You're only allowed to stay here with me and not move back in with them because I promised to take care of you."

"I know. I know."

"You'll need to be at the museum working alongside Dr. Walker, isn't that so?"

"Okay, Gram. You're right, but it feels like so little compared to actual sleuthing."

"It is actual sleuthing. What we all do helps put together the pieces of a complicated puzzle."

"But the next case you and Zack take on, you'll let me help, won't you?"

"Next case. What next case? There is no next case."

Sara got up from the table and began to put the dishes in the dishwasher. "You don't know that."

I didn't, but between her and Jane, we'd soon have an entire private detective agency made up of women. Hmmm. Not such a bad idea. We would, of course, have Zack serve as a consultant to our group.

Sara drove to work the next morning in her own car. Zack picked me up a few minutes after she left.

"How's your daughter?" I asked.

"Fine. Fine." He didn't sound very certain of that, but I let it go.

"By the way, we need to make one stop here in town before we leave. Turn right here." I knew Zack wouldn't be pleased to have Jane accompany us.

"The house on the left, the white one." I pointed to Jane's place with her profusion of rose bushes climbing the fence in front.

Zack stopped the car and glared at me.

"She called last night, and I told her what we were doing today. She sounded so hurt at being left out, so . . ."

Zack gave a deep sigh and said something under his breath.

"Did you just mutter 'women'?"

"Maybe."

Jane opened the back door of the car and threw herself into the seat. "This is going to be fun, huh, Zack?"

"Sure."

Jane leaned forward and tapped me on the shoulder. "He sounds cranky. Didn't you give him coffee this morning?"

"That's his own responsibility. I don't take care of him, you know."

Chastened by my tone of voice, Jane settled back in her seat, crossed her arms over her chest and spent the remainder of our drive staring out the window.

Zack was silent until we reached the edge of the city. "Where is this place?"

I gave him directions. When we arrived at the strip mall, he pulled into a parking slot in front of the store, shut off the engine and gave me a stern look. "This is a lousy section of town and the three of you women came here alone?"

"No, we didn't. As you just pointed out. We weren't alone. There were three of us."

"Hey," said Jane. "There's our guy."

"What guy?" asked Zack.

"The fellow who had the bag from the museum."

Jane popped out of the back seat and sped over to the homeless man we had met yesterday. I couldn't hear what was being said, but the smiles on their faces told me it was a pleasant exchange. Jane held up her finger to signal the man to wait a minute and ran back to us. "Got a fiver?" she asked Zack.

"What for?" He said but took out his wallet and looked inside.

"Guy needs breakfast. All I've got is a twenty."

Zack scowled but held out a five to Jane who rushed back to her newly found friend and handed it to him.

"He'll just use it on booze," Zack said when Jane returned.

"Watch."

The guy took the five and entered the convenience store. He came out with a cup of coffee and a bagel, smiled and waved at Jane, then proceeded to join his friends at the tent area where he tore the bagel in pieces, handed them around to the other men and shared the cup of coffee.

"See?" Jane smirked at Zack. "You're not always right."

Zack cleared his throat and looked down at the ground. "Okay. But let's do what we came here to do." He held the door to the pawn shop open and ushered us in.

Dev looked up from behind the counter and the smile that flickered on his lips briefly was quickly replaced by a frown. "You two again. And this time you bring a guy with you. I would have preferred you bring back the pretty gal that was with you yesterday. Now what do you want?"

Zack flashed his private detective's license.

"So what? You think that's impressive? Not to me."

"Here's the thing. I'm working as an investigator on a case. A bag from the Meadowbrook Museum was found in your dumpster. You don't need to know the details, but we've traced it back to someone who works at the museum. There's recently been a murder there, and we believe that bag ties the perp to the killing. I'm sure you don't want to obstruct our case, do you?"

Dev thought for a moment. "Okay, what do you want from me?"

"I want the name of the individual pawning a certain broach which my friends here showed you a picture of yesterday. We know you bought the broach. Now we need your records for who the seller was."

Dev pulled out a ledger from his desk drawer and read the entries there. "Well, here you go, but I'm not certain it will be of any help." He held the book out to Zack.

"S. Smith? You thought that was a real name?"

"Nope, but the person gave me an address and a phone number, so who was I to question it?"

"You didn't question it because you were eager to take the merchandise and cheat the seller on the price." Zack started to hand the journal back to Dev but snatched it back and continued to read the entries. "Seems you have a lot of Smiths coming here to pawn or sell items."

I leaned over his shoulder and looked at the page. "Lots of Browns, too."

"And they all had IDs?" asked Zack.

"Sometimes."

We knew Dev was lying, but there wasn't much we could do about it.

"Could you identify the person if we showed you a picture?" Zack pulled a photo of Jeremy out of his pocket.

Dev looked at it and shook his head. "Nope."

Zack scowled. "I guess we need to bring in some other photos of people working at the museum. I'll be back tomorrow." He gestured for Jane and me to leave, but before I walked out, I turned.

"Uh, Mr. Dev. Was the person selling that broach a man or a woman?"

Dev looked momentarily taken aback. "Uh, well, let's see." He tried to look thoughtful, but I could tell he was considering telling us another lie.

Zack skewered Dev with his meanest cop look. "Accessory to murder. You really want that?"

"It was a woman."

"Describe her," I said.

"Well, let's see. She was young. A lot younger than you two." His eyes roamed over Jane and me. "Kinda tall, good figure, too thin for my liking, but a bit of a looker."

"Hair?" I asked.

Dev gave me a snarky grin. "Oh, yeah."

"Tell the lady what she wants to know," said Zack, his voice coming out as a low growl.

"Blonde."

"Any scars, moles, birthmarks that you could see. Did you see the car she drove?"

Dev shook his head. "Look, if that's all, I need to close the door for a coffee break."

Zack nodded. "I'll be back. Don't go anywhere."

"Blonde?" I said when we got back into the car. "That doesn't describe anyone at the museum."

"Except for Sara," said Zack. "And we know it wasn't her."

I caught my reflection in the rear-view mirror and noticed I needed a retouch of my hair roots. My change in color I had gotten done earlier in the summer covered most of my grey, but I could see white coming in around my hairline. What a stupid thing to be thinking about now. Why did hair color cross my mind now?

Oh, right. I got it. Hair color didn't define a woman. It could be changed by dye—or by a wig.

WE STOPPED FOR A COFFEE AT A DINER because I was ravenous, not having eaten breakfast.

"Are you taking care of yourself, Maddie?" asked Zack with concern.

"Certainly. No one else is doing it for me." My tone was snappish. I wanted Zack back in my life. I missed him. I knew being short with him was not the answer, and I was about to apologize when his cell rang.

"It's Mary, my daughter's friend."

And possibly the mother of the son you didn't know you had, I thought to myself.

Zack left the booth we were sitting at to take the call outside. I watched him through the diner's window and saw his face go white.

"C'mon, Jane. Let's go. Something's up."

I pulled Jane out of the booth, tossed a twenty on the table and we joined Zack outside.

"What's wrong" I asked.

"Is it something to do with the case?" Jane reached out and touched Zack's arm in concern.

"No. It's my daughter. Mary said she's been admitted to the hospital."

"Overdose?"

"I think so. I thought Mary was keeping a close eye on her. Where could she have gotten drugs?"

"Zack, you know better than that. There are drugs available everywhere." This did not bode well for his daughter's recovery program.

Zack shot me a look that said he knew what I was thinking. "Maddie, I should have listened to you. I never called that contact you gave me. I thought Mary could help her, but I don't think it's working."

"Never mind. Call him now. He can meet you at the hospital. Even if your daughter is in no shape to talk with him, you and Mary should. He can help you." I put my arm around Zack and hugged him. "You can drop both Jane and me at her house. I'll walk home from there."

"You could come with me to the hospital."

I shook my head. "No. You and Mary need to work this out. Of course I'm always here if you need me."

"I need you more than ever, Maddie."

His words sent a rush of love and desire through me, but his daughter came first; there was a discussion he needed to have with Mary also.

"Tell Mary I said the time has come to stop keeping secrets."

"What does that mean?" asked Zack, closing the car doors for Jane and me.

"Just tell her what I said." I should have said more to Zack, but I wanted Mary to talk with him. Maybe I should have given her a deadline for telling Zack about the baby or I would tell him—but I didn't. The farther Zack and I went down this road of not talking to one another, the more truths, unspoken but crucial to our relationship, lay between us.

CHAPTER 17

JANE AND I WATCHED ZACK'S CAR pull away from Jane's house.

"Come on in. I'll put a kettle on for tea. I made a batch of strawberry jam yesterday and some scones. We'll have an early tea."

"Thanks, Jane."

"You look like you need someone to talk to."

I reached out and put my arm around her as we walked up to her house. "I wish we had met sooner."

"No worries. We'll just talk faster and by the end of this year we'll know each other as well as if we had grown up together."

We both laughed.

"Let's take our tea out to my back porch. It's still warm enough to sit there and watch my garden weeds grow." Jane bustled around her kitchen preparing the tea, scones and jam.

Settled on her porch with our feast before us, we both munched away at the scones and sipped tea.

"So," Jane said, putting her cup down, "What's going on with you and Zack? The two of you act more distant from each other than you were this summer. And he's moved back into the B and B and out of your house." She looked at me with probing eyes.

"We're, uh, we're taking some time apart while he's with his daughter."

"And that woman. Mary?"

I had kept my feelings about the change in Zack and my relationship to myself for so long, the words rushed out of my mouth before I could pull them back. I told Jane everything about his daughter's drug use, Mary's past with Zack and his wife, even about Mary's assertion that she and Zack had had a son together.

"And Zack knows nothing about this son?"

I shook my head.

"He needs to be told."

"I know, but not by me. That's Mary's responsibility. That was my reference to keeping secrets on Mary's part."

Jane picked up the teapot and refreshed out cups. "And when do you think she will do this?"

I shrugged my shoulders.

"Do you think there's any truth in her story?"

I gazed into Jane's garden hoping something there would help me make up my mind about Mary. "I don't know if she's lying or not, but I am distraught about his daughter's reliance on Mary to help her with her drug problem. From what Zack has told me, there's no change in his daughter's addiction. So what is the woman doing for her?"

"You know perfectly well what she's doing. Keeping the daughter and Zack tied to her, just another form of dependency. Call your counselor friend, Maddie. I'll bet Zack hasn't called him. Send him over to the hospital. He'll know what to do to help."

"I'm not being too intrusive?"

"From what I've seen, Zack is crazy about you, and he needs you. I know you're trying to be fair to him and his daughter, but if he were my man, I'd be a bit more assertive. Where's your usual Maddie Sparks's gumption?" Jane banged her cup back down into the saucer with a clack.

"Don't break it." I reached out and touched the saucer.

"I'm going to make another pot. Where's your phone, Maddie? Make that call."

"No more tea. I've got to go, pick up my car and get to the museum. I have some people there I need to talk to."

"You mean 'interrogate' don't you?" Jane gave me an impish smile. "Go on then. You can make the call as you walk home."

I felt lighter having talked to Jane. I had forgotten how important women friends could be, and Jane was proving to be one of the best confidents I'd had, maybe ever. Funny how we can get older and think there's nothing new for us, but inside of a year I'd met a man I loved and respected and a woman I knew would be, as folks liked to say now, a "bestie."

I checked my cellphone directory and discovered I didn't have my friend John Tennent's number, but when I googled Project 400, the drug counseling center, and connected, I recognized the voice answering the phone.

"Hi, John. It's Maddie."

"It's been a long time, Maddie. How are you?"

"Fine. Well, I'm fine, but I have a friend who could use your help. You haven't heard from Zack Montgomery, have you?"

"Name sounds familiar. Wasn't he the fellow who took over as acting sheriff this summer?"

"Yep."

"And didn't I hear a rumor about the two of you?"

"Yes, to that also."

"So you're going into the crime fighting business, are you?"

"What? Oh, not really. I thought you meant about Zack and me personally."

John chuckled. "Maybe I heard something about that too."

"Setting that aside, here's why I called you." I told John about Zack's daughter.

John listened without interrupting while I explained the relationship between Zack, his daughter and Mary.

"So is Mary a drug counselor?"

"No, but the daughter is very dependent upon her. And,

there's something else. Mary has a thing for Zack, has had for a long time."

"Complicated, isn't it?"

"I'm staying out of this. In fact, Zack and I have called a temporary halt to our relationship until his daughter's problem is all sorted out."

"Do you think Zack would use my help if I offered it to him?"

"I don't know. He's just so twisted around with everything."

"Let me give it a try. I'll stop by the hospital and see what's up."

"Thanks, John."

"I'm not promising anything. Zack may tell me to get lost."

Zack would never be that rude, I thought as I disconnected, but Mary might be.

WITH DIFFICULTY I TURNED MY THOUGHTS to the murder of Mrs. Carlton. Convinced the theft of the broach was connected to the murder, I mulled over how I might determine who from the museum might have taken the broach to the pawn shop. We had a number of part-time volunteers who came in once each week to work for a few hours, but none of them was blonde. If the young woman who took the broach to be sold was from the museum, she had worn a wig to disguise herself. The sales receipt in the bag was from Jeremy Westin's purchase. So had he put the broach in the bag and then what? Given it to someone at the museum and told that individual to sell the broach?

I felt as if I was on to something, but nothing made much sense. Where to begin, I wondered as I pulled my car into a parking slot behind the museum.

When I entered the building, Ellie was at the desk, Jeremy leaning over her. It looked as if they were having a private conversation, a serious conversation. Neither of them was smiling and the tension between them felt as thick as maple syrup.

When they saw me enter, Jeremy stood and smiled. "Hi, Mrs. Sparks. How are you today?"

"What's up, you two? Secrets?" I asked.

Jeremy gave a nervous laugh. "Gosh, no."

Ellie blanched as if I had caught her out on something.

"So did you find reading about the Victorians enlightening?" I asked Jeremy.

"What?"

"You know. You bought the last book we had in the gift shop about that era. Francis is ordering more for the opening of 'Our Neighbors.'"

"Oh, that. I thought I should read up on the era since the museum has scheduled that show. I found the reading fascinating and if a visitor asks me anything about the Victorians, I can at least provide some information." Jeremy gave me his most open smile.

Was he lying or had I connected events that were unrelated?

"Good for you, Jeremy. That's the kind of dedication we like to see in our interns." Sara had come out of her office without any of us noticing. "You and Ellie can go downstairs into the work room and make certain the exhibit is ready to be displayed. And this will be a good opportunity for you, Jeremy, to teach some of what you learned to Ellie."

I noted neither Ellie nor Jeremy looked pleased at the assignment Sara had given them, but Jeremy put his best face on it by nodding and guiding Ellie toward the stairway.

"That was a good play on your part, Sara."

"Well, I didn't know what you and Zack had found this morning at the pawn shop, so when I overheard your question to Jeremy and his reply, I decided it best to follow your lead." Sara looked around to see if anyone was listening. "What did you discover?"

"Well, Jeremy didn't bring the broach in for sale. The pawnshop owner said it was a young woman, blonde, tall and slender."

"So Jeremy wasn't connected to the broach?"

"I don't know. Any of our female volunteers could have worn a wig."

"That sounds sneaky, as if someone is hiding something if what you say is true."

I also told Sara about the call Zack received about his daughter. "Do you want to go to the hospital to be with him?"

"Thanks, but he has Mary there. And I called my friend, John Tennent who works at Project 400. John said he'd see what he could do to help."

The front door opened.

"I'll let you get back to your job. We can talk later." Sara returned to her office.

I looked up into the face of the individual entering to see it was Agnes Danderfield.

"Can you get away for a minute, Maddie? I need to talk to you."

I spotted Harold at the top of the stairs and called to him. "Could you mind the desk for five minutes, Harold?"

"Not my job," he said.

"I know. I'm asking you to do me a favor. Only five minutes."

"Seems like you spend more time away from the desk than you do at it. You were gone all morning. That sweet little gal, what's her name, uh, Ellie took over for you. Now you want me to do your job."

"Fine, Harold. I'll find someone else." I put a call in to the workroom downstairs. Ellie answered. When I told her I needed her back upstairs at the desk again, she sounded relieved and eager to help me.

Within minutes Ellie appeared at the desk breathless from running up the stairs.

"I'm sorry to take you away from what you and Jeremy were working on, but I need to talk with Agnes."

"Oh, no problem. I'm more than happy to help. Take as much time as you need."

I thought Ellie was sweet on Jeremy, but her attitude toward him today didn't indicate she had a crush on him. Had I misinterpreted her attraction to him on other occasions or had she rethought her feelings toward him because he had tried to use her as an alibi the day of Mrs. Carlton's murder? Perhaps there was something else going on.

Agnes and I walked out onto the lawn and sat on one of the benches there under a large maple now glowing in the sunlight, its leaves falling softly to the ground.

Agnes plunged right into her story. "I had hoped this situation could be resolved when my friend Mrs. Carlton was alive and I thought it was, but I'm not certain she had the opportunity to act on it."

"Agnes, I have no idea what you're talking about."

"Let me explain then. It's about an unsafe work environment."

"'Unsafe?' What do you mean?"

"Toxic."

It too me several moments to catch on, but then I understood. "Sexual harassment."

"Yes. The newspaper got a call from a woman who said she wanted to talk with someone from the paper about inappropriate behavior she had experienced in her job. I took the call and encouraged her to meet with me, but she refused. Instead she sent me a detailed account of incidents she had experienced at the museum. She refused to reveal her identity and said she had reported it to the museum's director who had spoken to the person involved, but the harassment continued."

"What did she want you to do?"

"She wanted a story in the newspaper."

"But without her name?"

Agnes nodded.

"But if you published the story, even without her name, wouldn't the harasser know who it was?"

"She contended that other women received similar treatment, but no one wanted her name made public. My boss, however, was keen on putting together a story even without any names."

"Are you going to publish the story?"

"Since the victim indicated she had spoken to the director and because Brenda Carlson and I were friends of sorts, I went to her to tell her about the story and about the newspaper's intention to publish it."

"When was this?"

"You saw me on the front lawn. It was the day unrest broke out among the people protesting the return of the nations' collections."

"I saw you go into Mrs. Carlton's office. I wondered what the two of you were talking about. How did she respond to your story?"

"She told me she knew all about the harassment, had had a number of reports on it and had called the individual into her office and let him know she would be putting a report of the behavior into his personnel file. And, if it happened again, she would terminate his employment at the museum. But it did happen again, so she had notified him she was meeting with the board and considering firing him."

"Names?"

"Mrs. Carlton wouldn't give me the name of the woman and she didn't reveal her identity to the harasser. She said she was giving him a few days to think it over before she took action. You can see why I've been struggling with this."

"If he didn't want Mrs. Carlton to take the story beyond her office, he could have killed her to make certain it didn't. Agnes, you have to go to the sheriff about this."

"I don't have any names. I really don't know who the people involved are." Agnes wrung her hands and leaned forward on the bench. "Talking to the sheriff could put me in danger."

"Maybe, but the man responsible wouldn't know Mrs. Carlton told you about this."

"That's true." Agnes leaned back onto the bench and sighed.

"If the guy killed to keep Director Carlton from talking to the board, he may try to silence the women he harassed. That puts many, if not all the women working at the museum in danger. You have to tell the sheriff what you know."

My cell rang. It was Zack. "I need to take this. I'll be just a minute." I connected and said, "Zack. How is your daughter?"

"She's gone."

"Zack, Oh, no. I'm so sorry. They weren't able to save her?"

"No, Maddie. I mean she left the hospital, and no one knows where she went."

CHAPTER 18

"WHERE ARE YOU NOW?" I asked Zack.
"I'm still at the hospital. John Tennet showed up here. Mary is with me."

"I'll be right there." I ended the call and turned to Agnes. "Tell the sheriff what you know. Now. I have a situation I have to deal with."

I left Agnes, hoping she would notify the authorities, and hurried back into the museum. I held up my finger to Ellie as I raced by the front desk, rapped on Sara's door and pushed the door open.

Sara saw the expression on my face and came around the desk to put her arms around me. "What's wrong, Grammie?"

I explained to her about Zack's daughter, Amy.

"Go, go. I'll take care of everything here."

I was on my way out of her office, but I turned back. "Listen, Agnes Danderfield spoke to me just now about a troubling situation which involves the museum. If you hurry, you can stop her before she leaves." I thought back to comments Sara had made about Harold and how he didn't understand personal space. "It's something I think you might already know about. And encourage her to talk with the sheriff. I'll call you when I know more about Zack's daughter."

I jumped into my car and sped off to the hospital. When I got there Zack, Mary and my friend John were standing outside the entrance.

"Any idea where she might go?" asked John.

"Mary is always with her," said Zack.

Mary shuffled uncomfortably and cleared her throat.

"Not always, I'd guess," said John, "Not if she found a way to get drugs."

"Well, she liked to take a walk by herself in the afternoon." Finally understanding what she was saying, Mary's eyes grew round with concern. "I didn't want to treat her like a prisoner, so I let her."

"Do you know where she went on her walks?" asked John.

"I don't. Maybe to the library or across the bridge to the cemetery."

"But she left her room here at the hospital in Stone Side. This is over ten miles from Butternut Falls. Mary and Zack, recheck the hospital in case she's hiding out here somewhere. Then take your car and start cruising the streets in Stone Side. Maddie and I will search the other side of town near the river. Keep in touch by phone. We may need to broaden our areas." John knew what he was doing and knew the small city of Stone Side better than we did.

We took my car. John directed me down Main Street and toward the bridge that crossed the river. Just before the road went over the bridge, John told me to pull over next to the gas station there. We parked the car and got out.

"Come with me. And let me do the talking. These folks aren't very trusting of strangers."

We headed under the bridge toward the riverbank. I was surprised to see a number of tents set up there. Shopping carts filled with bags, clothing and other items sat near the tents. A firepit smoldered in the middle of the encampment—a homeless encampment, something I didn't know existed in this small city, although

I'd heard rumors that it was here. John approached several people sitting near the firepit. They greeted him as if they knew him.

He signaled me to approach.

"This is a friend of mine. We're looking for her partner's daughter who ran off from the hospital and she needs our help."

The folks, all men, nodded at me and I smiled at them.

"So you're talking about drugs, I'd guess," said one of the men, thin face covered by a long grey beard. "You know we're not into that, so we can't be of any help."

"Look, I know you have rules against drugs of any kind here. You like to keep the place clean so the cops don't try to move you out of your homes here, but I also know you hear things and might know folks around who do deal in drugs."

The man didn't speak for a minute, simply stared at John, then at me.

"You can trust her. She's just worried about her friend's daughter. The young woman has a problem and is trying to clean herself up, and she was on her way until she found a source around here, probably over in Butternut Falls, who supplied her with the stuff."

"Butternut Falls, eh?" The man looked at his comrades and a silent conversation among them seemed to occur.

"She like to read?" asked another man, this one young, wearing a striped shirt and ripped jeans.

"Yes, I believe she does." I remembered Mary saying she thought Amy took her walks to the library some afternoons. Maybe that was a lie, but it was what we had to go on at this point.

"Check the upstairs reading room in the library there," the young man said.

"What?" I said. "That just can't be. Drugs in our little library? Why Mrs. Holmes the librarian wouldn't allow it."

"She doesn't know about it," he replied. "You think these drug suppliers are stupid enough to let the librarian know what they're up to?"

"So tell me how Amy might be getting drugs in the reading room."

"Put money in a book one day, next day the same book contains product." The man smiled. "Clever, huh?"

"How do you know about this?" I asked.

The men's friendly demeanor disappeared, and his eyes grew hooded with dislike.

"We don't question the sources of the information we get here, Maddie," warned John.

"Of course. I understand. The most important thing is to find Amy and help her. I don't care where a lead comes from and I'm not about to reveal the source of the information. I apologize. I'm just frantic with worry, that's all."

"Forgiven," said the young man.

"I do have another question, however."

"Ask it," said John.

"What if someone not looking for drugs picks up the wrong book and finds money or drugs. What then?"

"The supplier has people to keep an eye on the library. If that happens, it's taken care of." He gave me a pointed look.

I didn't like the sounds of "taken care of."

"Once your friend's daughter is safe, you can use this information any way you want. Just keep all of us out of it," the older, bearded man said.

"I will. Thanks for your help."

John exchanged a few more words with the men and then he and I left.

"So?" I asked.

"I'm assuming she wants to get back to her contact which means she's probably hitching a ride to Butternut Falls."

I looked at my watch. "The problem is that the library closes today soon. What then?"

"I think you know. We need to find Amy before desperation forces her to break into the library looking for her 'book' and she gets caught by the police."

"I'll call Zack." I started to punch Zack's contact into my cell.

"Don't do that. Let's keep Zack out of this or he'll have to make a decision which might put Amy square in the sights of the authorities. We'll find her before she can do anything foolish."

"You drive, John." I handed my keys to him.

He nodded and pulled onto the road, making a U-turn to head back to Butternut Falls. A fast trip later, we pulled up in front of the library to see the librarian about to lock the front door.

"Eleanor," I shouted to Eleanor Holmes, our town librarian, as I jumped out of the car and ran up the sidewalk. "Have you seen a young woman, slender, brown hair, dressed in ripped jeans and a tee-shirt here this afternoon?"

"Oh, her. She comes here a few times every week. She's up in the reading room. Oh, here she is now. I told her I was closing in a few minutes, but she told me she had left a package upstairs when she was here the other day."

Through the door I saw Amy on the steps to the reading area on the second floor. She paused midway down the stairs, undecided if she should continue on down.

"Hi, Amy," I said. "I'm delighted you like to read. I'm a writer, you know, and I worked here at the library for years. I love this place."

At first Amy's eyes jumped back and forth like a cornered animal, but then my words calmed her.

"I guess my dad is furious with me for running off."

"No, he's just worried. How about you come with me back to my place? I can make tea and I have some cookies, or we could have toast and marmalade."

Eleanor appeared to catch some of the awkward tension between Amy and me, so she withdrew into the library and let us continue talking in the entryway.

"Did you find what you were looking for?" I asked.

Amy shook her head. "It's not there. I knew it wouldn't be. I didn't have the money to pay the other day, so all they left was a note saying the price was double now. They know I don't have that kind of money." Amy sunk down onto the bottom step and put her hands over her face. "I'm so messed up."

John had slowly approached us. "Hi, Amy. My name is John and I think I can help. I've been where you are, so I know what you're going through. I think Mrs. Sparks is right. A good, hot cup of tea would be just the thing." He held out his hand to her. She looked up at him and took his hand. He pulled her off the steps and walked her out of the building to my car.

I caught Eleanor's eye as she reappeared from behind the checkout counter. "Thanks, Eleanor. I'll get back with you and tell you what this is all about."

As we proceeded down the sidewalk to the car, I caught movement at the corner of the building. Someone had been spying on us. I wondered what the person heard. I walked around the side of the building and saw a car pull off down the alleyway at the back of the library. John's friends at the tent city were right. The drug dealers were keeping an eye on the library. As soon as we could help Amy, I needed to let the sheriff know what was going on here.

Back at my house, Amy settled onto the couch. There were dark circles under her eyes and her skin was unnaturally white. I shot John a concerned look and signaled him to join me at the sink. "Does she need to go back to the hospital? Or should we call emergency services?"

"She's been through a lot, but I think all she needs is something in her stomach and a cup of well-sugared tea. And this is probably the time to call her father, so he won't worry any longer."

John went back to the couch to talk with Amy, and I put in the call to Zack. "We found her. We're at my place, having tea."

"Tea? What do you mean, tea? She should be back here at the hospital."

"John says she needs rest more than anything."

"What does he know?" Zack's tone was angry and sharp.

"He deals with these situations a lot, Zack. I trust him. I suggest you and Mary get here before I put Amy to bed in the spare bedroom. And, Zack, don't come in with guns blazing. She's fragile and she needs your support, not your wrath." I disconnected before he could say anything that might set me off.

I served the tea and scones and left John and Amy alone to talk, I went outside to sit on my back deck which overlooked the stream. From here I would be able to see up the street when Zack's car arrived. I wanted to stop him before he came into the house in case he was still hyped up.

When he and Mary arrived, I met them when they got out of the car.

"We're here to take her back to the B and B," said Mary who tried to push past me into the house.

I grabbed her arm. "Settle down. Amy's talking to my friend John right now. I'm sure Zack told you about him. Meantime, let's sit out back until John lets us know if Amy wants to talk with us."

"Why wouldn't she want to talk with me? I take care of her. I love her." Anger filled Mary's voice and she grabbed Zack's arm and tried to pull him toward the front door.

"I think Maddie's right. Let's allow John time with Amy and she can decide what she needs." Zack took Mary's arm and walked her toward my back deck.

"What she needs," said Mary, "is to come home to Seattle and for you to come back with us. Why are you here, anyway?"

Zack looked at me.

"Her? You prefer her over your daughter? What kind of a father are you? Maybe I should think twice about introducing you to our son."

Zack dropped her arm and stepped back, a startled look on his face. "What son?"

"I should have told you sooner, I know, but I didn't. I gave him up for adoption when he was born, but now I know where he is, and I want to contact him. We can be family, you, me, Amy and our son."

The woman was the queen of bad timing. She had only added to the crisis Zack was experiencing.

At that moment, John appeared at the back door. "Amy would like to talk to you."

I opened the door for Zack and Mary to join John.

"Amy wants to talk to you also, Maddie."

"There's no reason to include this woman in our family issues," said Mary.

"You may not think so, but it's what Amy wants." John held out his hand to me and we all entered the house.

Amy got off the couch and hugged her father and Mary. She also smiled at me. "You're so kind. Thanks for the tea, Maddie. It was just what I needed. No wonder my dad is in love with you."

"He's not in love with her." Mary dropped onto my couch, her arms crossed over her chest.

Amy shook her head. "Mary, you know how much I care about you. You've been by my side since Mom died. I can't express how much that has meant to me. And I want you in my life whatever happens, but leaning on you and on Dad isn't going to get me better. I need professional intervention."

Mary grabbed Amy's arms and pulled her down on the couch beside her "But we tried that, and it didn't work. I can help you. I know I can." Mary's voice rose in pitch, and she began to sob.

"John knows an excellent rehab center near here and he can get me in there probably today. That's what I want to do. I'll make it work this time. I promise." Amy squeezed Mary's shoulders and looked pleadingly at her father.

"If that's what is best for you, honey, then let's go for it." Zack leaned over and kissed his daughter's cheek.

"No, no, no," said Mary. "I won't have it. I won't."

"This isn't about you, Mary. It's about Amy and her life," said John.

"You're just an old drug addict who's peddling a program that might have worked for you, but it's not the kind of place for Amy."

"You don't know that, Mary. Amy wants to give it a chance. I say we trust her on this," Zack said.

"But I love her. I need her!" Mary cried.

"And she loves you, Mary. Do what's best for her. Let her go for now," Zack said.

"Is that what you're going to do? Just let her run off to this drug rehab place. Don't you care about her?" Mary said, her crying now so wild that her words were almost incomprehensible.

"I care for both of you. I always have." Zack said.

Did he mean that? Did he care equally for both of them? Did he believe Mary was the mother of his son?

I sighed in despair. Amy might find a new life as a result of the rehab center, but I felt as if the life I tried to create with Zack was gone. His new life was just beginning, with his daughter, a son he'd never met and the woman he'd known for many years.

Time was my enemy. Time had drawn these people together and I had no place in the life they would soon begin.

"I'll take you wherever you want to go," Zack said to Amy. He put his arm around Amy and his other arm around Mary who leaned into him, her sobbing less now. I watched the three of them walk through my front door.

John patted me on the arm. "I'll catch a ride with them. I called the rehab center, and they expect us there."

"Thanks for your help, John." I stood on tiptoe and kissed his cheek.

He opened the door to follow them but turned back to me.

"He's a good man, Maddie. I see why you love him. And, by the way, Maddie, he loves you, too."

Did he?

John was right. Zack was a good man, but good men did not walk out on their family.

CHAPTER 19

I HAD LOST THE ONLY MAN I genuinely loved. Something inside of me felt broken, bruised, a wound that could never heal. John said Zack loved me, and perhaps he did, but his responsibility now was to his daughter, and perhaps to a son he'd never met. I sat on the couch and stared across the room, for how long, I didn't know, but I finally got up and went into the bathroom to wash my face. There were no tears. This feeling of emptiness was too deep for tears.

Maddie, I said, to my reflection in the mirror, pick yourself up. You have responsibilities to your family, to Sara, to help Richard make certain his client Mr. Powles won't end up back in jail. Something tickled the back of my brain, and although it was late afternoon, something told me I should get back to the museum and talk with a few people there. Would pursuing clues to Mrs. Carlton's murder take my thoughts off Zack? I didn't know, but the family I loved and the manuscript I was working on were all I had now. They would have to do.

ELLIE LOOKED UP FROM HER WORK at the desk as I entered the museum. "Is everything all right?"

"Yes, yes. Fine. Can one of the other volunteers spell you at the desk for a few minutes? I'd like to have a few words with you." I had wondered if Ellie, perhaps wearing a blonde wig, had been the young woman selling the broach in the pawn shop. The receipt in the museum bag found in the pawn shop's dumpster connected Jeremy to the sale. Had he somehow convinced Ellie to sell the broach for him? I decided it was time to confront her about my suspicions.

Before she could get up from her chair to come with me, Harold walked up, a scowl on his face.

"Finally back, are you? The rest of us working here would like to have as much time off from our duties as you have. Must be nice to have your granddaughter running the show so you can have all the privileges she grants you."

"Oh, Harold, just leave it would you. If you must know I was trying to help a young woman who had overdosed. It's been an exhausting day." Then I turned to Ellie. "I'll find another volunteer to take the desk. Meet me in a few minutes in the break room." Before I took the stairs, I tapped on Sara's office door to tell her I was back.

She looked up at me, her brow wrinkled in consternation. "Grammie, come in for a minute, would you? I found something."

"I'm on my way to talk with Ellie."

"Can it wait for a minute? I think you'll want to see this." Excitement as well as concern wrinkled Sara's forehead.

"Sure."

"Good. Mrs. Carlton had a large desk calendar that sat on her desk, you know the old-fashioned kind that used to serve as a blotter. I thought I'd remove it. It's not something I like to use. I put all my information on my laptop, but when I took it off the desk, I found a scrap of paper underneath it. I was about to toss the scrap away, but I was curious about what was written on it. It appeared to be Mrs. Carlton's writing. I can't really understand what it means. Here, you take a look at it." Sara handed me the paper.

It read, "Agnes" with a dash after that followed by "Sexual harassment."

"Odd, don't you think, Grammie?"

But I knew what it meant. "Sit down, Sara. I need to tell you something." I repeated the conversation Agnes and I had about reports of sexual harassment here at the museum.

"Agnes had already driven off, so I didn't get a chance to talk with her earlier. Does she intend to publish that story?" asked Sara.

"I don't know, but I think you should talk to her about it. I'm assuming the harasser is Harold. I've seen how he violates the personal space of the young women who work here. And didn't you talk to Mrs. Carlton about his touching you in an inappropriate manner?"

"Yes, and she told me she would talk to Harold about it, but I wasn't the woman who talked with the Agnes about him."

"Have you found any reports in Mrs. Carlton's office pertaining to Harold?"

"No, but if she wanted to put anything in writing, I'd guess it would be in his personnel file. I haven't gone through any employees' files since I took over here."

"I think it's time you do that now."

Sara looked uncomfortable. "Is an anonymous phone call to the newspaper and this scrap of paper enough for me to go through Harold's file?"

"You experienced his behavior yourself. What do you think?"

"Maybe." Sara didn't look convinced.

"Look, Sara, if some woman here reported harassment to the newspaper, then we have a hostile work environment. I'll tell you what I'll do. I'm going to talk with Ellie right now about a different matter but let me ask her if she's had trouble with Harold."

"The board should know about this," Sara said.

I nodded. "But let me see what I can find out first."

"You never had trouble with Harold, did you, Grammie?"

I chuckled. "I think all of us have found the man difficult to deal with, but no. From what I've observed Harold prefers younger women."

"He's probably scared of you." Sara smiled. "I'll let you do your thing."

I didn't share with Sara that all this might be more than a sexual harassment issue. If Mrs. Carlton threatened to fire Harold for his behavior, was that a motive for murder? Harold? I wondered, but I began to look at him in a different light—not simply obnoxious Harold, but perhaps dangerous Harold.

WHEN I ENTERED THE BREAK ROOM, Ellie sat at the table fidgeting with the bracelet on her arm, turning it around and around. I wanted to talk with her about two issues: first, the matter of sexual harassment and then her possible role in selling the broach.

"Ellie, what I'm about to ask you will stay between us, although, if I'm right about your answer, you should report it to the authorities."

At my words, Ellie stopped toying with her bracelet and her eyes got wide.

"Wha . . . what do you mean, Mrs. Sparks?"

"Harold and his behavior toward you. It's called sexual harassment and it's against the law, you know. You should have reported it to Mrs. Carlton, but I guess you didn't think it was serious enough." I wanted to be gentle with her. She was such a naïve young woman who probably wasn't clear about the law. "You didn't talk to anyone else about it, did you? You didn't call the newspaper?'

"No! I'd never talk about anything that happened here to anyone outside work." Ellie began twisting the bracelet around her arm again.

Jeremy appeared in the doorway. "Hey, you two. Girl talk? Again?"

"Is that all, Mrs. Sparks?" asked Ellie.

I could hardly ask Ellie if she was responsible for selling the broach to the pawn shop with Jeremy right here, so I decided it was time I confronted Jeremy.

"That book you bought, Jeremy?"

"You mean the one on the Victorian era?"

I nodded.

"Well, Ellie was interested in the book, but it was the last one in the gift shop, so I gave the book to Ellie to read." Jeffrey looked to her for confirmation.

Ellie hesitated, then nodded. "I left the book downstairs on the break room table. I don't know what happened to it. With the protests and Mrs. Carlton's murder, I forgot all about it."

"And the bag it was in?"

Jeremy looked at Ellie. "It was just one of the plastic bags we use here. What's so special about it?"

"Maybe nothing, but I'd like to know where that bag went."

Ellie shrugged. "I think I tossed it into the trash." She turned to Jeremy. "I'm sorry I lost your book. It's bound to be around here somewhere. If I can't locate it, I'll buy you a new one," Ellie said.

"What's this all about? Why are you questioning us?" There was defensiveness in Jeremy's voice, and he stepped toward me in what felt like an aggressive move.

"Oh, nothing, really." I pushed a whisp of hair off my forehead and gave them an innocent smile.

Jeremy grabbed Ellie's hand and pulled her out of the room and with him down the hall.

I gave a deep sigh and sank into the chair I had vacated. Really smooth, I said to myself. I certainly hadn't done a very good job of that. If I thought I'd mastered some skills as a sleuth, this encounter told me I was lying to myself. I thought Zack and I had made a great sleuthing team, and perhaps we had, but I was missing the key person in the team—Zack.

I trudged back up the stairs to my desk and took over from the young woman minding it for me. A glance at my watch said it was late afternoon, almost time for the museum to close.

After I cashed out for the night, I wanted to take a quick look downstairs in that wastebin. Ellie said she thought she had thrown the bag that had contained the book into the trash. Could it still be there? But then what of the other bag and the receipt found in the dumpster by the pawn shop? I watched the hands of the clock in the hallway slowly creep toward five, then, as the museum guards began their survey of the building, I finished my work and sped downstairs to the break room, but, of course, the trash bin there was empty, probably dumped out for evidence after the murder. Hmmm. If she did toss the bag in the trash, perhaps she used the bin in the women's room.

The trashcan sitting outside the stalls appeared to be filled with paper towels and other trash. I poured everything out onto the floor and began sorting through it. I found several museum bags, both empty, but one contained a receipt from the gift shop. I put them to one side and continued my search, carefully sorting through the paper towels. Most of them were still damp and all had been crumpled by their users. Yuck! Germey! But my diligence paid off in an odd way. No more museum bags but crumpled up inside one of the crumpled paper towels was an old photograph. Odd . . . I smoothed it out. It was a picture of a woven basket. Odd . . . what was it doing here?

I dashed back up the stairs to Sara's office to reveal to her my finds.

"How long do you think the photo has been in that trash container?" Sara held the photo under her desk lamp to get a better look at it.

"The sheriff needs to see this." I said. "This could be the 'proof' Mr. Powles gave to Mrs. Carlton, a photo of the basket he claims belongs to his family." I slapped my hand against my hip. "Why can't Mr. Powles be more forthcoming about this?" If he had been in the room, I would have shaken him and demanded the truth.

"You know why he's so reticent to talk." Sara looked closely at the photo. "It looks like baskets in the nations collection."

"Can we take a look at the baskets?" I asked.

Sara nodded. We headed toward the stairs leading down to the room where the collection was stored.

She unlocked the door to the room and hit the light switch. The shelves dedicated to our holdings were illuminated by the over-head lights.

"Have you ever been in here before, Gram" asked Sara.

I shook my head. "I had no reason to be here."

Sara turned left before she and I encountered the shelving, then took a right at the last shelving row and proceeded down the row toward the far corner of the room. The shelves there were dedi-cated to the nations pieces. Low on the last shelf stood a number of baskets. Sara scanned each of them, finally carefully picking one up. "Doesn't this one look like the basket in the photo?"

"The photo is old, cracked from having been wadded up with the trash and in black and white, but it certainly could be that basket."

Sara and I stood there silently for a while, both of us contem-plating what the photo might mean for Mr. Powles's claim. Then Sara reshelved the basket and we headed upstairs to her office.

"How often are the trashcans emptied?" I asked.

"The authorities have been all over this place because of the murder, so the cleaners haven't been in here for over a week." Sara reached for her phone. "Let me just verify that with our cleaning company." She punched the contact into her phone, talked for a moment, then disconnected. "The trash cans haven't been emptied since Mrs. Carlton's murder. The cleaners are due in here tonight."

"Good. But wait. I can't believe the forensic team didn't go through all the trash."

"The photo could have been tossed in there after the murder."

"By whom and for what reason?"

Sara slid the photo into a clear plastic bag. "So who do we notify first? The sheriff or Uncle Richard?"

"Maybe both of them might coincidentally arrive here at the same time," I said.

"Can we arrange that?" Sara asked.

"Why not? I'll see what Richard's schedule is. Maybe he can drop by now. I'm sure he'll tell us we should call the sheriff and we will."

"We know that already, don't we?" Sara gave me a crooked smile.

"We'll tell the sheriff Richard came by to say hello right after we found the photo and he told us to call her."

"Will Sheriff Burroughs buy that story?" Sara sked.

"Probably not. She knows I have a sneaky side, but let's give it a shot. How good are you at looking dumb?"

"Grammie! How dare you ask that of a woman with blonde hair who's been fighting the stereotype for years?" Although Sara sounded insulted by my suggestion, the twinkle in her eyes said she wasn't.

Richard was in court, but his secretary told me she'd get a message to him as soon as he returned to the office, and she expected him back soon.

"I'll go talk with our guards to make certain all the visitors are out." Sara left me in her office pondering all the clues uncovered in Mrs. Carlton's murder so far. None of them made a whole story that made any sense.

"Look who I found on the front steps?" Sara led Zack into the office.

"Zack!" I said.

"Maddie. I hoped I'd find you here. We need to talk."

"Do we? What is there to say?"

"I talked with Mary, and she told me about the baby."

"Your son."

"You believed her story?"

Sara cleared her throat. "Uh, why don't I wait for Uncle Richard on the steps and leave the two of you to talk here?" Sara slipped out the door.

"I've only known you a short time, Zack, but what she told me didn't fit with the kind of man I thought you were. If you made love

to her, I was certain you would have been careful. You're a passionate fella—I know that—but I couldn't believe you'd ever let your
desire for a woman put her at risk."

Zack reached out and took my hand. "I've tried to win your
love and trust over these past few months, Maddie."

"You have won it, but you and Mary once meant something
to each other another. And she has tried for years to rescue your
daughter. You owe her, don't you?"

"Yes, I do owe her, but I don't love her." Whatever Zack wanted
to say after that was interrupted by a knock on the door.

Sara stuck her head in. "Sorry to intrude but Uncle Richard is
here."

I stepped away from Zack. "Our conversation can wait. There's
something important Richard needs to know. It may be related to
Mrs. Carlton's murder. We've also called Sheriff Burroughs."

Zack raised my hand to his lips and placed a gentle kiss on my
palm. "There's plenty of time for us, Maddie."

Richard entered the office behind Sara, gave a nod to us and
said, "You have information that has bearing on the murder?"

"Do we wait for the sheriff or tell Uncle Richard now?" asked
Sara.

"Show him the photo," I said.

She removed it from her desk where she had laid it and handed
it to Richard. Zack stepped forward to look at it.

They both looked a bit puzzled.

I explained where I had found it and our discovery that it
appeared to match one of the baskets in the nations collection.

"We don't know how it got in the trash or when it was placed
there, but don't you think the forensic investigators would have
gone through every bin in the museum right after the murder?"
I asked.

"Let's ask Anita when she gets here." Richard handed the picture back to Sara. "And I need to talk with Mr. Powles about this.
Meantime, Sara, can you make a copy of this photo? Be careful not

to smudge any fingerprints that might be on it." Richard handed the photo back to Sara and punched a button on his phone. "Mr. Powles? I wonder if it would be convenient for you to come to the museum. Now, please. It's closed, but I have something you will want to see."

Richard ended his call. "Suspicious fellow. He wanted me to tell him what was happening, but I don't feel comfortable talking with him about this until Anita's been informed about the picture. Although it looks old, we'll need more than this to establish ownership."

"Maybe that's what Mrs. Carlton thought also if he showed it to her. She could have tossed it into the garbage as irrelevant," said Zack. "If she did that, Mr. Powles might have been so incensed that he grabbed the sword, found her in the break room and killed her."

Sara shook her head. "I can't believe that of him."

"Sara. Sweeetie. Just because you love his son and want to believe he raised someone as bright and kind as Leonard doesn't mean he's not capable of violence. This is his family's history we're talking about." I put my arm around her.

"No." Sara pulled away from me and turned her back on us. I could tell she was fighting tears.

"I'll head out to the entrance and wait to let Anita in when she arrives." I reached for Sara's hand and squeezed it.

"I'll come with you," said Zack.

We left the office and headed down the hall to the entrance.

"Do you really believe what you said, that Mr. Powles might have been so furious at Mrs. Carlton's reaction to the photo that he killed her?"

"I don't know, Maddie." He shook his head. "What other suspects do we have?"

"About that . . ." I began and told him about the sexual harassment issue. "And don't forget the thefts and the sale of the broach from the collection. Someone is responsible and it isn't Mr. Powles."

"I'm having difficulty linking sexual harassment and theft to killing Mrs. Carlton unless . . ."

"Unless she knew who was involved and the person killed her to keep her quiet." I leaned against the wall next to the entrance. "And then there's the individual who was at Sara's back window the same night someone attempted to break into the museum."

"How do you put all those together with the murder?"

I shrugged my shoulders. "I can't. Not yet."

When Sheriff Burroughs' police cruiser pulled up in front of the museum, Zack said, "I know Mrs. Carlton's funeral has been postponed until her two daughters could arrange to travel here. When is it scheduled for?"

"Actually, tomorrow. Why do you ask?"

"Sometimes funerals attract more than mourners."

"Oh. You mean potential suspects, don't you?"

He nodded as we greeted the sheriff.

"What's up folks? I was trying to fit in an early dinner before I began my night shift."

"Sorry to keep you from your food, but we have something we think you should see."

Anita gave Zack and me a wary look as we led her into the building and then Sara's office. "I assume 'we' means both of you and who else? And hello to you, Richard. Why am I the last to know when Zack and the Sparks family are busy ferreting out clues.?"

"Sara and I just found this. Just this minute. And we called you right off." I gave her a disingenuous smile.

"Uh, huh, but Zack and Richard just happened to be around." She returned my look with a suspicious one.

"Something like that," I said and tried to hide my embarrassment.

"Okay. You first." She gestured for Zack and me to enter before her. "I'll just tag along behind." I caught the note of sarcasm in her voice, but when I turned to look at her, I could see the side of her mouth quiver in a smile she tried hard to hide. Whew. I didn't want to make an enemy of Sheriff Burroughs.

Sara held out the photo to her. "We found this in the ladies' room trash."

"I assumed your forensic team went through all the trash right after the murder," Richard said.

Anita turned the photo over in her hand. "So what is this? Why do you think it's so important?"

"We think it's a picture of the basket Mr. Powles contends belongs to his family. It matches one of the baskets in the collection we are holding to be turned over to the nations people soon," Sara said. "Mr. Powles told Mrs. Carlson he had proof that the basket belonged to his family. This old picture could be that proof."

Anita shook her head. "Well, maybe something finally makes sense. My forensics people found a number of old photos of Native American objects in Mrs. Carlton's purse. We didn't know what to make of them, but obviously she'd stowed them there. We didn't think much of it, but . . ."

"Of course not. You already had the man you were certain was the murderer. Why examine some old photos . . ." Richard said.

Anita whirled around to face him. "That's not the way I run an investigation. You know that."

Oops. Richard's words had offended Anita. I couldn't blame her for being angry.

"What I meant was old photos of artifacts in a museum director's purse wouldn't set off alarm bells. They would have been seen as pertaining to her work."

Anita gave Richard a thin smile. "Of course that's what you meant, Richard."

Richard cleared his throat. "I just called Mr. Powles to ask him to come to the museum so I could ask him about the picture," Richard said.

Anita continued to examine the photo. "I don't get it. Why all those photos in Mrs. Carlton's purse, but the picture of the basket in the downstairs ladies' room trash?"

But Sara had put some of the clues together. "I think Mrs. Carlton received the photos from Mr. Powles as evidence that his relatives took pictures of their treasured objects. She would have only been interested in the basket because it was the evidence she needed to show to the nations people to establish Mr. Powles's claim on the basket."

"How did it end up in the ladies' room trash then?" asked Zack.

"Because she ran in there on her way to the break room. She knew someone was after her and she worried the person wanted that picture, so she crumpled it up in a paper towel to disguise it and tossed it into the trash," I said.

"Then someone pursued her down the hall and into the break room, grabbing the sword as they ran past. They stabbed her, tried to search her for the picture, but the killer heard someone coming, so they dashed out moments before Mr. Powles entered the room," Zack said.

"That doesn't bring us any closer to the identity of the killer," said Anita. "And this is all speculation."

"Maybe," said Richard, "but let's get Mr. Powles in here, and without letting him know what we suspect, you can ask him about the proof he gave Mrs. Carlton when he met her in her office."

"Assuming," said Sara, "that he's now willing to talk to us."

"But if he knows we found the photos, then he has everything to gain. His family gets their basket back," I said.

"He's still a murder suspect. The less he knows about what we know, the better. I say we show him this photo and see what he says about it," said Anita.

We were at an impasse. How could we convince a possible murder suspect that he should cooperate with the authorities, especially one as mistrusting of the legal system as Mr. Powles?

Chapter 20

"You called Mr. Powles and asked him to meet us here, right?" asked Anita.

"We'll work out a story that will convince him we're playing straight," said Richard.

"How about the truth?" I said.

Everyone looked at me as if I had lost my mind, but Sara added her support.

"I think the truth about the picture and the other photos is the only way he'll believe we're trying to help him," she said. "How can he deny the photos belong to him if he wants to claim the basket?"

We waited for Mr. Powles's arrival, but after ten minutes, I began to worry he might not show. "Maybe he thinks it's a trap to get him to admit to something associated with the murder."

"Let me call Leonard to see if he knows if his father has left yet."

Sara stepped out of the office to talk with Leonard.

"If Mr. Powles is questioning why we want him here, perhaps Sara can convince Leonard that we mean well and want to help him gain possession of the basket," I said.

Sara stepped back into the room with a frightened look on her face. "Leonard told me his father left the house over a half hour ago, saying he needed to find someplace safe, that the authorities were after him again."

"So he's gone then?" Anita's face registered both disbelief and anger. Just when we thought we could obtain Mr. Powles's cooperation, he fled.

"Now what?" From the tone of Richard's voice it was clear he already knew what Anita was about to do.

"ABP," she said. "The man is still a person of interest in a murder case. Until we talk with him, we don't know if our speculations about the photos are valid." She grabbed the plastic bag with the photo inside, turned on her heel and left, calling her office as she made her way outside to her car.

"She's not happy," said Richard. "She wanted us to call her first and then have her get in touch with Mr. Powles."

"That wouldn't have worked any better than what we did. He doesn't trust white people. And with the authorities looking for him, he has no reason to believe we're trying to help him." I felt a sense of despair. We were so close to an answer in Mrs. Carlton's murder and how it might be connected to other happenings. Mr. Powles could have helped us and himself. We still had one chance to reach him. "Sara, call Leonard back and see if you can convince him we only want to talk to his father."

"I don't think he'll believe me, Gram, not with an alert out to local authorities."

"Try, honey. If only we could discover what place Mr. Powles sees as a "safe" place," I said.

Sara nodded and left the room once more to try to convince her boyfriend our intentions weren't bad. I gave a deep sigh. Would I trust the police if I was in his shoes? Probably not.

"I'll be back in a minute." I rushed out of the office and found Sara in the hallway talking on her cell to Leonard. "Let me talk to him."

I took the phone from Sara's hand. "I'm not supposed to tell you this, but we need your father's cooperation if he wants that basket back in the family. Tell him we found the pictures and we know they're proof the family has the right to the basket. I'm willing to talk with him without the police or other authorities in on the discussion. He can name the time and the place."

I handed the phone back to Sara.

"Boy, are you in trouble, Gram."

"Yes, I know I shouldn't have told him about the photos, but sometimes secrets harm more than they help. Let me have the copy you made of the photo. I want to show it to Mr. Powles when I meet with him . . . if I meet with him. When you finish with your call, let's go home. I'm exhausted, hungry and thirsty."

I stepped outside into the dark. I could feel the weather beginning to change. The nights were no longer filled with the leftover heat of summer, but now the wind signaled the cold to come. I pulled my sweater tighter around me and made a mental note to remove my wool coat from the upstairs hall closet. Winter was on its way.

Sara, Zack and Richard exited the museum to join me. From the lights on the front of the building I could see the discouragement on everyone's faces. Sara and I turned down the sidewalk leading to the back parking area. Richard and Zack had parked their cars in front of the building.

"Maddie," said Zack.

"Later, Zack. We can talk later. Right now I want to go home."

"Night, Mom, Sara." Richard got into his car and pulled out.

We left Zack standing in the light that pooled at the bottom of the museum stairs. He looked so lonely and defeated. I wanted to run back to him and hold him, but I couldn't.

THE MUSEUM WAS CLOSED THE NEXT DAY for Mrs. Carlton's funeral. The event was held in the large Unitarian Church in Stone Side because the building had space for over a hundred mourners. As the director of the museum, Mrs. Carlton was well known in the area, and many people would want to attend including state officials, representatives from other museums, local residents, family members and nations leaders and their members. I spotted Leonard walking into the church with the Onondaga and Oneida Nations members. Beside him stood a tall, slender woman, her silver hair pulled back from her face with a tortoise shell barrette. She wore traditional Nation's clothing, a brightly patterned skirt and blouse and soft leather boots on her feet.

Leonard led her over to me. "This is my mother. She and I are here to represent our family."

She held out her hand and enclosed mine in her small, warm one. "My husband has spoken of you. Mrs. Sparks. I have a message I need to deliver to you from him."

"Yes?" I said excitedly.

She smiled. "You must come to our house this afternoon for tea. We will talk then." She and Leonard joined the nations members who moved toward the front of the church.

Sara stood at my side and heard what Leonard's mother said. "Have you met her before?" I asked.

"Yes, several times. She makes a good cuppa, Gram."

I turned my attention to the two women who sat in the first row in front of the casket.

"Mrs. Carlton's daughters," I told Sara. "I met them several years ago at an event at the museum before you began your internship there."

Sara and I approached them, paid our respects and shook hands with the men beside them who identified themselves as the daughters' husbands.

"Any information about Mrs. Carlton's ex-husband?" asked Sara.

"He's deceased. No other family except for . . ." Just as I was to reveal to Sara that Mrs. Carlton had a half-brother, Agnes Danderfield's old boyfriend, Zack waved at me. He and Richard had saved seats for us at the back of the church. As I scanned the crowd, I saw that everyone who worked at the museum was in attendance. Harold sat toward the far-left side of the room next to his cousin, Graham, head of the museum board of directors. Next to them were the board members. Someone tapped me on the shoulder, Agnes Danderfield.

"Are you here as a friend or is this part of your newspaper assignment?" I asked.

She scowled at me. "Friend, of course but I'm as curious about who's here as you are."

There was no sign of her Al Lawton.

"Al didn't come with you?"

"No, but he's here someplace." She looked around searching for him. "Ah, he just came in. He's going up front to sit with the family. We decided we didn't belong together after all. Oh, and you might want this. He asked me to give it to you." Agnes handed me a boarding pass for an airline ticket with Lawton's name on it.

"The day after Mrs. Carlton's death, I see." Good. I wouldn't have to search the internet for information on the time of his arrival here.

"I knew you added him to your list of suspects, Maddie. Brenda was right. He's not the man for me. Too unreliable. But he's no killer."

She turned on her heel and found a seat on the other side of the room before I could thank her.

FOLLOWING THE SERVICE, THE MOURNERS LEFT to follow the hearse to the Butternut Falls cemetery, the one across the stream from my cottage. As we stood in front of the grave, I caught the eye of Jeremy Westin, who nodded at me and Sara. A young woman stood at his side—a girlfriend, I wondered? I hoped they were planning to attend the get-together after the internment. The Historical Society had opened their newly renovated building for the event. I wanted to meet Jeremy's companion, not only because I had never seen her before but because she had beautiful blonde hair, and she was, as Dev had described the young woman who sold him the broach, "a looker."

The people who came to the after-funeral event were about half that at the church and gravesite. None of the nations people attended and I didn't spot Jeremy and the blonde women I was so curious to meet. Sara, Zack, Richard and I mingled with some of the attendees for half an hour then we took leave, once more expressing our sympathies to Mrs. Carlton's daughters and their husbands.

"See anyone interesting?" asked Zack.

I shared with him my curiosity about the woman with Jeremy.

"Should I pay him a visit?" Zack asked.

"Not just yet. Jeremy's already suspicious about my questioning him and Ellie yesterday about the book. Let's let him think no one found his date's presence today unusual. Tomorrow at the museum I can talk with him."

"You mean 'pounce' on him, don't you Gram?" Sara gave me a quirky smile.

"Exactly," said Richard and Zack together.

"Is this a good time for us to talk, Maddie?" asked Zack.

"Sorry, but I have an invitation to tea."

"Oh. Anyone I know?" he asked.

I didn't want Zack to know I had been invited to the Powles house by Mrs. Powles. "I don't think so."

I gave him a smile and waved goodbye. Sara and I walked to my car.

"I'm glad you're not saying anything to Zack about Mrs. Powles's invitation. He could be waiting for you at his house, and you promised to meet with him without the authorities in tow."

"Yes, but I'm certain neither of Leonard's parents would see you as an interloper."

"Perhaps not, but let's not take that chance. Drop me off at Mom and Dad's. I'll use this opportunity to catch up with them."

"You're such a good daughter." I reached over and patted Sara's hand.

Sara gave me directions to Mr. Powles's house, which was located several miles outside Butternut Falls on a gravel road which led up the hill off the main highway out of town. The road curved around and around climbing the hill until I came out at a clearing with a log house in it. Beyond the house stood an area enclosed with a fence. Two black horses within the enclosure flicked flies off their backs with their tails as they grazed the abundant grass. Mrs. Powles stepped out of the front door to greet me as I opened my car door.

She took my hand and led me through the doorway into the house. I looked up into her brown eyes which were filled with warmth as if I were an old friend she was eager to see. I don't know what I expected, but not what greeted me in the house. While the outside was made of hewn logs, stripped of their bark, the inside belied that frontier look. An open staircase led to a second story balcony while the first story of the house was open— kitchen, dining area and living room flowing into each other. A large window in the living room looked into the hills beyond the house, an area shadowed in the late afternoon sun by blues, grays and purples.

"So lovely." The sight took my breath away.

"Please," Mrs. Powles gestured to a large sofa, "sit. I'll bring over the tea."

I sank into the sofa and felt as if I was being enveloped by its softness. "I don't know if I'll be able to get myself out of here." My feet barely touched the floor.

Mrs. Powles smiled. "You are a tiny woman, Mrs. Sharps, but I'm sure we can help you out."

"Call me Maddie."

"And I'm Kate."

The tea service looked like fine porcelain with tiny blue painted flowers adorning the pot, cups and saucers.

I took a sip of the tea. It was strong black English breakfast tea, a bracing brew which I preferred in the afternoon, and which fit my need for comfort after the funeral. "Lovely." I sighed and sank back into the couch.

"Here." Mrs. Powles shoved a footstool under my feet. "Isn't that more comfortable than having your feet dangle?"

Kate looked as if she was in no hurry to deliver whatever message her husband had for me, so after a few more sips of tea and a bite of a spiced cake, which I complimented her on, I decided to take the initiative. I extracted a copy of the picture of the basket.

"The original of this was found in the trash in the women's restroom in the basement of the museum. There were other photos also. It's old and I'm assuming together the photos constitute proof the basket belongs to your family. I believe Mr. Powles gave it to Mrs. Carlton to share with the nations people."

She took the photo from me and examined it. "Albert. Can you come downstairs?"

I hadn't noticed the figure who stood gazing down on us from the second-floor balcony. Albert Powles strode down the stairs and approached us. His expression was as usual unreadable. He took the copied photo from his wife's hand.

"I gave Mrs. Carlton a number of photos the day of her murder. I don't know what she did with them, but I hoped she would show them to the nations leaders, and they would agree with her that my family should be the recipients of what is rightfully theirs. Why did the authorities not tell me they found the photos?"

Now I understood some of his suspicion and why he chose not to meet us yesterday at the museum.

"You thought the photos had purposely been taken, perhaps by the authorities or someone at the museum. Not true. They only came to our attention yesterday." I recounted to him how the photo of the basket had been found as well as the others. "I suspect Mrs. Carlton took the original photo of the basket with her and headed downstairs to the break room where she, the nations representatives and you were to meet. Before she entered the breakroom, she saw someone in there, not you, not the nations people, but someone she didn't trust. She turned and quietly fled down the hall toward the women's restroom where she tossed the picture in the trash to hide it. The person waited for her to appear in the breakroom, not knowing she had secreted the photo. The killer, having seen the photo in her hand when she left her office and knowing that the two of you had met there and you had given her the evidence she was about to present to the nations people of your right to the basket, was certain the photo had to be somewhere on her person. Her killer stabbed her with the sword taken off the wall in the hallway and was about to search her when he heard someone approaching, you, Mr. Powles. With no time to search her body, the killer fled but worried there might be other photos, so he decided to break into the museum to make a thorough search of Mrs. Carlton's office. Unfortunately for him, the break-in was unsuccessful."

Mr. Powles continued to hold the copy of the photo then raised his glance to meet mine. "You've thought a lot about this, haven't you?"

"I have, well, not just me, but Sara, Zack and Richard also."

"And what does the sheriff think?" he asked.

"The sheriff thinks the photo is real and that it establishes your claim on the basket. So, you see, we only wanted to talk with you about the photo yesterday at the museum."

"And that's why the police and other law enforcement agencies are looking for me." He almost spit out these words.

"You didn't show up for the meeting."

"Why would I? Nothing was said about finding the photos. I assumed the authorities wanted to question me again, perhaps arrest me again."

"Well, now we know your claim to the basket is genuine."

"And do you know the identity of the killer?" he asked.

"No, but we have some leads."

"That simply takes us back to the beginning but raises another question which no one has considered yet."

"Which is what?" I asked.

"Why would someone go to such lengths to keep my family from claiming the basket?"

I felt so stupid. I hadn't given any thought as to who would kill to keep Mr. Powles from claiming the basket. Mrs. Carlton must have known or suspected why, but she was dead, unable to reveal the reason.

He handed the photo back to his wife. "I won't be here if you tell the authorities you met with me, so don't waste their time and effort coming here to bother my wife and search my house." He turned on his heel and left.

I had thought I was so smart working through the events surrounding Mrs. Carlton's murder, but I had missed the most critical issue, the one which must point to the identity of the killer—who didn't want Mr. Powles to claim the basket?

I pondered this as I drove down the hill away from the house. By the time I reached the highway, all I knew was that I wasn't such a clever detective as I thought. It had crossed my mind that the finger of suspicion pointed to either the Onondaga or Oneida people, but neither of their leaders seemed interested in claiming the basket. Someone did not want Mr. Powles to claim the basket. That's what my gut told me. But why? My gut was silent on that issue.

CHAPTER 21

B ACK AT HOME, I THREW MYSELF onto the couch where Spike joined me and crawled into my lap. As I absentmindedly petted him, my brain struggled with everything that had happened surrounding Mrs. Carlton's murder, the thefts from the museum and possible break-ins at Sara's house and at the museum.

The blinking light on my answering machine caught my attention. I dumped Spike onto the floor to go answer it, a move he did not take kindly. He stalked off, tail thrashing in anger and made his way to the kitchen where he stood over his food bowl and gave me dirty looks and loud yowls.

"Soon, buddy." I punched the listen button and heard Sara's voice.

"Hi, Gram. I didn't want to call your cell because I thought it wasn't wise to interrupt your meeting with Mrs. Powles. I'm at Mom and Dad's having dinner here and staying the night with them. I'll have Dad drop me at your place tomorrow and we can share a ride into museum if you like. Oh, and tomorrow night, I've made plans to stay at my apartment with Leonard. I should be perfectly safe with him there also. I've been neglecting him lately. I think we need some together time. See you tomorrow."

Spike called to me from in front of his dinner dish. My stomach rumbled. Except for the small piece of cake I ate with my tea at the

Powles's house, I'd eaten nothing since the small salad I had for lunch. Both Spike and I needed food, him because it would quiet his nagging and me because I couldn't ponder the elements of the conundrum of murder and thefts without fuel for my brain.

I poured some kibbles in Spike's bowl, then I checked the refrigerator: nothing much there. I opened the freezer and peered in at something in a plastic bag. Should I defrost it and take my chances? The thought of fried chicken made my mouth water. The convenience store sold fast food dinners like pizza, deli sandwiches and, if a person got there early enough in the evening, fried chicken. It wasn't as good as the Kentucky colonel's, but it was fried, and fat was what I craved. I threw on my sweater, grabbed my bag and keys and told Spike I'd be right back. He didn't care how long I would be gone as long as it didn't extend beyond his next meal.

I got lucky and snagged the last box of fried chicken. When I got in the car to drive home with my dinner, I decided to eat the chicken, sitting in front of the store so that I wouldn't have to deal with Spike nagging me for some of it. I gobbled a thigh, drumstick and wing and left the breast for later. Maybe I'd make chicken salad with celery and grapes and serve it on a bed of lettuce for tomorrow's dinner, my homage to eating healthy after my fried dinner. I pulled up in front of my house and when I got out of the car and walked up the sidewalk, I felt something was wrong inside. I didn't remember turning the light on in my office.

When I inserted the key into the lock and twisted the knob before I turned the key, the door opened. I was certain I had locked it when I left. Sara had a key to the house. Maybe she came back here instead of spending the evening with her parents. But where was her car? I hadn't seen it out front.

"Hello." I stuck my head in the door. "Sara? Are you here?"

I heard noises coming from my tiny office off the living room.

"Sara. Are you in there?"

Now the office was dark. I reached around the door to flip the wall switch just as someone grabbed me, flung me to one side and ran out of the office. I fell backward into the wall, tried to catch myself, but tumbled onto the floor. Before I could pick myself up, the intruder ran into the living room. I heard the front door slam. I got off the floor and heard a plaintive meow from my desk. Spike was huddled on my keyboard, one of his favorite places to nap.

The fur on his back and tail stood on end and he'd pulled his whiskers back toward the sides of his face. He was upset. I noticed blood on one of his paws. I picked up his paw and examined it. He wasn't hurt, but he was indignant. Someone had disturbed his nap.

"Catch yourself a robber?" I asked him.

He'd had a go at the person who'd entered the house and disturbed his after kibbles nap. Obviously, Spike had taken a swipe at the individual and scratched him or her enough to draw blood. Probably the uninvited visitor had tried to push Spike off my desk because the papers on the desk were in disarray. I always kept everything there in neat stacks. Someone was looking for something but hadn't found it because Spike interfered, and then I had returned home.

"You're quite the watch cat, aren't you? For that you deserve a snack."

At the word "snack" Spike jumped off my desk and headed out the office door toward the kitchen. I tossed my sweater, bag and box of chicken on a kitchen chair and headed toward the pantry to grab the bag of snacks I kept there for him.

"Here you go, you brave fella." I held out the treat to him, but he hesitated. "C'mon. I'm not bringing it to you."

I moved toward him, but he backed up startled as I was by the sound of the kitchen door opening. Before I could turn to see what was happening, everything went black.

"GRAM, GRAM. WAKE UP." SARA BENT OVER ME, her hand caressing my face. "I called an ambulance. It's on its way."

Next to her stood Zack, his face filled with concern.

"I tried to reach you by phone, Gram, but there was no answer. The only place I could think of where you might be was with Zack, so I called his cell. He told me he would come over to check on you, but I got here first. Mom and Dad are on their way also."

Wow. Did my head hurt. "Someone was here when I got home. They were in my office looking for something. Spike confronted them and they ran out when I came into the office, but then I think I was hit on the head when I came in here to give Spike a treat."

"I checked the house. It appears the intruder reentered the house after they ran out the front door. The kitchen door was open," Zack said. "I called Sheriff Burroughs. She should be here any minute."

Spike appeared at my side and let out a yowl.

"Will someone please give him a treat?" I reached my hand to the back of my head and felt something sticky there.

"Leave it alone, Gram."

I closed my eyes for a moment and when I opened them again, the room was filled with people—Abigail, Geoffrey, Sara, Zack, EMTs, police officers. I groaned as the EMTs lifted me onto a stretcher. As they rolled me to the door, I turned my head and noticed my sweater and container of chicken were where I had tossed them on the kitchen chair when I went to get Spike's treats, but it wasn't what was there that worried me. My bag was missing.

Sara drove to the hospital behind the ambulance. We left Zack and the sheriff at the house to take a closer look at what had happened there. I was wheeled into an examining room where Sara held my hand until the doctor on duty came in.

"I'm Doctor Jacobs. I understand you got hit on the head by an intruder and lost consciousness. That's not a good ign. We're talking about a possible concussion here. We'll want to keep you overnight for observation and take a few pictures of your head."

"Speaking of pictures," I said to Sara as they took me off to radiology, "A copy of the picture was in my purse and my purse is gone. I think that's what the intruder was looking for. Tell Zack, will you? And could someone put the leftover chicken in the fridge?"

And off I went for X-Rays and an MRI. After the hospital put me in a room for the night, Zack accompanied by Anita came in to talk with me.

"We found your bag tossed onto the side of the road just down the street from your house," said Zack. "Everything was still in it, wallet, keys, credit cards and money. And the copy of the photo of the basket was there also."

Whether I had had a concussion or not, my brain seemed to be functioning quite well. "So what were they looking for?"

"Don't worry about that for now. You need to rest for a while. A nurse will be in here to monitor you." Zack's wonderful blue eyes were filled with concern and worry.

"When can I go home?"

"Be a good girl and follow the doctor's orders, would you, Gram? Just this once?" Sara gave me one of her sweet smiles and smoothed my hair back from my forehead.

"Is my gray showing around the roots?" I asked her.

"Yup. She's going to be fine," said Abigail, standing behind Sara and holding Geoffrey's hand.

Geoffrey scowled. "I thought you told me everyone at the museum was safe. Look what happened, Mom."

I flapped my hand at him dismissively.

The nurse kept me up throughout the night. The doctor came in early in the morning and said I could finally get some sleep.

"But now I'm not tired," I whined at him.

And that's all I remembered until the light from the midmorning sun shined in my window and awoke me.

"I'm starving." I sat up in bed, visions of eggs, bacon and crispy buttered toast running through my head, which, by the way, still ached.

"Time for breakfast," announced an attendant, bringing in a tray.

Unfortunately, my earlier image of a hearty breakfast was erased by a presentation of oatmeal and weak coffee.

The hospital released me right after a late lunch (which consisted of a hamburger, no catsup, the ubiquitous hospital Jello and another cup of weak coffee) and told me to go home and rest. Sara was at the museum for the day, so Zack accompanied me to my house.

"I can't stay here for long, Maddie, but I want to make certain you're getting much needed rest and have everything you need to get through until Sara stops by after work." He carried me into the house and set me on the couch.

"Quit fussing over me. You're like a hen with new chicks." I tossed the blanket he had placed over me onto the floor. "Too hot."

Zack stood over me, a grave look on his face. "You will be good, won't you, Maddie? I don't want to be worrying about your health."

"I'm fine. Really." I grabbed the blanket from the floor and covered myself "Too cold."

"Maddie, pay attention. You got hit on the head and lost consciousness. You need to stay here and rest. Do you hear me? I want your butt on this couch for the rest of the day."

"What if I have to go to the bathroom?"

"You know what I mean. You are not to go anywhere, certainly not to the museum."

"Why would I do that?" I opened my eyes wide, hoping for a look of innocence.

It didn't work.

"I know you. You're thinking you should be questioning people at work, aren't' you?"

"No. Uh, maybe. Yes, of course." I sat up on the couch. "You know what I think?"

Zack sighed and shook his head. "No. What"

"The key to Mrs. Carlton's murder can be found in the answer to the question of why someone wanted to keep Mr. Powles from claiming the rights to that basket."

"And that person had to kill Mrs. Carlton to accomplish that?"

"I think so. Let me think on it for a while. Meantime, could you make me a pot of tea, and find Spike, would you? I know he had to be upset over the intruder and my not being here with him."

"Is that all you need.?"

"Spike is probably hiding under my bed."

"No, he's in the kitchen sitting patiently in front of his bowl."

"Not yowling? Oh, he must really be upset."

ZACK LEFT ME WITH SPIKE BESIDE ME on the couch, a pot of tea on the coffee table and my laptop on the end table in case I wanted to do some writing.

"Sara said she'd be home early today, so stay put."

"Yes, yes," I replied. I heard Zack close the front door and had just put one foot on the floor when the door reopened.

"I locked the back door and I'm locking this one. Stay put."

"What about visitors?"

"Everyone who should be visiting has a key to get in. Stay put."

"Don't patronize me," I yelled at him as he pressed the lock and closed the door for the final time, I hoped.

"Let's see that paw of yours, Spike." I maneuvered him around so that I could hold his leg and examine his paw to make sure I was right about what happened last night. There was no sign his paw was injured, and he'd obviously licked it clean of the blood he'd drawn when the intruder had disturbed his nap on my desk.

Someone had a nasty scratch on their arm or hand, I thought to myself. I wonder who?

I'd polished off the entire pot of tea, eaten the snack of cookies Jake had left on a plate for me and opened my laptop to work on my manuscript. But I couldn't write a thing. I was too restless. I moved Spike off the end of the couch, grabbed my sweater and bag, which had been returned to the house, probably by Anita, and opened the front door.

Seated on a lawn chair on my front porch was my friend Jane.

"What are you doing out here?" I asked.

"Babysitting you, like Zack asked me to do."

"You could have come in and kept me company. I'm going crazy in there with nothing to do."

"I was told you needed rest, so Zack borrowed a chair from your garage and put it here for me." She held a swath of material. "Crocheting to keep me busy."

"Come in here. I need to talk to someone to help me put together what's happening."

Jane made another pot of tea and located a fresh bag of cookies in my pantry. Jane and I put our heads together. I caught her up on the photos and the break-in last night at my house. We brainstormed for over an hour.

"I've got nada," she said.

"Me either, but I can't sit here for one more minute."

"You can't leave."

"I'm going to the museum. You can come with me, or I go alone."

Jane tossed her crocheting on the couch. "You think returning to the scene of the crime will jog something loose in your brain?"

"No. I just need some fresh air and a close look at some hands and arms."

"GRAM," SAID SARA WHEN I WALKED into her office. "You're not supposed to be here And, Jane. Aren't you supposed to be looking after her this afternoon?"

"She threatened me."

"How?"

"She said she'd lock me in a closet."

Sara gave Jane and me a stern look. "Don't be silly. Gram is half your size. How could she wrangle you into a closet?"

"She couldn't, but I was worried she's spread rumors I was having an affair with a younger man."

"You wish," I said, then added, "I won't stay long. I just need to take a look at all our volunteers and employees here."

Sara's mouth gaped open. She cast a look of concern at Jane.

"Must be the effects of the blow on the head," said Jane. "I have no idea what she's up to and I didn't ask."

"Okay, Gram, but I'm coming with you. Both of us are in case you stumble and fall or lose consciousness."

"C'mon then." I started out of the office, Sara and Jane close behind.

As soon as I got out of the elevator on the third floor, I realized how futile my task was. All the guards wore jackets covering their arms and none of them had any scratch marks on their hands. The same was true of the guard on the second floor. I ran into Harold and Jeremy talking in the hallway outside Sara's office; same deal. Jackets covering their arms and their hands showed no wounds. Francis in the gift shop had on her long-sleeved sweater for autumn. Ellie and Debra James, the acquisitions director, weren't in this afternoon.

I was stumped. Unless. I asked Sara to do me a favor, but she was reluctant. "If I do that, it may have a negative impact on our collections."

"It will be for only a few minutes. The museum will close in a half hour, then you can return everything to normal."

"Fine." Sara grabbed her keys from her desk and, checking the hall to make certain no one was watching, she inserted a key into the plastic covering the temperature control box outside her office and turned the thermostat to eighty-five degrees.

Soon museum employees came to Sara's office to complain of the heat.

Sara gave everyone a comforting smile "I know it's uncomfortable. I tried to adjust it, but there's something wrong with the thermostat. I've called our heating and cooling company and they're on their way. Take off your jackets and sweaters and roll up your sleeves. It's only a half hour of discomfort until the museum closes."

"Well, it better be fixed by tomorrow or I'm not coming in to work," said Harold.

Where I would have bitten off Harold's nose, Sara gave him a comforting smile. "I'm sorry this is happening, Harold. Everyone is overheated. If it can't be fixed by then, we'll close for the day."

Jeremy stood by Harold's side and the two of them pulled off their jackets and headed down the hall toward the gift shop.

"Okay, Gram. You've got the employees disrobing. What now?"

"I'll take a look at them again."

"What are you looking for?" asked Sara.

"The mark of the cat." I winked at her and headed off to re-examine arms and hands.

The employees gave me odd looks when I appeared again, following them around and staring at them. I heard one of the guards whisper to another, "That bump on Mrs. Sparks' head must have done some damage." The other guard nodded in agreement.

It took me over twenty minutes to cover all the floors and the basement area. No one had any suspicious marks on either their hands or arms, but I had missed two key employees.

"Sara, have you seen either Jeremy or Harold?"

"They went off together a few minutes ago toward the gift shop."

"I know. I looked there but I can't find them."

Francis, locking up the gift shop heard me and said, "I heard Harold say he was getting out of here early. He couldn't stand the heat. Jeremy went with him. Maybe you can catch them in the parking lot."

I looked out the entryway glass doors and spotted two cars drive past, one with Jeremy in it, the other driven by Harold.

They were awfully eager to leave the museum.

CHAPTER 22

"Sorry I put you to so much trouble, Sara."

"Could you explain what you were up to?" Sara reset the building's air conditioning.

"The intruder last night disturbed poor Spike who lashed out and scratched the person. I was looking for that scratch to establish the identity of the intruder."

"No luck?"

"My money is on either Harold or Jeremy, but they left before I could check their arms. That scratch won't last forever. The identity of my intruder is key to Mrs. Carlton's murder. I don't know how. Not yet, but I will."

"Next step?" asked Jane, as she, Sara and I locked up and left the museum.

"I think I need to pay a visit to each of them. Let's begin with Jeremy. He lives near here."

"Gram, you know Zack is not going to like your running around trying to track down clues. And I can't say I'm in support either. Go home and get some rest." Sara exchanged glances with Jane.

"She won't, you know. I'll accompany her and try to keep her out of trouble."

"Good luck," said Sara.

JANE AND I PULLED UP IN FRONT of an apartment complex not far from the museum. I checked the address Sara had provided. Jeremy's apartment was 301. The signage on the side of the building indicated the apartment was on the third floor at the end of the building. We rang the bell and heard voices inside. After a minute, the door opened.

"Yes?" said a tall, blonde woman, the one I'd seen Jeremy with at the funeral.

"Is Jeremy in?"

"Who's asking?"

"Maddie Sparks. We work together. And you are?"

"Candy. I'm his girlfriend. He's not here."

Jane, standing behind me, came forward. "I'm sure we heard voices when we rang the bell."

"Oh, that was me talking to my dog."

"Dog?"

"Come here, Bub," she called. A chihuahua ran out into the room from the kitchen area.

"Cute." I bent over and held out my hand.

The dog growled.

"He's not fond of strangers." She picked him up. He continued to growl.

"Do you expect Jeremy back soon?" I asked.

"Yes, of course. He always comes right home after his day at the museum. Oh, here he is now."

Jane and I turned our heads to see Jeremy heading down the hallway toward us. He had his jacket slung over his shoulder and his shirt sleeves rolled up. As he got closer, I spied a long scratch on his right arm.

"Wow. That looks like a nasty scratch," said Jane.

Jeremy leaned past us and gave the young woman a kiss on the cheek, then reached out to Bub, the dog. The dog growled.

"This little bugger scratched me last night." Jeremy said.

"Bub doesn't really like men." Candy pulled the dog closer to her and gave it a kiss on the head.

I was of the opinion that Bub didn't much like anyone other than Candy, but maybe that was because I was more of a cat person than a dog person, unless the dog was larger than Bub. I was fine with a Great Pyrenees.

I took Jeremy's arm and examined it. "Looks bad. Maybe you should see a doctor. It could get infected."

He quickly pulled his arm back. "What is it you want?"

"Do you know if Harold was in Mrs. Carlton's office the morning of her death?"

Jeremy's eyes grew wide with surprise. "Do you think he had something to do with her death? And why come here to ask me?"

I thought fast for a cover story.

"Uhm, I don't want to alert Harold. I was going to ask you this afternoon, but the two of you were together, so I didn't get the chance."

"You suspect something." Jeremy pulled his sleeve down to cover his scratch.

"Well, we all know he didn't like Mrs. Carlton very much, and someone at the museum called the newspaper and reported sexual harassment was going on there. He probably was on the verge of losing his job."

Jeremy nodded and continued to look at his feet. When he looked up his expression had changed. "Harold was always bothering the young women employees, wasn't he? But is that a reason to kill Mrs. Carlton, you think?"

"What do you think?"

"I don't know, but isn't this line of exploration the business of the sheriff's department? Why are you asking these questions?"

"Well, you know me, Jeremy. I'm just an old busybody, nothing better to do, I guess. But keep this under your hat, would you? Better not to let Harold know we're on to him."

"Sure."

Candy leaned into Jeremy and whispered something in his ear.

"Right." He put his arm around her waist, provoking another growl from Bub. "Uh, I'd ask you in, but Candy and I have someplace we need to be in a few minutes."

"Didn't mean to take up your evening."

Jane and I smiled and turned to go. Before the door closed, I spun around and asked, "You wouldn't have any ideas about items missing from the 'Our Neighbors' collection, would you?"

He shook his head and closed the door.

As we walked to the car, Jane said, "Do you think you should have been asking Jeremy those questions? Those are leads in the case."

"Leads, yes, but they lead nowhere right now. However, the scratch on his arm was telling, don't you think?"

"You heard him say it was from that beastly little Bub's nails."

"Was it? Well, I did what I intended to do, put pressure on him and indirectly on Harold. I've seen the two of them with their heads together more often than I'd like. There's something going on there."

"Why not just tell Anita about the scratch?" asked Jane.

"I don't think that will work. You heard him. He will say it's a scratch from the dog and I'll bet Candy will back him up on that."

"This could get you into a lot of trouble especially from Zack." Jane shook her finger at me.

"I know, but we're getting nowhere in this investigation. Someone needs to give it a nudge."

"That someone needs to be you?"

I shrugged. "Why not? No one sees me as much of a threat. A little pressure might convince someone to do something incriminating."

"I just hope what you did won't get you into trouble with anyone else, like Mrs. Carlton's killer."

Me, too, I thought. I agreed with Jane. If Zack found out I'd spoken to Jeremy and what I'd said, he wouldn't be happy.

"Let's call it a day. Jeremy may tell Harold I suspect him of Mrs. Carlton's murder. I think Jeremy was the individual who broke into my house last night, and his fiancé fits the description of the woman selling the brooch to the pawn shop. Who better to hassle these people than me? We'll see what happens tomorrow."

"Are you going to tell Zack what you did?"

I thought about it. Should I tell Zack? I knew he would be angry, but he needed to know what I had done and why.

"I suppose. I'll contact him later. I think he went to visit his daughter this afternoon."

"And shouldn't the sheriff know, too?"

"Don't nag me, Jane."

"Well, shouldn't she?" Jane insisted.

"Yes, yes. I'll have Zack tell her. Let's go home and have a nip of something."

"Something stronger than tea, I hope. At least for me. Maybe you shouldn't drink."

I put my arm around Jane's shoulder. "Don't be silly."

JANE AND I EACH ENJOYED A GLASS OF WINE at her house and talked about the possibility that I had set a fire under Jeremy by asking questions about Harold.

"We'll see what tomorrow brings." I hugged Jane goodbye and headed home to feed Spike and eat that left-over chicken breast and a small salad—and, of course, call Zack, a conversation I wasn't looking forward to. When I pulled into my drive, I saw a car I did not recognize parked out front. I unlocked my front door and went inside.

"I'm on your back deck," a female voice called.

I opened the kitchen door leading out to my deck. Mary sat on one of my chairs there. "That's my rental out front. I came over for a chat about Zack."

"Does he know you're here?"

"No, but I'm sure he won't mind. We're all friends, aren't we?"

Well, no we weren't, but something in her voice warned me I should tread carefully around her.

"I did something I maybe shouldn't have." Instead of her eyes registering remorse for what she did, there was a malicious twinkle in them.

"What was that?"

"I let your nasty cat out when I arrived. Shooed him off. He won't be back anytime soon. Just another homeless stray."

"That isn't true, Mary. You don't have a key to get into the house."

"Oh, but I do." She held up a housekey dangling from a keyring made of leather with a bank logo on it. I recognized it. It was the house key I gave to Zack.

My heart did a thud of fear. Spike had been a housecat since I got him. He'd never been out in this neighborhood. What had this looney woman done? Before I could go into a full-blown panic, reason took over. Spike wouldn't have gotten anywhere near Mary when she entered the house, and he certainly would have put up a fight if she had tried to grab him. No, I assured myself, the big fella was hiding somewhere in the house, probably under my bed. He was clever enough to know who the good guys were.

"Why would you do that, Mary?"

"Just to see the frightened look on your face, the one you have there now."

"You're mistaken. This is not the look of fear. It's disgust. Get off my porch! We have nothing to 'chat' about."

"What about Zack and me and our son?"

"You know, that's an interesting story. If you were talking about most men, I might believe you, but not Zack. If the two of you got together, which I doubt, he would have wanted to protect both of you. You know what I mean. But I don't think it happened. I don't think Zack ever had feelings for you. In fact, he told me you were always 'odd'" Well, okay. Zack never used that word, but he had described Mary as difficult for him to feel comfortable with. "I think you were as delusional back then as you are now. There was no Zack and you, and no baby. And you know there will be no Zack and you now."

"You don't understand, do you, Maddie? I'm the only one who can save his daughter."

"I think we know that's not true. She's going to save herself because she's got professional help now."

Mary smirked. "I don't think she likes the program she's in. She's left it."

"Left?'

"Oh, yes. Right after Zack visited this afternoon. I stayed there with her, and we talked. She hates the program. She wants to be with me."

I took a deep breath to calm myself. Had Mary taken Amy out of the drug rehab facility?

"Oh, I know what you're thinking. That this is another bluff. Call the facility. They'll tell you she's not there."

I didn't have the number of the facility on my cell, so I called John Tennet instead. He would know what was happening.

"Maddie. So glad you called. Amy left the facility late this afternoon."

"I know. And I know why. She's with Mary."

There was a moment's silence on the line. "Do you know where they are?"

"Maybe. Don't worry. Mary won't harm her. She only wants the best for her." Lies I hoped would reassure Mary and win her confidence in me. I caught Mary's eye and smiled at her. "I'll get back to you."

I had to step carefully here. I was certain Mary wouldn't harm her, but I wasn't convinced Mary knew when she was helping and when she was doing harm.

"See? I told you. She's fine, sleeping quietly."

"What did you do? Where is she?"

"She just needed a slow transition off those drugs not a lot of mumbo jumbo about how she would help herself talking to a bunch of ex addicts."

I lost it. "What did you do?" I yelled.

Mary flinched at my tone. "I knew how she got her drugs, so I went to the library and got some for her."

"You planned this when she went into the facility, didn't you?"

"I wanted to help her. Yes."

"Tell me where she is, Mary. Sleeping? You may have overdosed her. She needs help."

Mary gave me a sly look. "I'll tell you where she is, but first we talk. Promise me you'll give up Zack, let him go, tell him you don't love him so he and I can contact my son."

"I may believe you have a son, Mary, but I don't believe Zack is his father."

"That's my business. Just stay out of our lives. Promise me and I'll tell you where Amy is."

"I can't do that."

"No, you just won't. You want to keep him for yourself, but he doesn't love you. Do you want Amy to die?"

"Maddie. Mary." It was Zack.

"I didn't hear you pull up," I said.

Zack held up his hand to let me know he was in control of the situation. "I overheard what you said, Mary. Now tell me where you've hidden my daughter." His expression was grim, but he spoke in a friendly, yet firm manner to Mary.

Mary got out of her chair and rushed down the deck steps and into Zack's arms. "Of course I'll tell you. And then we'll all be together."

From the embattled expression on Zack's face I knew he wanted to fling Mary away from him, but he knew his daughter's life was at stake.

He looked down at Mary and quietly said, "Let's go get her, shall we?"

"She's right here. In the car."

Zack set Mary away from him and ran to the front of the house where Mary had parked her car. He opened the back door. "She's here, but her breathing is shallow. Call 9-1-1, Maddie."

I ran to join Zack to see how I could help. By the time the ambulance arrived, Amy was unconscious. Two EMTs rushed to her side. "We're losing her," one said. The other ran to the ambulance and came back with a box. I couldn't see what it was, but he inserted what looked like a nasal inhaler into her nose.

"Narcan," he said.

We waited, but he shook his head. "No reaction."

"Let's give her a second dose." He pulled the second inhaler out of the box and sprayed it into the other nostril. Suddenly Amy made a gulping sound, her eyes opened wide, and she tried to sit up.

"Dad?"

Zack threw his arms around his daughter. "Honey. Are you okay?"

"Yes. Oh, Maddie. You're here too." She held out her hand to me. I took it and squeezed.

"We're so relieved." I said.

Mary pushed forward. "I'm here, too. I told you everything would be better once I got you out of that place."

"You lied to me and then gave me drugs. You tried to kill me. I thought you loved me!"

Mary tried to envelope Amy in her arms. "Oh, no. I made a mistake, but now you're doing better. Your dad, you and I can go home, back to Seattle."

Amy pushed her away. "No. I don't want you in my life anymore. Go away."

Mary's hands flew to her face, and she began to weep.

Zack, still holding his daughter tightly to him, said, "Maddie, could you all the sheriff?"

The ambulance took Amy to the hospital. Zack followed them in his car after checking that I didn't mind waiting with Mary until the sheriff arrived. I agreed. At this point Mary seemed to withdraw into herself. Anita arrived a few minutes later. I took her to one side and explained to her what happened.

Head down, Mary got into the sheriff's car. I watched the car speed away from the house.

I went inside to be greeted by Spike who meowed grumpily at me for his dinner. Everything seemed back to normal, but it wasn't.

CHAPTER 23

I DIDN'T EXPECT TO HEAR FROM ZACK that evening. I knew he would want time to spend with his daughter. Sara arrived a half hour after the sheriff had driven Mary off.

"You look beat, Gram. What's up?"

"I think I need someone to put their arms around me and hold me."

Sara rushed across the room and pulled me to her on the couch. "Tell me."

I told her everything about Mary's visit and the situation with Zack's daughter.

"I can't believe after the emotional ups and downs today that I'm saying this, but I'm hungry. Are you, Sara?"

"Sure. What's in the fridge?"

I pulled out the leftover chicken breast from yesterday which we shared and split the last pint of chocolate ice cream in my freezer, all the food groups that counted when a person had experienced a distressing day. Sara drew a bath for me and filled the tub with lavender bath beads.

"I'll let you soak for a while." She tiptoed out the door. When she returned the bath water was beginning to lose its warmth, but I felt almost completely recovered from the day's events.

"Tomorrow," I told Sara, as I wrapped myself in my terry robe and started down the stairs where Sara had prepared hot cocoa for us, "tomorrow, we begin to make sense out of everything we know about the break-ins, thefts and murder."

"Are you really up to that after the days you've had?"

"Yes, I am. I really, really am." I might have sounded more confident that I should have, but I had started something today I had to finish. Tomorrow Harold and I would have a talk.

When I arose the next morning, I felt as if someone had used me as their punching bag.

"It's the aftermath of the past two days," Sara said as we were drinking our morning coffee.

"Yeh, I know. I don't bounce back as readily now as I did when I was younger."

"Look, why don't you stay home today? Get some rest or work on your writing."

That sounded appealing. I hadn't spent much time on my manuscript since the murder. But on second thought, I needed to talk with Harold today. I was certain Jeremy would have told him about the questions I'd asked yesterday. If Harold thought we were onto him, he might get jittery. I wanted to keep up the pressure on him hoping he'd break and tell us something we needed to know. I was certain we could use Jeremy and Harold against each other and find out the truth.

"The weekend is usually our busiest time at the museum. Besides, I'll be fine once I move around a little, get the blood flowing, unkink my back."

"It's your call, Gram. Share a ride this morning?"

"Let's take both cars in case I change my mind about staying the entire day. I can come home early if I feel the need."

I arrived at work before we opened the museum. "Have you seen Harold this morning," I asked Jeremy who came up the stairs from the basement floor.

"I think he went to the breakroom for coffee."

"Beautiful woman, your fiancée. Lovely hair."

"Uh, thanks." Jeremy quickened his pace past me.

Since I didn't need to be at the desk until we opened the front doors, I went looking for Harold. Instead I found Ellie, sitting at the break room table and crying.

I rushed over to her and put my arm around her shoulders. "Ellie, dear. What's wrong?"

"Men. You just can't trust them, can you? From the old guys to the young. They're both alike."

"Anyone I know?"

"You already know Jeremy has tried to use me as an alibi for Mrs. Carlton's murder. He then led me to believe he wanted a relationship with me, but I heard him talking with someone on the phone this morning. It had to be a woman. He said he loved her and would be home early tonight. And then there's Harold. I have asked him not to stand so close to me and not to put his arms around me or to touch me. I reported him to Mrs. Carlton, and she said she would have a talk with him. I think she did, but her reprimand didn't stop him. He just did it again. Backed me against the table and tried to kiss me. I feel used by both of them."

"This has gone far enough. We're going to talk with Sara about Harold. What he's doing is sexual harassment."

"But it will be my word against his. No one saw him."

I laughed as I grabbed her hand and helped her up from the table. "I'll bet most of the people in this museum have seen how Harold behaves and will back up your story. In fact, I'm sure of it because someone working here reported the behavior to Agnes Dangerfield at the newspaper."

"Really?" Elie stopped crying and looked happy to hear that news. She blew her nose and went into the bathroom to splash water on her face then joined me at the door to Sara's office. We knocked and went in.

After Ellie had told Sara what had happened and how often it happened, Sara gave a deep sigh. "I know Mrs. Carlton reprimanded Harold and hoped it would change his behavior, but clearly it didn't. Harold pulled the same thing with me, not since I took over this position, of course, but on earlier occasions. And I'm certain that several employees, all younger women, who worked here as interns and have now left, experienced the same thing. I'll bet it was one of them who went to the newspaper. You were right, Gram. This has to end right now, or this workplace will get a reputation for being an unsafe place for women to work."

"What are you going to do?" asked Ellie in a quavering voice.

"I'm calling Mr. Graham, director of our board, to get his input on the next steps to take. If it was solely up to me, I'd toss Harold out on his butt." Sara reddened. "Sorry. I mean I'd have the museum take some, uh, legal action."

"Mr. Graham and Harold are cousins, you know," I said.

"I don't care. He'll have to take some kind of action. If he doesn't, then he can find another museum director and I'll go to the newspaper myself." Sara rose from behind her desk. "Now, let's open the doors and look forward to a busy day. We have a few groups coming in for tours. I'll assign all the tours to Harold. That should keep him busy enough he won't have time to harass anyone."

Several minutes later as I settled into my chair at the front desk, Harold walked by, his face a dark cloud of anger.

"Morning, Harold. When you have a minute, I'd like a word."

"Not today. I'm too busy." He stormed off down the hall.

A few minutes later Graham, the board director, entered and strode past me. "Morning, Mr. Graham. Lovely fall day, isn't it?"

He grunted and headed down the hall, knocked and entered Sara's office. Ten minutes later, Graham opened the office door, turned back and said, "I'll take care of this. Your job is to function as the museum's director and that's all." He slammed the door and walked over to me. "Have you seen Harold?"

"I think he's heading a tour group."

"Where? Where is the group now?"

"I think they're on the third floor."

He punched the elevator button once and waited, then pushed it again. When the elevator didn't arrive, he punched the button again and again. "Why won't this damn thing work?" Several more angry pushes and he started toward the stairs. I heard him mutter, "Stupid, stupid man."

I smiled to myself. What better time to have a talk with Harold than now, after his cousin had dealt with him, when the pressure was on. I waited in eager anticipation for Graham to finish with Harold and for Harold to come downstairs.

The tour members emerged from the elevator several minutes later, and they didn't look happy. One of the group came over to me. "Both those men were so rude to us."

"I'm so sorry. We're a little short staffed today, but, if you don't mind, I can have one of our interns show you around."

The group agreed. I could hear angry voices coming from up the stair well.

Not very professional, Mr. Graham, I said to myself, and then got out of my chair and went to the stairs to see if I could hear what was being said.

"You idiot," Graham's voice. "How could you do this to me? I counted on you. Get out of my sight."

"What about my job? You can't fire me, you know." That was Harold.

"Is that a threat?" Graham roared back at him.

Graham descended the stairs first and stalked out of the building. Harold followed. I expected him to look chagrined, but he didn't. "Stupid man."

"That's what he said about you." I gave Harold one of my most innocent smiles. "I thought the two of you were close."

"We are. That was just a little spat. We always fought when we were kids. Still do it." Harold returned my smile.

"So everything's okay?"

"Of course."

"Good, because I think Sara would like to see you in her office."

"Graham already talked to me."

"No. No. This is about something else I believe. Something about a broach? I think she wondered if you took it or was it Jeremy?"

"Mind your own business, Mrs. Sparks." He stomped by me and headed toward Sara's office. I quickly picked up the phone and called her. "Incoming."

I WAS ON MY MORNING TEA BREAK when Harold left Sara's office, so I had no idea of his demeanor. No matter. Sara would share everything with me later today. But we were so busy at the museum she and I didn't make contact until just before we closed the doors.

"I hope you don't mind, Gram, but Leonard and I are meeting for dinner tonight at his parent's house."

"Do you think Mr. Powles might put in an appearance?"

"I have no idea, but I doubt it. He knows Leonard and I love each other, but he also doesn't trust me. I don't think he'd take the chance I might call either you or Richard or Zack and tell one of you if he came home. I know we haven't had the chance to talk today because I've been so busy, but I'll catch you up when I get home later. If you're still awake, that is."

On the way home I mused over the past few days' events. Had I jabbed a stick in a hornet's nest or merely bothered annoying people who had nothing to do with theft and murder? Just because I found Jeremy and Harold unpleasant didn't mean they were guilty. Nah, I shook my head. They were guilty of something, something that had to do with the museum and its collection. I hadn't been able to look through all the photos because Anita's forensic team had taken them when they were discovered in Mrs. Carlton's purse. I wondered what the other pictures showed.

I punched in the connection to Anita's cell.

"Hi. I hope I'm not bothering you. You have all those photos, don't you? Could I stop by and take a look at them? I know you examined them, but I'd just like to see if there's anything that jumps out at me, anything we haven't considered yet."

Anita agreed, so I took the highway to the county office building to prowl through the photos.

Anita led me to the evidence room and pulled the box containing the photos off the shelf.

"Here's the one we found in the bathroom waste bin. There are a number of fingerprints on it, all of them smudged, but one clear one. It's Mrs. Carlton's."

I looked at the photo of the basket again, peering closely at it as I had done the first time. In the foreground was the basket. What I hadn't noticed before because the photo was so wrinkled from being in the trash was the blurry figure of a young Native American woman. Perhaps the person who wove the basket?

"Your speculation, Maddie, that Mrs. Carlton tossed it into the trash is probably correct." Anita cleared her throat in embarrassment. "My officers should have done a better search."

Anita reached into the box and pulled out another evidence bag. "Here are the photos found in Mrs. Carlton's purse."

"She was going to show the photo of the basket to the nations leaders at the meeting she called for them and Mr. Powles. It would have been the proof needed to assure them the basket belonged to his family." I began to go through the photographs one by one. None of them were of good quality. It was difficult to make out specific designs on the objects. Mr. Powles must have brought all these photos to Mrs. Carlton, hoping that together they might establish his claim on the basket. She had chosen to use only the clearest picture of the basket to show to the nations leaders.

"Old black and white photographs. Really old. I'd guess from the late nineteenth or early twentieth century," said Anita.

"We'd have to check with Mr. Powles when we find him, but I'd guess the woman with the basket is an ancestor, probably his great grandmother."

"She appears in some of the other photos of smaller baskets, pots and beaded work." I looked through them and stopped at one that caught my eye. "But this photograph is of two people. The same woman, the basket at her feet, but she is holding the hand of a man. He appears to be white. But look at the expression on her face." I looked up in surprise. "I know what I see there. What do you see?"

"Some kind of personal connection between the two?"

"Very personal. I think they may be lovers."

Anita scrutinized the photograph. "Maybe. There's a story there. I wonder what it is. I'd like to question Mr. Powles. Dang that man for running off!"

"I may know someone who can tell us more about these photos."

"Who?"

"His wife."

"Let's go then." Anita placed the pictures back into the evidence box and started to leave.

I grabbed her arm. "Let's back up a minute. None of Mr. Powles's family much like white people and have special enmity toward authorities. Could you give me copies of these and I'll take them to her and ask her what she knows."

"Why do you think she'd tell you?"

"We had tea together after Mrs. Carlton's funeral."

"Bonded over a cuppa, did you?" asked Anita.

"Something like that."

Anita considered her options. "Okay then. Come with me. I'll get you the copies."

IT WAS GETTING DARK AS I ROUNDED THE CURVE up the hill to the Powles property. I spotted Sara's car parked in front as well as a beat-up Jeep SUV beside it. I guessed that car belonged to Leonard.

I knocked on the door. Kate Powles opened it and didn't look surprised to see me standing in her doorway. She did seem pleased to see me.

"Come in and join us."

I looked around the room. Sara and Leonard sat together on the couch holding hands. Kate gestured for me to take the over-stuffed chair across from them. Her husband was not in the room.

"Did you expect him to be here?" his wife asked.

"No." I replied. "I think you can answer all my questions."

"Coffee?" she asked.

I shook my head. "It's too late for caffeine for me."

"It's decaf," she said. "We're just about to have dessert. Pie made from the apples from our orchard."

After we'd all eaten our slices of pie and had our coffee, I reached into my bag and extracted the copies of the photos. I placed them on the coffee table, spreading them out so we all could see each one.

I pointed to the photo of the two people and the basket. "You know who she is, don't you?"

Kate picked up the photo and looked at it, a tiny smile lifting the corners of her mouth. "A great woman, a woman heartbroken, but so strong, talented and brave."

"Tell me her story."

"It is a long tale."

"I have all night."

She began the story, the flames from the fire in the fireplace casting shadows on her face. The story was not at all what I expected to hear.

CHAPTER 24

"THE WOMAN YOU SEE HERE WITH THE BASKET was my husband's great grandmother. Stories tell she was the most talented basket maker in the family, perhaps the most talented one in the entire Haudenosaunee Confederacy. Before the white invasion, all the land around us belonged to the Haudenosaunee Confederacy. My husband's family claimed the land we now live and farm, all the land you see when you drive up here, across to the hills beyond our buildings and down to the valley below." She swept her hand toward the window. "But a white settler moved us off our land and claimed we had no right to it. After many years, we got it back, but a white family came again and tried to take it from us. They were unsuccessful. The white man was terribly angry. His anger came between his son and my husband's great grandmother. She, called Maria Phillips, and the white man's son were in love and wanted to be married, but his father said no, and our family agreed with him. She married a member of our family, a man distantly related to her. From all I hear in stories from the old ones the marriage was happy, so perhaps it was meant to be. The old ones say she wove the basket for her white lover but was forbidden to give it to him. Yet, somehow, the basket disappeared. Perhaps stolen from our family? Or sold to a white man when money was scarce.

We do not know, but we know the basket found its way into the Taylor collection and from there into your museum. My husband found out it was in your collection, the one about to be returned to the Onondaga and the Oneida. This was an opportunity to bring it home to us where it belongs. These old photos prove it is ours."

We were all silent at the end of her story. The fire had burned low and the shadows on Kate's face had deepened, hiding her expression, yet the sadness she felt relating this tale enveloped the entire room and left us filled with the hollowness that came from hopes not yet realized.

"What was the name of the white man who filed the claim against this land?"

"I do not know. The name of the white man was never mentioned in the old ones' stories," she replied.

I wanted to know that man's name which meant I needed to research some land records in the county office building. Tracing the history of the basket could help lead to Mrs. Carlton's killer and an understanding of the events surrounding it.

"Perhaps I can help you discover what happened to the basket and how it ended up in the Taylor collection. That is, if you think the family would like to know."

"Of course, but . . ."

"But clearly the basket belongs to your family, and it will be returned later this fall at the ceremony when the museum turns over the collection to the nations members and your family."

"Will finding out how the basket left its home and ended up in a white man's collection help solve Mrs. Carlton's murder and establish finally my husband's innocence?"

"I hope so."

What I also hoped as I looked at Sara and Leonard's faces was that similar forces separating Marie and her lover back then didn't find their way into the love I saw on my granddaughter's face.

As if reading my mind, Kate said, "But Marie made a good marriage that produced strong sons and daughters."

"I know, but I want things to be different now. I want love to be enough." I meant that not only for Sara and Leonard but for Zack and me.

I got up, thanked her for telling me the story of the basket and embraced her. Sara followed me out of the house after saying good night to Leonard and his mother. Leonard had decided to stay overnight at his parents' house.

Sara followed my car back down the mountain.

"Do you drink brandy?" I asked when we arrived home and walked into the house.

"I do now." She threw herself onto the couch while I took my grandfather's brandy decanter from the carved liquor cabinet that stood at the bottom of my stairs. The decanter was heavy glass and I had wielded it against a killer only this past summer. I poured a bit of the amber liquid in it into two snifters.

We held our glasses aloft and saluted each other.

"Do you think Mrs. Powles is part white?" asked Sara.

"If she is, then you're thinking she would understand how you and Leonard feel about each other, right?"

"Maybe." She took a sip of her brandy and screwed up her face. "I don't think it's for me."

"Do you want anything else?"

"No. I think I'll go on up to bed. This evening and everything leading up to it from the day of Mrs. Carlton's death has exhausted me."

Spike followed her up the stairs. I guess he was exhausted also because he didn't bother me about food although his dish was empty, or perhaps, the cat understood what Sara was feeling—the possibility that the love she felt for Leonard wouldn't be enough to keep the two of them together.

I took Sara's snifter and poured the contents of it into mine, drank it down in two gulps and slumped back onto the couch.

"GRAM!" SAID SARA "DID YOU SPEND the entire night down here?" I opened my eyes to daylight. "What time is it?"

"Seven."

I tried to move, but my old bones felt creaky and stiff. Stupid of me to sleep on the couch when I had a nice, comfy bed upstairs.

"I made coffee," said Sara. "I'm going to skip breakfast here, but I'll grab a bagel sandwich on the way in. If you want, I'll make you something to eat before I go."

I could tell she was eager to be out the door. "Never mind. I'll just have coffee and then jump into the shower. I'll see you at work."

The bright, sunny day drew a large number of visitors to the museum. We were busy with small tour groups as well as family groups. It was as if everyone knew this might be the last lovely fall day before colder weather set in. Unfortunately, both Jeremy and Ellie called in sick, so the rest of us hustled the entire day to cover their work. There was no time for me to question anyone, so the day passed like a usual busy workday. It almost felt like we were back to normal, but I knew in my bones we were not. There was work ahead for me to do, sleuthing work.

MONDAY MORNING I WAS OUT THE DOOR within a half hour of Sara leaving, but I didn't intend to go straight to the museum. Instead I headed north to the county seat where the county office building and the land records office were located.

"Dorie," I said to the young woman behind the counter of the land office. "I need to see some old land records."

"Oh, hi., Mrs. Sparks. I haven't seen you for a while."

"Busy, you know. And I guess you have been also." I looked at her expanding stomach. "I heard you and your hubby were expecting."

"Yup. Our first and we're so excited." She smoothed the bulge in her dress and smiled. "So what exactly are you looking for? I can bring you the appropriate books and you can sit at the table over there and go through them. That way, if you need help, I'm right here."

I described the location of the land. Dorie went into the back where the records were kept and soon came back out with several heavy volumes.

"Here you go. I think that's what you need. If not, let me know."

It took a few minutes for me to find the correct page and trace the history of the Powles family land. The records indicated it was part of nations land in the early nineteenth century but then had passed into a white family's hands for over fifty years. By the latter part of the century it had been deeded through a court action back to the Powles family. Kate's story was true.

I got up from the table on shaky legs. Was a more than century old dispute over a piece of land motive enough for murder? But why Mrs. Carlton? I still couldn't make any sense out of her death. I had no choice but talk with the descendants of the white family who tried to claim the land. I could think of no reason the man who was the descendent of those who claimed the Powles's land would agree to talk with me. He probably didn't even know his ancestors once had possession of the property. I would have to use Sara's connection at the museum to get additional information. I hated to get her involved.

I parked my car in the employees' lot behind the museum and entered the front door. The first person I encountered was Harold who appeared to be on his way out, and he was not happy.

"I'll bet you're behind this," he said to me as he stormed past me.

"What did I do?"

"You got me fired."

Uh, oh. Harold's lecherous ways had finally caught up with him.

"Well, maybe you deserved to be fired."

"For touching some young thing's bootie? How is that a crime?"

"It's called sexual harassment, Harold, and it is a crime as I'm sure you were told."

"Well, I'm suing this place, you, that granddaughter of yours who thinks she runs the place and . . ."

At that moment Sara emerged from her office. "You're not being fired, Harold," she said. "You've been put on leave pending the board's review."

"My cousin won't stand for this." He slammed through the front door.

We hadn't yet opened the door to visitors, so the only people who observed the exchange were employees—Francis from the gift shop, Murray the guard, Ellie and Jeremy.

I caught a tiny smile cross Ellie's face and she and I exchanged pleased glances. Francis also looked happy to see the back of Harold, but Jeremy's face registered both surprise and concern.

"I don't get it," said Jeremy. "Harold was just a fun kind of guy. Just kidding around mostly."

"That kind of kidding isn't needed from anyone," said Sara and gave Jeremy a pointed look. He shuffled off down the hall.

"Got a minute, Gram?" She waved me into her office. "Putting him on leave was Mr. Graham's idea. We talked this morning. He's coming over around noon so we can discuss the next steps."

I nodded. "I have some news for you, Sara."

"What?"

I told her about my search among the land records at the county courthouse this morning.

"So . . ." I began, but a commotion caught our attention.

We went to the door and opened it to see Harold back in the building, this time holding an antique pistol, and threatening to shoot anyone who got in his way.

"I think he's come unhinged," I said.

Harold pushed through the door of Sara's office and confronted us. "Call my cousin and tell him he needs to come here now, right now, to settle this thing. I won't have some girl telling me what or what I can't do." He slammed the office door behind him and stood in front of it preventing us from getting out.

"But Harold. It was your cousin who recommended I put you on leave," said Sara.

I stepped in front of her. "Where did you get that pistol?" I asked Harold. "It looks like one from our revolutionary war collection. Lifted it, did you? What else did you lift from here?"

Harold's mouth dropped open at my accusation. "You think you know something, but you don't. I'll tell you who's the thief."

"Let's see. Would that be the only friend you have around here? Jeremy?" I was guessing, but I could tell from the look of surprise on Harold's face that I was right. "He conned you into stealing that broach from the museum and then replacing it with a fake, didn't he?

Harold was about to reply when the office door banged open, knocking him to his knees. The pistol flew from his hand.

"Zack! What are you doing here?" I kicked the gun out of Harold's reach.

"I stopped by your house this morning, but you weren't home, so I went to Anita's office to confer with her about the murder. She said she'd seen you drive out of the county office building parking lot. We were both kind of curious about what you were doing there, obviously not to see her. Dorie Haines came down the hall on her coffee break and told us you'd been there checking some records. I was curious about what records. So here I am and just in time, I see."

"Harold likes to defend his stupid behavior with antique weapons, swords, guns. He'd probably find a dagger or a catapult useful." I handed the pistol to Zack. "And you're an idiot, Harold. That pistol can't be loaded. There's no ammunition here for it."

Harold remained on the floor and started crying. "It wasn't my fault, any of it. Like you said. It was Jeremy."

"The two of you were in on it together," Zack said.

"It was his idea, all his. He kept the bracelet to give to his fiancé."

Anita entered the office. One of the museum employees had called her when Harold had reentered the museum and began his threats.

"Good to hear, Harold. Come with me. You'll answer for your part in the murder of Mrs. Carlton and for the theft of that broach and bracelet as well as attempts to break into Maddie and Sara's homes and the museum."

"Murder? No way."

"I'll also be taking Jeremy into custody." Anita put cuffs on Harold.

"Well, not now, you won't," said Sara, looking out her office window. "There goes Jeremy in his car." Jeremy, intently leaning forward over the wheel of his car, drove down the driveway of the museum and shot out into the road.

"I'll get him. I'm parked out front." Zack ran out of the office to pursue Jeremy while Anita put a call in to her officers in the field to detain Jeremy if they encountered him.

"Where do you think he'd run to?" Anita asked me.

"Probably to his apartment to hide," I said.

"I'll send two of my officers there." Anita led Harold out of the office.

"I'm not saying anything more without a lawyer," said Harold. "Maddie, can you call your son for me?"

"Get your own lawyer, Harold." The nerve of that guy.

Sara talked with each of the employees at the museum to make certain no one needed medical attention. Everyone said they had been frightened but Harold hadn't harmed anyone.

"Regardless," Sara said, "I'm closing the museum for the day. Go home, everyone. We'll open tomorrow as usual."

Sara checked the doors to make certain they were locked after everyone left.

"I'm curious, Gram. What did you find among the land records?"

"I discovered the name of the white family who tried to lay a claim to the Powles land."

"Which was what?"

"Graham."

"You think it was our board of director's family?"

"I thought I might ask him when I ran into him. Didn't you say he was coming here today?"

"Oh, gosh. I totally forgot he wanted to confer with me about the case with Harold. It's almost noon. He should be here any minute. We can talk with him then."

"Except the museum is locked up."

"Oh, as the board director he has the combination to all the doors in the museum, internal and entrances."

Did he? Suddenly that along with other pieces of information about Mr. Graham began to form a pattern in my mind.

"Call him and tell him what happened with Harold and that you'll confer with him tomorrow."

"I'm sure he's already on his way."

"Stall him."

Sara gave me a puzzled look. "Ooops. Too late. The security panel just lit up indicating someone has entered the front door. It has to be Mr. Graham. What's up, Gram? Why don't you want to talk with him?"

"I think he may be dangerous."

CHAPTER 25

SOMEONE KNOCKED ON SARA'S DOOR.

"Don't open it."

"He must know I'm in here waiting for him. I have to answer the door." Sara opened the door to the hall where Mr. Graham stood, a look of impatience on his face.

"Why is the museum closed?" asked Graham. When his gaze fell on me behind Sara, he didn't look pleased at my presence.

"We had an incident with Harold. The sheriff took him into custody and now is looking for Jeremy," Sara said.

Graham looked puzzled by what Sara said, but he also tilted his head to one side in curiosity. "So are you saying the mystery surrounding Mrs. Carlton's murder has been cleared up."

I stepped in front of Sara. "I'm not certain of that. Maybe. I don't think we have all the evidence we need to accuse them of killing her."

"Them?" he said.

"We think Harold and Jeremy may have been in on everything together." Sara's eyes darted between Mr. Graham and me. My warning her not to let him in had made her nervous, and I was afraid Mr. Graham would pick that up from her.

"Look," I said to Mr. Graham, "Given everything that has

happened around here today, Sara needs some time to pull herself together. Why don't the two of you discuss Harold's situation tomorrow?"

"Sure. Why not? But while I'm here, I might as well check the collections room. There's something in the 'Our Neighbors' objects that I'd like to take another look at, if that's okay with you, Sara. You two go on ahead. I'll only be a minute. I can lock up after I finish."

"Let's get you home, Sara. Leave your car here. I'll drive you."

By now I knew I had completely confused Sara with my mixed messages about Graham.

"Okay. I guess." Sara grabbed her purse from her desk drawer and followed Graham and me out of the office. He walked us to the front entrance where Sara and I stepped out the door. We turned and waved at Graham through the windows and started around the back of the building toward the parking area.

"What is going on, Gram?" Sara asked.

"Maybe nothing, but I've got a funny feeling about him. Give me the security code to get back into the building. You wait here and if I'm not out in five minutes, call the sheriff. And Zack."

"What are you doing, Gram?"

"I want to see what in the 'Our Neighbors' collection needs his attention. Go on now. I won't' be long."

I punched the security code into the panel by the front door, hoping Graham was already heading downstairs and wouldn't yet have access to a security read-out letting him know someone had entered the museum. I wanted him to believe he was alone and safe, free to do what he wanted without scrutiny from others . . . like me.

I tiptoed to the railing at the top of the stairs to the basement level and caught sight of Graham passing the interactive soft animals displays in the open area below. As he turned the corner into the collection storage area, I ran down the stairs to follow. He had entered the room and left the door ajar. The overhead light was on, and I could see Graham pulling a storage box from the shelves.

What surprised me, but probably shouldn't if I had had time to think all this through thoroughly, was he was not in the row of shelves housing the "Our Neighbors" items but rather farther back in the collections room in the far corner where the nations objects were stored. I hid behind the shelving watching Graham as he opened the box and removed a basket. I didn't have any doubt whose it was. Mr. Powles's basket. The look on Graham's face as he examined it was disturbing. His eyes narrowed, and I heard him mutter, "Finally, you'll be mine."

I put my hand over my mouth to stifle the gasp of shock that rushed out, but I was too late. Graham heard me and turned.

The two of us froze in place and stared at each other.

"You have no way of proving it, Mrs. Sparks."

"Are you so certain of that, Director Graham?"

"I was careful, very careful."

"Except for the photograph of the basket. And there were other photos also."

"Yes, I worried about all of that, but they really prove nothing."

"They were of enough concern to you for you to try to obtain the one Mrs. Carlton was planning to show to the nations leaders to prove Mr. Powles's claim on it. I thought you planned this so carefully?"

"I had to improvise."

"You wiped the hilt of the sword clean, but then you heard someone coming and didn't have time to search Mrs. Carlton or the room for the photo."

"Maybe. As I said it really didn't matter, except . . ."

"Except that photo can prove the basket belongs to the Powles family."

"But you see, Mrs. Sparks, that photo won't match the basket here because I'm taking it. I wanted to replace it with another basket when I found out Mrs. Carlton had the photo of it, but I haven't had the opportunity. Until now."

"You tried to replace it by breaking into the museum, but the code you used that night was the one Mrs. Carlton had given you and you didn't count on Sara changing the code when she took over Mrs. Carlton's position." I wanted to keep him talking. The longer we were here, the more likely Sara would worry and call the sheriff and Zack as I had told her to do.

He pulled another basket from behind boxes on the bottom shelf. "And here is the replacement. So like the original, don't you think? But don't forget, Dr. Walker examined the collection after the murder and authenticated all the objects."

"So at some point you hid the other basket in here."

"Don't be silly, Mrs. Sharpes. I wouldn't expose myself that way. I had Jeremy hide the basket here. I wanted to stay far away from this collection until the time was right."

Thoughts tumbled around in my mind, but Graham's words brought me a moment of clarity and revealed to me how devious he was. "You knew Geroge and Jeremy has taken items from the museum. You used that information to threaten them with exposure if they didn't do as you said."

"Yes, but I was smart enough not to let Jeremy know why I wanted that fake basket nearby. He might have wondered, but the boy is not smart enough to figure anything out. And even if he did, I would say he was trying to replace the genuine basket with a fake just like he did that broach. It wouldn't prove he killed Mrs. Carlton, but it would strongly implicate him as well as his partner, my dear cousin Geroge." Graham rocked back on his heels and smiled, a smile of profound satisfaction.

"But here's what you overlooked. If you replace Mr. Powles's basket with that one, when the day for returning the objects comes, Mr. Powles will say the basket is not his and he has that picture to prove it."

Mr. Graham chuckled. "Well, it isn't, is it? It was meant as a gift from his great grandmother to her lover, my great grandfather, but Powles's family wouldn't allow that. Then his family also took my ancestor's land."

"The land never belonged to your ancestors."

Graham waved away my assertion.

"Mr. Powles will certainly contend that the basket is not his. But after he's made such a fuss about the basket? And the photo? But the photo doesn't match any basket in the collection. A photo of a basket that no one can find because the real basket will be in my private collection. Who will believe anything Powles says? He's a troublemaker and he's an Indian."

I was surprised at Graham's racist remark. "But you collect and cherish Native artifacts. You brag that yours were all gifts from natives, not stolen or purchased illegally."

"I'm not what I appear to be, am I?" He set the original basket on the shelf and his shoulders lifted in a deep sigh. "And now let's see about you, Mrs. Sparks." He started toward me, but I had already read his intention and had turned to flee out of the collections room. I ran out the door, down the hallway and up the stairs, Mr. Graham only steps behind me. At the top of the stairs, he grabbed my arm and shoved me toward the railing, pressing himself against me. He then lifted me onto the railing.

"This will be a fatal fall for you, an unfortunate accident."

"Gram!" Sara had come through the front door and ran down the hall toward me.

Mr. Graham's face darkened with anger. "Two unfortunate accidents."

Sara pounded Graham's back with her fists. "Let go!"

But he tipped me backwards and I could feel my feet lift off the floor. I grabbed for the railing, but I couldn't reach it. Instead I threw my arms around Graham's neck and pulled him toward me. And down we both plunged.

CHAPTER 26

*T*HUD.

I couldn't breathe. Something soft enveloped me, like clouds of cotton. Could I have gone to heaven so soon after I died? I opened my eyes and stared into a pair of round black eyes, not at all how I envisioned the gaze of an angel.

"Gram!" Are you okay?" It was Sara's voice. Had Graham pulled her off the railing with him also?

"I'm glad I'm in heaven with you. We can be together through eternity." I rolled to my side and reached out to embrace my granddaughter.

"Gram, we're not in heaven. You fell when Mr. Graham tried to throw you over the railing, but you reached out and grabbed him and the two of you fell together. You're not dead."

"But I should be." I gazed into those black eyes again.

"You fell onto the soft sculpture exhibit, into the arms of the koala bear to be exact."

"Did you go over, too? Are you okay/"

"I'm fine. I didn't fall."

"Where's Graham?" I asked.

"He's over there. He fell beside you and landed half on the giraffe's neck, half on the floor. The animal helped break his fall, but not enough. I think he has a broken collar bone and maybe a leg, too."

Graham moaned. "Help me."

I rolled to my side and tried to get up, but I couldn't get enough leverage. I sank farther into the stuffing of the koala.

"Take my hand, Gram. I'll help you to your feet." Sara pulled me up, held me for a moment then let go. I wobbled back and forth several times then got my legs under me.

"Come over here and sit down for a minute." Sara led me to one of the benches against the wall near the soft sculptures. "I'll call an ambulance to take care of Mr. Graham."

"As far as I'm concerned you can just leave him there. He's a murderer."

Graham groaned again and tried to move. His cries of pain became louder. "Help me. Help me. Now!"

Sara cast a glance at him. "I'll bet you have a story to tell me, huh, Gram?"

"Graham killed Mrs. Carlton, but I only began to put it together when I found out his family had tried to claim the land that rightfully belonged to Mr. Powles's family . . ."

"Stop jabbering and get me a doctor. I'm dying." Graham let out another cry of pain.

"Do you think he's dying?" Sara asked.

"No, but he seems to be in a lot of pain."

Before Sara and I could consider Mr. Graham's situation in greater detail, we heard banging at the front entrance door.

"I'll go." Sara ran up the stairs. I heard voices and then Zack's head appeared looking over the balcony.

"Zack." I held my arms out to him.

"Maddie." He ran down the stairs and grabbed me in a tight embrace.

"Ouch."

"Sorry, Maddie. Are you hurt? Where?" Zack began to run his hands over me searching for bruises and breaks.

Graham ceased his yelling long enough to hiss at us. "Do your snuggling another time. I need a doctor."

Zack and I ignored him and embraced each other tightly.

"Too tight, Maddie?"

"No. I love it."

"Umph," said Graham and then there was silence.

"Oh, no. He really was hurt. He's dead." I felt a horror at having ignored his pleas even though I also knew he deserved whatever pain he had suffered.

"He just passed out, Maddie. And I hear the sirens now. The EMTs will take care of him." Zack continued to hold me.

Sara had waited at the door to let emergency services in then she raced down the stairs ahead of the EMTs carrying the stretcher. "Down here."

"I called the sheriff just as you told me to, Gram. She should be here soon." Sara took a seat beside me on the bench. "Is Gram really alright, Zack?"

"She's fine, but I think she should go to the hospital to be checked over."

"Get me away from that woman. She's ruined my life." Graham freed himself from the EMTs and started to crawl out of the pile of soft sculpture animals and down the hall toward the side exit, but the EMTs stopped him and began their examination. Graham thrashed around, trying again to push away the EMTs.

I looked up to see that Anita had arrived. "A quick rundown on what's going on?"

"He killed Mrs. Carlton," I said.

"Mr. Graham then tried to keep us from talking by trying to toss Gram over the railing. I'm sure he planned some kind of accident for me also," Sara said.

"You can fill me in on the details later." Anita reached for her handcuffs and walked toward the stretcher.

I felt the presence of someone behind me.

"Mr. Powles," said Zack. "What are you doing here?"

"My wife told me this morning that she had related the story about the land and the basket to Mrs. Sparks and Sara last night. I thought it was time I talked to the old one and her granddaughter about those events, so I came here to finally speak about our history." He turned his dark eyes on Mr. Graham. "Is this man the killer of Mrs. Carlton?"

I nodded. "His name is Graham. He's the head of the board of directors at the museum and a descendent of the family who tried to take your land as well as your basket."

Powles stared hard at Graham. "My family never spoke the name of the white man who tried to take our land away, but it appears now you will be named as a killer and a thief. You will face white man's justice as you should."

"I just discovered Graham attempting to replace your basket with another, an idea he got when he discovered Harold and Jeremy had replaced the broach with a fake. Graham knew a lot of what went on at the museum not only as the director of the board, but because he was always around, spying on people like Jeremy and Harold and everyone he thought he might be able to use to get the basket back. None of us at the museum took note of his presence because he was the board director and we expected him to be here. Things just didn't go as planned. He didn't know you had the pictures as proof of your claim. He thought only Mrs. Carlton could identify the right basket. Graham must have been listening outside her office when you gave her the pictures. When she left with the picture in her hand to meet with you and the nations leaders, he thought he had to silence her and get rid of the photo. After her murder, Sara brought in an expert, Dr. Walker, to authenticate the nations collection. Graham realized that was no problem. He could replace the basket after Dr. Walker's work and that you and your evidence would mean nothing if there was no basket to compare the photo to." I turned to Graham. "You decided to sit tight and wait until you could replace the basket with one of your own, one that didn't mean as much to you as the Powles basket."

"It was meant to be in my family." Graham spoke through his pain, the bitterness evident in his voice.

"But," Zack said, "Mr. Powles could identify the original basket. He would know it had been replaced."

"Who would believe him? He wasn't white and he was still under suspicion for Mrs. Carlton's murder. The fake basket would be in the collection, placed there after Dr. Walker verified its originality. Once the replacement had been made, with Mrs. Carlton dead, the museum would vouch for its authenticity."

Graham tried to laugh, but it came out in a strangled cough. "I don't get any of this. Photos? A broach? It sounds far-fetched to me."

"Does it, Mr. Graham? Your ancestors stole the land from Mr. Powles's family."

"Whites stole land around here from all the nations people. They got it back, didn't they?" he said, his words breathy.

"Oh, yes. In the case of your family it took a court battle for Mr. Powles's family to have the land returned. You couldn't get the land, but you could steal the basket. In fact, you were passionate about the idea, a way for you to hurt the Powles family after all these years." I said.

Graham propped himself up on his elbow and glared at Mr. Powles. "I needed to right a wrong. I wanted you and your so-called family to know what it feels like to lose what belongs to you. You took my family's land, land we plowed and planted and worked for years.so I wanted to take the basket from you. It was actually mine anyway." With these bitter words, he fell back on the stretcher, and the EMTs carried him off, Anita close behind.

For several minutes no one had anything to say.

"The basket was meant as a gift, but prejudice got in the way and then, over a century later, prejudice again intervenes, and this time the result is murder." My gaze met that of Mr. Powles's.

"Grandmother," he said, tipping his head to me. "Thank you for believing me and my family."

Zack's eyes lit up. "You found the account in the land records office this morning, didn't you, Maddie?"

I nodded. "After I saw those land records, I suspected Graham killed Mrs. Carlton. Once Mr. Powles claimed the basket belonged to his family, Graham became obsessed with obtaining it. He thought he could take his time, but when Mrs. Carlton announced her intention to follow the law and return the collection to the nations and Mr. Powles's family, Graham knew he had to act."

"The basket meant revenge. He doesn't have any respect for Native American artifacts. He only wants to own them." Sara said.

"And he used Jeremy and Harold's larcenous intentions to help him get away with murder. I'm sure both of them had every intention of continuing to lift articles from the museum and make money off them." I shifted around on the bench to alleviate the soreness I felt creeping into my back.

"Let's get you medical attention, Maddie." Zack gently pulled me up and steered me toward the stairs.

"Uhm, let's take the elevator," I said. "No doctors, no hospital. I want to go home. With you."

"My poor, sweet Maddie. Your body has taken a beating over these past weeks, hasn't it? I'll tell you what. I'll make you a cup of tea when we get to your place." Zack smiled down at me and touched my face with his finger.

"You'll do no such thing. You'll make me a martini. A double!"

CHAPTER 27

As Zack busied himself making our drinks in the kitchen, he told me he had caught up to Jeremy at his apartment where Zack talked him into going into the sheriff's department for questioning.

"I think I'll hear from Sheriff Burroughs tomorrow and find out what Jeremy had to say about the thefts and break-ins. For now let's put the case aside, my love, and enjoy our martinis." He brought me a frosty stemmed glass and joined me on the couch with his drink. We clinked glasses, and I took a sip.

"You make a mean martini, my dear." I leaned back on the couch into Zack's arms.

"And you make a fine detective." He kissed me on the mouth, a gentle kiss, filled with promise. I settled deeper into his arms, and we sipped our drinks. I could feel my limbs relax, and for the first time in days, my mind let go of its worries.

Drinks finished, Zack grabbed both our glasses and started for the kitchen.

"No more for me. I'll just fall asleep. Besides, I think it's time for you to head out to the B and B."

"I think it's time I explained everything about Mary and me to you. I've been a real fool."

"And so have I. I should have told you that Mary came to see me, spinning that story about the baby. I thought she should talk to you. Maybe I was right, but I shouldn't have hidden her threats against me. I knew she was dangerous."

Zack's eyes lit up. "We should have talked to each other sooner. I wanted to, you know."

"Pride, stubbornness." I reached out to him and caressed his cheek. "But let's leave that discussion for another time, when I'm not so sore and tired or feeling so numb from this hefty drink."

I knew he was disappointed, but he didn't argue with me. "I assume Sara is back at her apartment tonight." Zack donned his hat and opened the door to leave.

"And I'll bet she has company."

"She probably is going to let him stay the night." Zack's lips curved downward in a frown, but I could see a twinkle in his blue eyes.

"Soon." I closed the door, waited until I heard his car drive away, then turned off the porch light.

Spike encircled my legs and looked up at me with a demanding meow.

"I'll give you a snack and then it's off to bed for both of us."

He meowed, more softly this time as if he knew his request was going to be granted.

WE BOTH SLEPT IN, UNTIL I was awakened by a phone call the next morning.

"Not awake yet, Maddie?" It was Zack. "I thought you might like to come with me to the sheriff's office. Anita has some information I'm sure you'd like to hear."

"Yes! I'll jump in the shower and grab . . ."

"Never mind the coffee. I'll bring you a cup and a donut. Be there in fifteen minutes."

I called Sara to say I wouldn't be in today for work. "I hope that won't be an inconvenience."

"You deserve time off after what you've been through. Take all the time you need. I'll work it out here."

Anita had been a very busy and persuasive woman last night. She looked tired but happy this morning and, hearing what she found out from Jeremy and Harold, she had reason to be proud of herself.

"Graham caught Jeremy and Harold one afternoon going through items in the collections room, talking about which ones they could nab without getting caught. From then on, he owned them. They took the broach and the bracelet, finding that they could easily substitute a similar broach for the real one, but the bracelet was too difficult because its design was so unique. They took a chance on it anyway, and only grew concerned about the thefts when Mrs. Carlton decided to mount the 'Our Neighbors' collection earlier than they anticipated. They had planned to take other items, but Mrs. Carlton's murder threw such a spotlight on the museum, they decided to call a halt to their thievery."

"So what Graham told me yesterday was the truth. He was solely responsible for Mrs. Carlton's murder."

"Yup. And he did try to use the old key code to enter the museum. He took out his frustration at not being able to get in by beating on the door, almost cracking the glass."

"I have no doubt about that. I saw him try to annihilate an elevator button when the car didn't immediately respond. That was just yesterday when Harold tried to use an antique pistol to threaten all of us."

"And what about the person peeking into Sara's windows and the individual who hit Maddie over the head and took her purse? We can speculate, but what did Jeremy and Geroge tell you?" asked Zack.

"Well, both Jeremy and Geroge deny responsibility for those incidents," said Anita.

"Do you believe them?" asked Zack.

"I think Graham was the person who broke into my house. He just wanted to assure himself there was nothing I had in my possession that would implicate him in Mrs. Carlton's murder."

"But the copies of the photos were in your purse," said Anita.

"He didn't really care about them and leaving them in the purse would lead us to believe none of the photos meant anything important to the murder," I said.

"Maybe. I'd like to know for certain if Graham was the person who attacked you. It would mean another charge of attempted murder."

A chill took over my body and I began to tremble.

Zack noticed. "Are you okay, Maddie?"

"Yes. It's just that the man killed once and it's just now sinking in that he tried it again, two more times with me. I wonder, do I need some medication to get beyond all this?"

"Like what?" asked Zack.

"Another one of your marvelous martinis?" I laughed.

"It's too early." He sounded relieved that I could joke about what had happened.

We heard voices coming from outside Anita's door.

"I need to talk to her. I know stuff that might be important in the museum case." It was the shrill voice of a woman.

What now?

The door banged open and Jeremy's girlfriend, Candy, pushed her way into the office.

"Oh, hi, Mrs. Sparks. I didn't know you would be here. Well, no matter. What I'm about to say isn't confidential. It's about Jeremy. I should have known better. He's not the man I thought he was. I mean, he did give me this bracelet." She took a quick breath and held out her arm to reveal the bracelet that had been stolen from the "Our Neighbors" collection, "But I ran into Sara just now outside of the building as I was about to visit Jeremy. I was wearing the bracelet and she saw it. She told me it was stolen from the museum. Stolen! Can you imagine?"

Zack and I exchanged glances.

"I hope she told you you'll have to give it back," I said.

"Yes, I know. That's fine with me. It's old, probably junk." She tore it off her wrist and tossed it on Anita's desk. "There. Take it."

But she wasn't finished with her rant. "I suspected Jeremy for months of not being faithful to me. He was always going on about Sara, how smart she was and how beautiful. I suspected him of cheating on me with her, so one night when he was gone, I sneaked over to her apartment and looked in the windows certain I'd catch them together. I didn't, but that didn't mean he wasn't with somebody that night, and probably other nights, too."

Well, that cleared up the window peeker at Sara's.

She was about to leave, but spun around and said, "And I'm willing to testify against the jerk, if you need me."

"Jeremy, you mean?" asked Anita.

"Yes, Jeremy the Jerk." She stood in front of Anita's desk, blinking her eyes as if she had more to say.

We waited, but she remained silent. We exchanged glances with one another.

Candy turned to leave then appeared to get a second wind. "Oh, and what's more, not only was Jeremy always hitting on other women, he also didn't treat my dog very well." She took a quick breath. "I guess that's all."

Anita frowned. "Not quite. Peeking in windows is against the law. I could arrest you."

"Gads. Trying to check up on that cad means I'll be occupying the cell next to his. I have bad taste in men." Candy looked as if she was about to break into tears.

"Why don't you take a seat in the hall, and we'll talk about this when I'm finished here," said Anita.

Candy retreated into the hallway and plopped down on a bench. Anita closed the door.

"I followed up on your lead on drugs at the library and caught a guy hanging around there. Did your daughter ever contact her supplier?" Anita asked Zack. "Could she identify him?"

"I'll ask her."

"And what about Mary" I asked.

"She will undergo a psych evaluation, but everything points to her spending some time in a facility until the doctors deem her mentally healthy enough to face charges."

"My daughter will be devastated to hear about Mary," said Zack. I wanted to keep my mouth shut, but I couldn't help myself. I blurted out, "Will Amy return to Seattle? And will you go with her?"

Zack reached out to take my hand. "As you can tell, Sheriff Burroughs, my gal and I have some issues to discuss. Will you excuse us if we leave so we can talk in private?"

"You've earned it, both of you. Thanks for your help."

"Oh, no," Zack said. "We didn't help you. Maddie did. It was all her work."

Back at my house, Zack and I settled on my back deck, listening to the water ripple over the stones in the creek as it made its way south toward the river. I wrapped my heavy wool sweater tightly around me but was glad of the additional warmth provided by Zack's body as he pulled me toward him. I held my breath as Zack began talking.

"Amy called this morning from the rehab facility. She wants to remain here to complete her stay at the facility. As for after that, she may go back to Seattle or remain in this area. I hope she decides on the latter. It will give us a chance to get to know each other better."

I let out my breath, happy to hear Zack would be near.

"I won't be moving back in with you, Maddie. You know that."

"Of course. We need to get to know each other again, too."

"No more secrets," I said.

"No more secrets," he agreed.

"How about dinner at the Billinghouse tonight?"

I kissed him on the cheek. "Just like our first date. I'll wear the dress I wore that night." But something worried me. "Would you mind leaving? I have some things I need to do."

He looked surprised, but we agreed he would pick me up around seven tonight. Once Zack left, I took a look at myself in the entryway mirror. I was right. I needed a root touch up. I called the salon and scheduled for later this afternoon, then I called Sara.

"Gram. Is everything alright?"

"Everything is fine, but I'm calling about you. And Leonard." I heard Sara sigh.

"We're fine, too."

"And your position at the museum?"

"I still have my thesis for my degree to write and two courses to finish this summer. I'll be here for a while. I haven't made up my mind about the position yet."

"Oh."

Sara chuckled. "Why don't you just ask me what you want to?"

"Okay then. What about you and Leonard and the possibility that you might leave here for a position elsewhere?"

"That's my gram. Straight and to the point. Leonard and I have time to work out our future. We'll take these months to see what we can do."

"Oh, good. I worried that . . ."

"You worried that I had found the love of my life in a partner and in my career and that the two wouldn't be compatible. Don't worry, Gram. We'll do our best."

I was pleased with Sara's answer especially that she talked about "we," her and Leonard. Young people were so smart nowadays.

Like Sara I had found someone I loved and I also was devoted to my writing and, of course, my sleuthing—but if I wanted to keep writing romance, I'd better get to it. The deadline for my manuscript was March, only months away.

"I hope this won't make your decision about working at the museum more difficult, Sara. I know you're down volunteers with Jeremy and Harold gone, but I'm going to cut back on my volunteer hours there. I have a book to complete."

Sara groaned. "I'd love to have you here, Gram, but I understand. You mentioned your friend Jane. Do you think she'd like to volunteer at the museum?"

"I'm sure she would love it. Call her."

"Will do. Gotta run. I've got some last minute paperwork to do and then Leonard and I and his parents are off to Mom and Dad's for dinner."

"Nervous?"

"A little."

"Everything will go fine, I'm sure."

"I hope so. I'll talk with you tomorrow."

"Bye, Sara."

I looked at my watch. I had several hours before my hair appointment, so I decided to make good on my promise to myself to work on my manuscript.

After a satisfying hour at my keyboard, my phone rang.

"Sheriff Burroughs. Not bad news, is it?"

"I just thought you'd like to know. Graham had a nasty scratch on his arm and the doctor told me it's gotten infected. Cat scratch fever, I believe."

I chuckled. "You can add the additional charge of attempted murder now. You know Spike scratched the person who broke into my house and hit me over the head. This proves it. Or is a cat scratch inadmissible as evidence?"

Anita laughed. "We'll find a way to make it work."

I disconnected and felt Spike rub against my legs, blink his golden eyes at me, a cat's way of saying "I love you," and begin his deep purr.

"Well, you did it again, you rascal. Helped your mama tag a murderer."

Extra tuna treats for my boy and a fancy dinner with the man I loved. Perhaps no overnight passion tonight, but soon. Very soon. I was too old, or was it too impatient, to wait long.

Tap, tap, tap on my keyboard. *And he kissed her deep and long . . .*

Cows, Lesley learned growing up on a farm, have a twisted sense of humor. They chased her when she went to the field to herd them in for milking, and one ate the lovely red mitten her grandmother knitted for her. Determining that agriculture wasn't a good career choice, instead she uses her country roots and her training as a psychologist to concoct stories designed to make people laugh in the face of murder. "A good chuckle," says Lesley, "keeps us emotionally well-oiled long into our old age." She is the author of the Eve Appel mysteries from Camel Press as well as several cozy mystery series and numerous short stories. Go to her webpage to find out more: www.lesleyadiehl.com.

www.ingramcontent.com/pod-product-compliance
Lightning Source LLC
Chambersburg PA
CBHW011513100726
47899CB00010BD/3344